THREADS OF CONNECTION

THREADS OF CONNECTION

JANE SHEARER

Published 2025

by 3Eyes Publishing

ISBN: 978-0-473-73925-6

© Copyright 2025

To Chris. For everything.

AUTHOR'S NOTE

'Threads of Connection' is written in response to the global, existential threat represented by climate change. While parts of New Zealand will be flooded, or experience extreme drought, higher winds and higher temperatures, our country is relatively lucky compared with the growing impacts of climate instability being seen around the planet.

What can and should people do in the face of such an overwhelming crisis? This is the question I ask myself, and readers. Is doing the best we can – buying electric vehicles, reducing meat consumption, recycling our waste, eschewing overseas travel – going to cut it? Or do we need stronger action?

New Zealand had its 'nuclear moment' in February 1985 when Prime Minister David Lange demanded America confirm or deny whether its submarines were nuclear-armed as well as nuclear-powered. They refused to confirm and US Secretary of State George Shultz revoked New Zealand's security guarantee and the country suffered trade losses as relations with the USA foundered.

Later in the same year, New Zealand was in the nuclear spotlight again. We had campaigned against French nuclear weapons testing in the Pacific from 1966. In July 1985, the Greenpeace ship Rainbow Warrior was sunk in Auckland Harbour by French agents behaving so unprofessionally the story sounded more like a spoof thriller than a real act of terrorism. However, one crew member died, so terrorism it was.

As a country, we punched above our weight with our protests against global nuclear proliferation. Could the same happen again if New Zealand made a concerted stand against drivers of climate change? And could individuals make the difference themselves, rather than requiring government to take a stance, at a time when governments are not taking the level of action people know is required to prevent catastrophic planetary warming.

This book is inspired by the way the Rainbow Warrior bombing became an action point and a symbol. It asks the question whether it is philosophically and morally acceptable to destroy property (not life) when your goal is saving the planet and your avenues of action are dwindling.

What do you think?

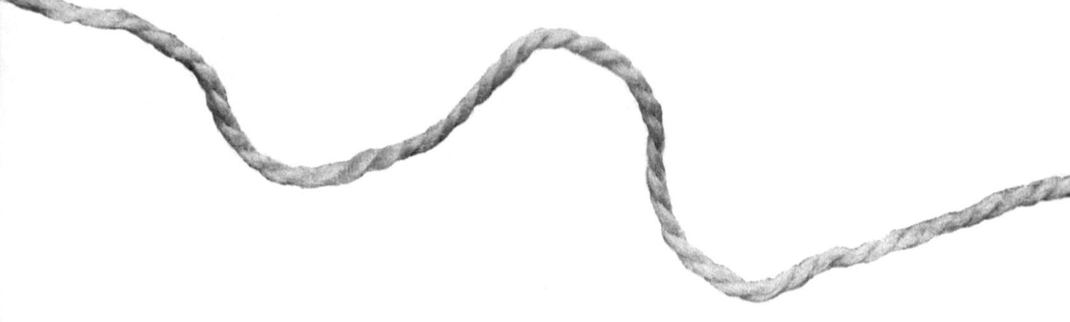

PROLOGUE

BREAKING NEWS 7:00AM 26 MAY 2030
TERRORIST ATTACK IN LYTTELTON HARBOUR

In the early hours of this morning, terrorists sank a foreign-owned coal ship in Ōhinehou (Lyttelton) Port, Aotearoa New Zealand, near Ōtautahi (Christchurch). Eleven crew members are reported missing although no one is yet confirmed dead. It is thought the sinking used a method similar to the 1985 bombing of the Rainbow Warrior in the Waitematā Harbour, Tāmaki Makarau (Auckland). Explosives were placed below the waterline and detonated remotely. The area is cordoned off in case of more explosions. Police are asking the public to stay away while they investigate the attack. Police report that an accident on Governors Bay Road, in which five teenagers were injured, may be linked to the bombing. The Prime Minister, Marama Wihongi, says she deplores terrorism in Aotearoa New Zealand. She deeply regrets any harm to the international crew and wishes to convey her sympathy to the crew members and their families.

COAL SHIP SUNK: Desperate Times Desperate Measures

A foreign-owned coal ship has been sunk in Ōhinehou (Lyttelton) Port, Ōtautahi (Christchurch), Aotearoa New Zealand. Ōhinehou residents report hearing explosions shortly before sunrise. "My dog woke me up to go out for a pee," said Mark of Gilmour Terrace. "I opened the door, then heard a muffled thud. I looked out the window but couldn't see anything. A few minutes later I heard another loud thud. Then I saw sirens and flashing lights headed to the port."

A spokesperson from Green Planet denied any involvement. "We have no connection with this incident. We extend our sympathies to those affected. We believe all crew and port staff are accounted for, despite some reports to the contrary." Green Planet also stated, "We emphasise this action is ecotage not eco-terrorism, given the focus on property rather than people. Ecotage is a last resort. However, coal shipments should have ended a decade ago. Exporting climate change is not a strategy. We must prevent further injury to our critically damaged planet."

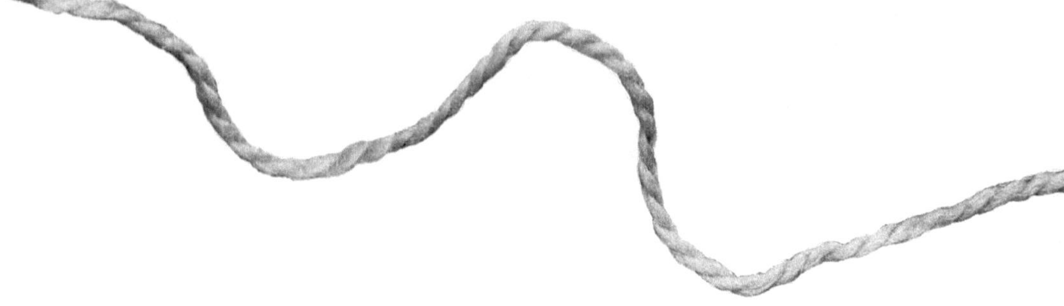

HUMANS WITH STORIES

February 2030

On the noticeboard of the Sumner Fresh Choice supermarket, Ōtautahi (Christchurch) Aotearoa New Zealand, February 2030:

LOOKING FOR CONNECTIONS?
TRY HUMANS WITH STORIES
Find the current state of the world overwhelming? Need some
support from people outside your whānau? Want to meet other people
in a nurturing atmosphere?
Come and join us at Humans with Stories, where we'll share
narratives to find our common threads.
Lynda 030 786 7437 (STORIES)

JULIA

November 2029

It's a stormy November night and my toilet is vomiting onto the floor. Fran, Lynda, and I are having one of our regular Dolls with Stories board meetings while the sea growls and rumbles three blocks from my house. Will tonight be another event where waves tear through the rip-rap wall protecting the Esplanade walkway from marine predation?

We should have connected on CryptoCast, rather than got together. However, we haven't caught up in person for weeks, and ten years of friendship have only enhanced how much we enjoy each other's company. Lynda, Fran, and I met at Obsessives Associated and, through sharing our stories there, became friends and started our Dolls with Stories social enterprise.

We are sitting in my living room drinking Kenya Bold tea out of my eclectic collection of mugs on my brightly re-covered easy chairs. I match the mug with the person drinking from it, rather than mugs with each other. Kenya Bold is my only addiction but it's getting ever harder to source, given the strained supply lines into New Zealand. My tea ritual centres around a brown Temuka teapot kept warm by a slightly misshapen tea cosy I knitted as a child. The pot and mugs are laid out on my gran's tray inlaid with swirling mother-of-pearl leaf patterns, and I pour milk into a Boris Johnson Toby jug Lynda gave me.

Today I give Lynda a mug decorated with 'Home is where the Mum is' in flowing, flowery text. Love hearts and roses sprinkle down between the letters. It's so not Lynda. Fran's drinking from a mug painted with a rainbow shaped like a wiggly slide, with stick figures leaping into the colour bands then launching off into the sky. I hold my own mug, decorated with a pumpkin saying, "I'm soup-er", and inhale the earthy scent of Kenya Bold.

"We have tea," Lynda says. "Time for business."

"Hang on," I say. "If you go to the toilet, please don't flush. When it's stormy, sewage spews back into the room."

"Really? Is that recent?" Lynda asks.

"It started a while ago, but now it's worryingly frequent. Apparently, groundwater is getting into the pipes because of the rising sea."

Lynda screws up her face. "Glad we live high on the hill."

"Yes, lucky you," I say.

"Okay girls," Fran says with a smile in her voice, "no bickering in a meeting." Fran's had many years' experience managing children in her teaching roles.

"Like we've talked about before," Lynda says, "I want to help more adults. Life is so stressful and getting worse. More need mental health support but fewer professionals are available. People wait months for an appointment with a counsellor. Our community needs to help itself."

Lynda is the CEO of Dolls with Stories, through which we help children by pairing them with a mentor and giving the child a special doll with amazing clothes and accessories made by volunteers. Each child and mentor jointly create stories for their doll, developing plotlines children can aspire to live. It's been a great success, and we have branches throughout New Zealand. To help fund Dolls with Stories, we make limited numbers of highly collectible dolls and sell them in international, online auctions. Lynda is always looking for the next great thing to improve or expand what we do.

"We don't need to help everyone," I say. "We're good at helping children, but we might not be the right people to help adults. Our Dolls with Stories workshops for adults were a complete disaster."

"That disaster is why we are thinking again," Lynda says. "We need to learn from our mistakes. Move on. Do better. We've learnt so much, I'm sure we can extend."

We trialled two workshops for adults last year which were painfully embarrassing and made me nervous about trying again. Imagine a group of adults sitting in a circle with dolls on their laps, making up stories for the dolls based on personal life experiences. How could we have thought that was a good idea? One of the guys walked out when we tried to hand him a doll. A couple of group members got into it, but most didn't come to the second session. We considered getting adults to create stories for dolls in pairs or groups but decided that might be worse and canned the whole idea.

"How about storytelling circles?" Fran suggests.

"Yes," Lynda says. "We could advertise using a picture of people sitting round a campfire."

"I don't think that's enough," I say. "People can tell each other stories whenever they want. And we shouldn't encourage people to light fires. Did you hear the government's reduced the fire service's energy quota by the national reduction target this year? Soon they'll be walking to fires and borrowing garden hoses."

Lynda rolls her eyes at me.

"How about telling each other stories with the goal of finding connections?" Fran says. "Isn't that what's missing since the pandemic? People feel divided and groups like Regain Your Power exacerbate things with their social media making people scared of each other. Storytelling helps everyone to discover common ground."

"If we just let people talk, some people might go on forever," I say.

"We'd have to manage them talking," Lynda says.

"You can't shut people down!" I exclaim.

"We get one person to tell a story each meeting," Fran says. "They tell a story important to them, but one they are comfortable telling to the group. We give them a set amount of time and a co-leader keeps them to time."

"That would be me," Lynda says, "seeing as Julia doesn't wear a watch and I always run meetings under time." It's true. Lynda would never be late for a meeting. I try to be prompt, but I don't like the constriction of a watch on my wrist or my life. I can forget to look at my cell phone for hours when wrapped up in a creative project. Lynda will pop in to find me immersed in a pile of creative debris, which I move to make us a cup of tea.

"Now, we need to figure out how people share their connection with the storyteller," Fran continues. "What ideas do you two have? I shouldn't have to invent everything."

I say, "People could write Post-it notes and put them on the wall."

"Post-it notes are so 2010s," Lynda says. "And we'd have to buy Post-its then throw them away. Wasteful. You can't even use both sides. And who writes on paper these days? Next you'll be wanting fountain pens and ink wells. We could do the obvious – people raise their hands and say what they have in common with the speaker?"

"Interrupting the speaker might make it hard for them to tell the story," I object.

Fran says, "How about we create a Buzz chat group for everyone in the workshop? People message their connection."

"Best not to use Buzz," says Lynda. "I've read you might as well broadcast your private thoughts to every nutcase in cyberspace. Warble has much better encryption."

"Sure, you know best about technology." Fran and Lynda pulled me out of a rabbit hole of online misinformation during the pandemic. I'm now terminally wary of getting too involved with the internet. "I agree we need to find connections during the meeting before people forget what's been said. But if workshoppers are using their phones, mightn't they look at funny cat videos rather than listening? And read other people's messages rather than writing their own?"

"All solvable problems," Lynda says. "Warble has a 'holding pen' function for group chats. Messages go to an admin who then releases them. Everyone can see who has sent messages, but no one can read messages until they're released. That way people can't copy each other."

"Perfect. You can be the admin and manage the messages, Lynda," I say.

"Oh, no. You're not getting off so easily," Lynda replies. "I've already volunteered for timekeeping. We can both be administrators, but you're the lead for messages."

"Okay, I'll manage messages," I agree. "But what about cat videos? Or Candy Crush?"

We sit contemplating the challenge. "I'll send our IT guru a message – he'll have a solution." Lynda's already typing rapidly with her thumbs.

Lynda's phone buzzes almost as soon as she finishes her message. "Of course, we use phone-to-phone connectivity without the internet. If everyone switches on flight mode, Warble will still work fine. We can also be old school and ask people to bring their phones to the front of the room once they've sent their connection."

"Good work," Fran says. "That's the start of a plan for running workshops. What about an introductory session to get people comfortable before they tell their stories?"

"Comfortable?" Lynda says. "Shouldn't we get people out of their comfort zones? Unsettle them so they'll talk to new people. Everyone similarly uncomfortable, you know?"

"What are you thinking of?" I ask.

"Twister? Get everyone moving and connected!" Lynda is an enthusiastic runner and biker; movement is part of her psyche.

I look at Lynda's eight-months-pregnant stomach. "How are you going to play Twister? And what if someone in the group isn't very flexible?"

"You have a point about the other people," Lynda says. "Fran?"

Fran tilts her head, and her dark chin-length curls swing with her face. Over the last ten years, those curls have accrued numerous grey strands. "How about the ball-of-wool intro?"

"I like wool; I've got some nice balls in my shed." I ended up at Obsessives Associated because my house had filled with broken objects together with a miscellany of materials for repairing them. These days, I keep favourite repair materials in my shed, but do most of my work at our Broken is Beautiful workshop in Ferrymead. Broken is Beautiful is the name of my repair and re-creation company which I manage jointly with Robbie, Lynda's partner. I ask, "How does the ball of wool work?"

Fran explains. "I hold the ball. I tell you about myself. If you have something in common with my statement, you put your hand up. Like, if I say I enjoy gardening and you enjoy gardening too, you raise your hand. I hold on to the end of the wool and pass you the ball. Next, it's your turn to tell the group about yourself until someone else puts their hand up. We keep going until everyone in the group has spoken. The line of yarn zig-zags across the group, creating a visual web of connections."

"Okay," I say, "I'll get some wool options and we can make a multicoloured ball."

"Nice, Julia. You are getting more proactive all the time," Lynda says, and I give her a wry smile.

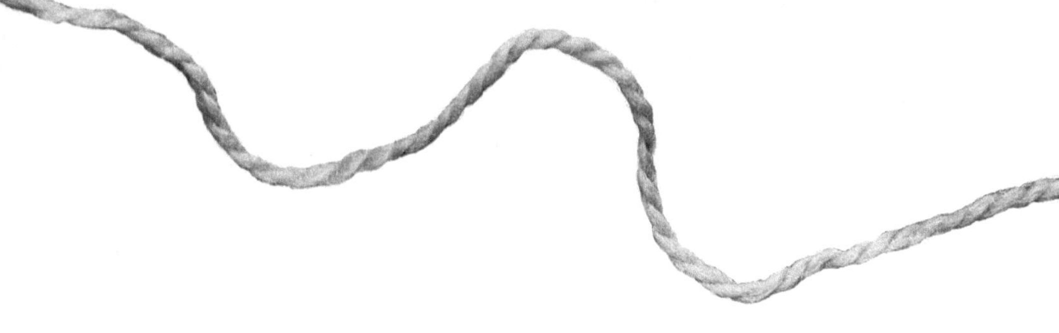

JULIA

7 March 2030

"Kia ora, hello, and welcome to our first Humans with Stories workshop. I'm Julia and this is Lynda." My mind precipitately goes blank, and my mouth is dry. What do I say next? We've been planning these workshops for nearly half a year; I should know! Ten years ago I attended my first Obsessives Associated meeting in this same room – the Sumner Surf Club – as an unwilling and unhappy participant. A decade on I'm a confident person, co-leading a workshop with Lynda, except I'm unexpectedly struggling to keep my gaze on the seven people sitting in a semicircle of brightly coloured plastic chairs and all looking intently at me.

Luckily, Lynda has never suffered from lack of confidence. She faces the room, bright-eyed and erect. "Hi, everyone, I'm Lynda. I'm so happy to meet you all. Julia and I are sitting up the front right now. But we're all in this together. Humans with Stories is a group of equals sharing stories to build connections. Life's tough. Community creates a safety net. We've helped children for a decade through our social enterprise Dolls with Stories. We want to help adults and we're excited to be sharing these workshops with you."

"Thanks, Lynda," I say. Her intercession allowed me brain space to remember my role. "Today in our kōrero we will find things we have in common using a ball of wool, then share kai brought by our mentor, Fran, sitting in the orange chair."

I see glances between participants and raised eyebrows. How does one find connections using a ball of wool? Fair enough, I'd wondered too when Fran suggested it.

"Let's all move to the open space by the windows so we've room to lay the wool down at the end of our exercise." Everyone shifts over to the floor-to-ceiling windows with a view of puffy clouds dressing an evening sky above a dark-blue sea. People jog along the narrow strip of sand between the waves and the Surf Club, weaving between dog walkers who launch balls for their running animals. When we've formed a circle, Fran gives everyone a smile. Her blood-red shirt looks great against her brown skin, and her matching red glass earrings catch the light.

"We'll start with a karakia. I've just sent the words to our Warble chat so you can read them," Fran says. "Today we'll say it in English. Next workshop we'll use te reo Māori. I'll send a YouLook link for anyone who'd like to practise."

I'd been resistant to including karakia in our meetings. "We aren't Māori and likely workshop participants aren't either," I said.

"Karakia are a normal part of meetings," said Fran. "They're a good formal recognition of the beginning and end of a group session. We could consider a waiata as well. People like singing together."

"Julia, which stone are you hiding under?" Lynda said.

"Well, I still can't speak Māori and I don't like prayers. I know I was supposed to do lessons, but learning languages has never been my thing. I'm not sure about mixing Māori words in with English, either, like you keep on suggesting."

"We can work on your pronunciation and vocab," Fran said. "And there might be Māori participants, even though Sumner is still awfully white compared with the rest of Ōtautahi. Languages constantly get new words. Modern English contains plenty of words from other languages."

"Yes, I know that," I say. "I'm not ignorant, even if I didn't go to university. Fine, karakia and random Māori words are in, and Fran will teach us the karakia. Do I have to say 'Ōtautahi' rather than 'Christchurch'?"

"Up to you," Fran said.

Fran leads off our first group karakia. "The sun has risen in the sky."

"Birds are singing, insects are moving, the world is alive!" The group responds, although most of the response is from me and Lynda.

"A new day is upon us, my friends …" Fran continues.

"So, grab your paddles," we chorus back.

"Is it decided?" Fran asks.

"It is," we all say together.

"Excellent," says Fran. "Now I'll hand the meeting back to Julia and Lynda."

"I'll start off holding the ball of wool and tell you some things about myself," I say. "If you have something in common with what I say, put your hand up. I don't want to be holding the ball too long – I want to hear about you.

"So, I'm Julia Stout, though I've always been thin." There's a burble of polite laughter. "I love to re-create broken objects to be better than they were before. Maybe you've heard of *kintsugi*? It's a Japanese art form. You glue broken ceramics back together then highlight the glued cracks with gold rather than trying to hide the breaks. That's the basis of what I do to re-create people's special things."

As yet, no takers for the wool.

"I started my business, Broken is Beautiful, by repairing things for Sumner locals. People were always grateful and, now it's hard to buy new things, repair is more important than ever. When I'm taking a break from repair and re-creation, I like to drink tea. My favourite is Kenya Bold, although I've been trying New Zealand-grown Zealong tea. I know I should swap completely to Zealong because buying local is more sustainable. But old habits and tastes die hard. Kenya Bold has helped me through too many crises; I won't desert it easily."

First wool taker. The large man opposite me in the circle has thrown his arm in the air.

"Andrey, what's your connection?" I'm grateful Lynda organised name tags so I could say 'Andrey' smoothly. Fran remembers names because she's a teacher and Lynda has lots of practise at meetings, but I usually only meet one person at a time.

I hold the end of the wool and throw the ball to Andrey; a thick purple length of yarn joins us. Andrey is an intense-looking guy in his early thirties who flamboyantly fills the space he occupies. He has an intriguing, colourful tattoo covering one arm, a thick mop of mid-brown wavy hair, an impressive handlebar moustache and bright orange shorts.

"Hello, I'm Andrey Putin. No relation to the former dictator. Although I am from Russia by way of Finland and Slovenia. Because I am Russian, my second-favourite drink is black tea. Like you, Julia, I am excellent at repairing things, and building. I am building a tiny house on wheels. I do everything myself. If I don't know how to do something, I learn. I love learning! I love many things! I love Aotearoa. I love Ōtautahi. I love freedom. I love IPA, my first-favourite drink. You know IPA? India Pale Ale? With great flavour. Not so very Russian, though. Vodka I can drink, but IPA I love. I learn about brewing in my work as a Production Assistant at Three Boys Brewery. When I'm not working at Three Boys or on my tiny house, I like to cycle around the Christchurch Port Hills."

Lynda puts her hand up and Andrey passes her the wool; a fuzzy yellow mohair thread joins them. "I'm a keen cyclist too. At least I was and will be again. I'm looking forward to welcoming my daughter into the world, so my knees don't hit my stomach when I get on my road bike."

The hands of two young women go up simultaneously. We didn't plan how to manage two people wanting to talk at the same time, but Lynda doesn't miss a beat handing over the wool. "Zahra and Victoria, one of you hold the strand and the other the ball." Zahra takes the ball and unrolls some wool so Victoria can hold it; a pink and blue piece of yarn connects them with Lynda.

Zahra looks at the wool. "How appropriate, or traditional, depending on how you think about such things. I'm Zahra Kämpfer and I work as an arborist. Victoria and I are also looking forward to our babies who will be born in August. We don't know their sex yet and we don't want to. We'll give our babies names that don't limit them by gender. Our goal is to create full human beings for whom sex is not a defining characteristic."

Zahra has stunning blonde dreadlocks down to her waist which hang heavy on her head. Zahra's clothing contrasts with her dreads; it's all sharp-edged. She has shiny pointed boots over jeggings and a square-cut jacket. She has a mouth that turns down at the corners even when she's smiling. Are some babies born with downturned mouths or do people develop them over time?

"I like recreational biking too. Perhaps you can give us tips on how to keep cycling for as long as possible when you are pregnant, Lynda? We have a tandem we will put kiddie seats on. Although, I'm much keener on biking than Victoria, aren't I, sweetie?"

This group is going to produce a lot of babies, although our workshops will finish in July, before Victoria and Zahra are due. Not so Lynda. She, Fran, and I discussed how our timing of this trial of Humans with Stories is not ideal, given Lynda's pregnancy. With typical Lynda determination and energy, she wanted to push ahead and co-facilitate.

"This is the next step beyond Dolls with Stories. It's time to get on with it. And I'm going to be part of it! When our baby is born, Robbie can look after her as much as me. We're both her parents."

"What about breast-feeding and not sleeping?" I asked.

"Julia, you know me better than that! Where there's a will, there's a way. I'm not lacking in will!"

Lynda's right: I would never criticise her determination.

Zahra continues. "We wondered if this is the right time to bring children into the world. So many challenges; so much uncertainty. But can there ever be a right time? What would the world be without children? We must have hope!"

One of the two remaining men puts his hand up at shoulder level.

"Zahra, can you please pass Eeman the ball of wool?" Zahra hands the wool over and a green length of garden twine connects her with Eeman. I realise, too late, Victoria didn't speak; Zahra did the talking for both of them.

Eeman has a friendly face and a warm smile. His white T-shirt and jeans are spotless, but well-worn.

"*Apa kabar? Saya* Eeman. Meaning, how's it going? My name is Eeman. Hope is a cornerstone of my life. Hope, faith and charity are the pillars of my Christian beliefs. I grew up on a volcano in the far north of Sulawesi, an Indonesian island where my family grows cabbages and carrots. I travelled to this beautiful country of New Zealand because I heard about it from cycle tourists who visited our village. After coming here I met a beautiful New Zealander who I love, but part of my heart remains in our volcanic highlands. I teach English. I help migrant children in Ōtautahi schools. With climate migration, there are many children to help."

Fran has raised her hand. Eeman passes Fran the ball of wool and a sparkly turquoise strand joins them. I particularly like this wool.

"Hi, I'm Fran Nobell and it's lovely to be in this diverse group of human beings. My connection with Eeman is I also teach children, tamariki. My speciality is tamariki with learning challenges – I create education programmes to suit each child. I have a daughter called Holly who is a hairdresser in Ōtautahi. However, what I really want to tell you about today is a special journey I am starting. I'm adopted and I'm looking for my birth whānau. I want to find my iwi and the marae I'm from. Literally, find my tribe."

How, in a decade of friendship, did I not recognise Fran is of Māori descent? Her hair is dark and curly, and her skin is brown. However, lots of different ethnicities have brown skin and dark curly hair. Don't Māori people normally have straight hair? I remember my comments about karakia and Māori with embarrassment. I look at Lynda, who raises her eyebrows. When we all became friends through OA, Fran told Lynda and me about her abusive birth mother and being in State care before she was adopted. She never mentioned being Māori and we never delved into that area of Fran's life again. Why not? Did Fran put us off? Why can't I remember something so important? And why has Fran now decided to find her birth family?

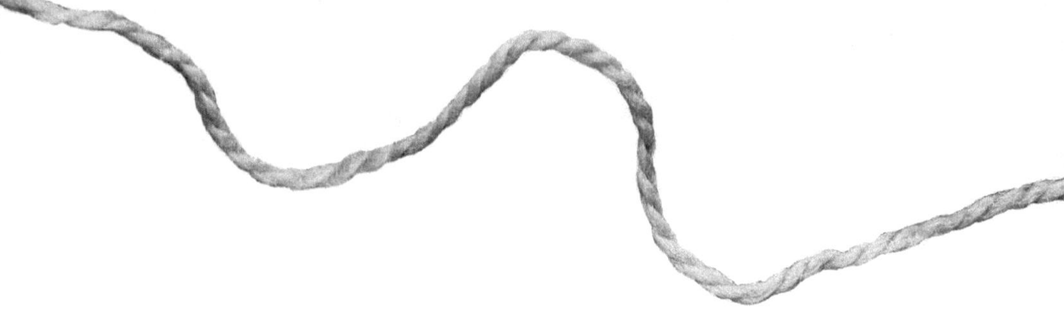

JULIA

7 March 2030

After Fran's surprise announcement, I would like a break to recover my equilibrium. However, ball-of-wool introductions demand seeing the exercise all the way through. It's hard to pick wool strands off the floor.

"Thank you, Fran, for sharing your news. What else would you like to tell us?" My words sound trite. I can't properly recognise Fran's announcement in a public forum.

"I became a teacher, a kaiako, because I wanted to help children. I still do, but it's getting so hard. Everyone's burnt out and no one listens when people say how hard it is. School management doesn't listen. The Ministry of Education doesn't listen. Kaiako aren't listening to each other. We don't have time for each other. We struggle to have time for the tamariki. Kaiako are leaving in droves and those of us still teaching wonder how long we can keep going."

Rosemary puts her hand up. I already know red-haired Rosemary, who had a brief relationship with Lynda's partner, Robbie, a decade ago. Robbie was staying at my house during the big COVID lockdown of 2020. To cut a long and embarrassing story short, I found Rosemary and Robbie kissing in my garden and behaved badly. I haven't forgotten and I doubt Rosemary will have, either. I'm surprised she joined a group with me as co-leader. Surely she hasn't forgotten my name? Though it was Lynda's name, not mine, on the notices we put up in local supermarkets and on notice boards.

Fran carefully passes the ball to Rosemary. An orange crocheted chain connects the two women. The chain dates from when I tried to teach Robbie to crochet as punishment for saying crocheting is something women do.

"Why anyone wants to make knots in perfectly good wool to create strange blankets and ugly decorations is beyond me," he'd said.

"Bet you can't do it," I laughed.

"Bet I can, lassie."

As it turned out, Robbie was good at crochet. Of course, he is good with his hands. Robbie runs the repair side of my Broken is Beautiful business. When my life got back on track, through my friendship with Fran and Lynda, Robbie took on repairs while I grew my re-creation activities. He has made a tremendous success of our local repair service. Although Robbie is Scottish and arrived in New Zealand in 2018, he now knows more people in the seaside suburbs than I do. After Robbie and Rosemary split up, he and Lynda got to know each other through mountain biking classes. They've been together ever since.

"Kia ora, I'm Rosemary Barne and I'm a doctor. Doctoring and teaching definitely have burnout in common. There aren't enough hours or minutes in the day to see all the patients wanting appointments, let alone get through our ever-increasing admin. As professionals, we're supposed to help patients and support each other. But we're all so exhausted we can't help ourselves, let alone each other.

"Enough about the miseries of medicine, though. I love cycling, like Lynda and Andrey. I try to bike regularly, though between my partner and two children and my job, I have minimal free time. I've had to give up mountain biking because I can't stay fit enough to enjoy the steep hills around Ōtautahi. I came here a decade ago to complete my medical training, loved the place and stayed on. Funnily enough, I met Julia early in my time here. Julia has the most amazing mosaic bench in her garden. You made it yourself, right, Julia?"

"Yes, out of crockery that broke during the earthquakes." The mosaic sofa was where I discovered Robbie and Rosemary kissing. "I should take the wool back from you, given our connection."

Rosemary hands me the ball of wool, unwinding black and white threads intertwined. This wool reminds me of the blackball sweets my gran kept in a jar which my brother, Johnno, and I would raid, hoping Gran wouldn't notice.

I stroke the black-and-white wool with my index finger. "I said I re-create objects, but I didn't explain properly. Right now I'm making a sculpture out of a piano; its soundboard cracked because the moisture in the air is changing so rapidly. It's a family heirloom the owners don't want to lose entirely so I'm making a clock out of the keys. The clock will have a different chime each hour – a musical clip from recordings the owners took of the piano being played before it cracked."

The remaining man puts his hand up and I throw the ball of wool across the centre of the circle to him. The strand that unrolls is the bright red of a love heart emoticon; I bought it for a scarf, but love heart emoticons aren't my style. The man fumbles the ball and drops it, saying, "Oops, sorry, how clumsy."

"It's my fault. I should have passed it more carefully," I say as he picks it up.

"Hi, everyone," says the apologiser, straightening up. "I'm Stephen John."

My brain glitches on Stephen's name. I will have to make an effort to remember whether he is called Stephen or John. Stephen looks a similar age to me, which is nearly sixty (I would prefer to forget how near sixty I am, as sixty is older than I want to be). He's wearing a blue merino T-shirt, faded jeans, and walking shoes that have seen plenty of kilometres. He has an approachable face with a trim beard and shaved head and only a tiny spare tyre around his middle. However, I'm in no position to comment on the spare tyres of others. Despite being thin, I can't stop weight accumulating around my mid-section these days.

"I like instruments and music," Stephen says. "I help people by singing their songs."

What an interesting-sounding job. Does he sing songs people have told him they like? On what occasions? Stephen pauses for so long I'm not sure he is going to explain.

"How do you sing people's songs? What sorts of songs?" I prompt.

"I work with people in hospice or hospital care. They tell me about their lives, and I help them create their own song."

"And then?" I ask.

"Some people don't want anyone else to hear their song. Some people want to record it and give it to their families. Some people ask me to come back and sing it with them as company. Some people want to throw a party where we sing their song before they die."

Stephen hesitates again.

"I've never heard of that sort of work," I say.

"Possibly not. I invented it."

"What else can you tell us about your life, or what you like or do, Stephen?"

"I live high on Scarborough Hill with my wife in a house we built," Stephen says, then grimaces in a strange way, as if he didn't want to tell us this very ordinary thing.

"We live on Scarborough too," Lynda says. "Though I'm already holding a strand of wool, so you don't have to pass me the ball."

However, Stephen rapidly passes the wool to Lynda and a grey strand unrolls, the colour of the sky when a cold nor'easterly wind blows through Sumner.

"Okay, some more about me," Lynda says. "I live on Scarborough Hill with my partner, Robbie, in a house we are doing up. I'm CEO of Dolls with Stories. It's a social enterprise Fran, Julia and I set up ten years ago. We help tamariki to have good lives."

Victoria has her hand up. Great. Although she's holding the wool from when Zahra took the ball, it's better she speaks too. She rolls out a smooth cream-coloured strand that looks like its purpose in life is to be a baby's bootie.

"Hello. I'm Victoria Harding. Giving tamariki the best life is so important. I'm very excited Zahra and I will have babies at the same time, so they grow up together in our family, our whānau."

Victoria is a Rubenesque blonde with flowing style. Her lipstick tones in with her glasses' frames and her floral scarf. Blonde braids circle her head. Her clothes flow around her body in an overlay of textures – velvet, linen and chiffon integrating artfully. There was a doctor at our OA support group who had the same ability as Victoria to wear unusual clothes with inimitable style.

"When I'm not working as a nurse, which takes far too much of my time right now, I like shopping for clothes in second-hand stores or making my own."

I put my hand up. It's time to cast off our wool for the evening, now everyone has contributed. When Victoria hands the wool over, the last connecting strand is a variegated yarn in all the colours of the rainbow.

"I make my own clothes too, Victoria, although you are much more skilled than me, judging by your beautiful outfit.

"Thank you, everyone, for your contributions. The last part of this exercise is putting our wool-web on the floor, so it reminds us of our connections as we eat the tasty-looking kai waiting for us on the bench, courtesy of Fran. Everyone please take a picture of the web and send them to our Warble group as a memory of how much we have in common from our different perspectives."

Everyone carefully puts the wool strands they're holding down at their feet, and we admire the colourful, star-shaped pattern on the floor.

"Some last reminders," I say. "I look forward to seeing you all again in two weeks. Like we said in our introductory email, the workshop will be one person telling a story from their lives each week. We'll send you a link tonight to the DonkeysRU app to pick the order in which people will speak at workshops. The shortest tail will go first."

Lynda's IT guru developed DonkeysRU as a fun and random way of sorting out who goes first. You create your virtual group and a paddock full of donkeys appears, one for each person. There are different coloured donkeys, donkeys with striped shirts, donkeys in high heels or hats, donkeys with musical instruments. Everyone chooses a donkey with the incentive to be quick, so you get your favourite donkey. Your name appears on your donkey and, once all the donkeys are taken, their tails unroll to a trumpet sound. Then the donkeys line up in order of tail length with tails held high. DonkeysRU makes me laugh every time we use it.

I hear snippets of animated conversation over herbal tea, hummus with a range of crackers for different dietary requirements, and vegan, gluten-free cake that looks dense and chocolatey and tastes even better than it looks. Fran offered to organise tonight's food to take the stress off Lynda and me. She's always so generous with her time and her energy. I watch her circulating the room. She looks more tired than I ever remember seeing her, with shoulders curved inwards. Lynda looks similarly exhausted; not surprising given her state of pregnancy and CEO role.

I do my best to talk with each group member, bringing up something shared in the workshop. I don't make it to Rosemary but absolve myself of guilt when I see her chatting with Fran and Lynda.

Before we leave, Fran brings us back together for our closing karakia. I know this one well because we used it at OA. It speaks of home, not least because it reminds me of my garden, originally created by my gran.

Fran leads off. "The sun has set upon our gathering for the day."

We follow on. "The birds are silent, the worms are still, the world is at rest."

"The night has arrived, my friends."

"So, tie up the waka."

"Have we landed?"

"We have landed."

As the group files out the door of the Surf Club into the late summer sun, I smile at Lynda and Fran with relief and satisfaction. Humans with Stories has attracted an interesting group of people with lots of potential for sharing. Although Rosemary's presence makes me nervous; I could have done without her being part of our workshops.

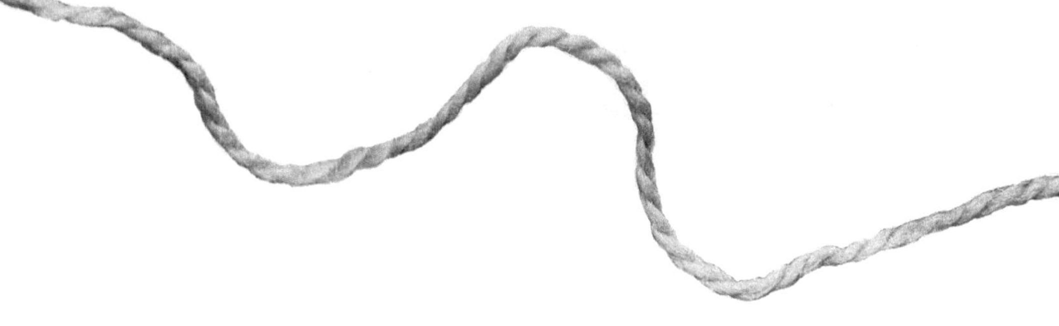

STEPHEN

7 March 2030

I'm sick of myself. How could I have thought going to the Humans with Stories group would be different? I can't change. I'm always the same old Stephen, making up a version of the world how I want it to be. A pretend world with a house and a wife. Not a lonely man in a caravan. I trudge along the Esplanade towards Scarborough Hill. I don't notice the sun or the salty waves breaking on the rocks.

I didn't know anyone at the workshop, which was a good start. Not surprising. It isn't like I hang out with people in Sumner, or anyone, except the people I write songs for. I've seen Julia cycling around but never spoken to her. I'm not a cyclist, I'm a walker. It's way too steep to cycle up Scarborough Hill. Walking is easy. I can take myself out the door straight onto the trails and forget about the world and the people in it.

Ouch! I just tripped on a rock. I need to pay more attention. The Esplanade used to be a wide pavement beside the sea where I avoided dog walkers and women with pushchairs while carrying my groceries home. Now it's full of potholes scoured out by the waves. The wall at the edge of the pavement is breaking down, dropping stones on the walking path. The council raised the wall a few years ago, but that didn't work. It's more broken than ever. Looks like the council has given up.

If I owned a house along the Esplanade road, on the other side of the wall, I'd be worried. Good thing my house is safe up on the hill. A while back, there were a lot of 'For Sale' signs on the Esplanade. 'House For Sale' is a well-used song title. 'House for sale, You can read it on the sign' is the start of Lucifer's chorus. More prosaic than usual real estate language. 'Enjoy the seaside every day of your existence', was one of my favourite signs. The seaside was trying to come in the door. Not so enjoyable. These days there are no signs. It's more like Bon Jovi's 'This House is Not For Sale'. 'Outside the sky is coal black, the streets are on fire. The picture window's cracked, and there's nowhere to run.'

No one buys houses along the Esplanade now because insurance companies finally smelled the ozone. No insurance. No mortgages. No sales. People were shocked. 'Government must step in', headlines blared. 'People betrayed by politicians.' The right-wing government coalition reviewed the Earthquake Commission insurance scheme but there was no spare money to extend it. The Finance Minister must have been desperate, or ready to quit politics, when she said, "Anyone want taxes to increase?"

As the 'For Sale' signs vanished, the Esplanade gardens withered and died. Salt water breaking over the road can't have helped. A few weathered signs still remain. Maybe forgotten. Maybe people still hopeful against the odds.

Maybe I can still tell the truth at the next workshop. Will anyone remember what I said in the first one? Do I remember what anyone else said? Maybe I should test myself. My memory doesn't seem to be what it was these days. I might need practise.

Fran, Lynda, and Julia sat together up the front. Three people seems like a lot to run a group. I don't remember what they wore. Clothing isn't something I spend time thinking about, it's not very interesting. And caravans don't have much wardrobe space. I wear this blue merino T-shirt every second day; I have a grey one for alternate days. I have two jackets which I also alternate and two pairs of jeans.

Lynda was both very pregnant and energetic. Julia was nervous. Fran was confident and in charge of the prayers at the beginning and end. Why do we need Māori prayers at a meeting? Fran is Māori but it's not like the rest of us are. I don't get the need for religion. It's just another story people tell, like about Father Christmas or the tooth fairy. The Indonesian guy was religious too. Even his name – something like 'Amen'. And people get so intense about religion. Not that Amen was intense. There was a big Russian guy who had enough intensity for everyone. Was his name Andy?

The woman doctor was named after a herb or a spice. Fennel? No, unlikely. Saffron? Poppy? Oh yes, Rosemary. She didn't give away much when she spoke. Doctors are useful to have around, as are nurses. Like the beautiful blonde woman who is having a baby with her severe partner. I don't remember what the partner does. If the severe one is a nurse, I wouldn't like her to be my nurse, I'd choose the blonde woman any day. She almost reminds me of Cynthia, my wife, except no one is the same as Cynthia.

Maybe I won't go to the next workshop. I'm not sure I see the point. Even if I tell the truth to this group, how will it make a difference? Who is going to be interested in my life? I'm barely interested in it. And the group has too many different people – there's sure to be conflict and I don't like conflict.

I hum song concepts as I walk to get my mind off conflict that might not arise. I've only got a couple of days before I see my current song client again and he hasn't got much time left. He's not a nice person, but I agreed to write his song. Writing people's songs gives me puzzles to solve, something focused to spend my time on. My client was an oil executive. He wants a song that makes him sound as big as he thought he was. He boasts about the corporate empire he created. He doesn't seem at all sorry about the damage his industry did and is still doing. He says climate change was always going to happen. Once humans discovered energy they weren't going to leave it in the ground – we might as well have a good time doing whatever we can while we can. My client's good time is over, however, because he's in hospice care.

What style will I make the oil exec's song? He played guitar in a rock and roll band when he was at uni; that's the only thing I really like about him. Strong beat. Virtuoso electric guitar riffs. They fit. I play riffs in my head as I walk up the Scarborough Hill tracks, my pace quickening as I match my step to the music. Now I'm keen to get home and play on my synth, guitar, and computer in my caravan. I haven't lived in a house since the 1990s, when Cynthia and I bought our Scarborough section at the wild southern end of the hill, rather than the upmarket northern end. We were going to build our dream home there.

To save money, we bought a small caravan and moved it onto the section. I tried to come up with a house plan because I was a software engineer while

Cynthia was an accountant and quilt maker. However, I got log-jammed. I kept on finding things I needed to know before I could start on a design. If we didn't properly think everything through we might get something wrong. However, there are so many parts of a house to think about that you can't think of all of them at once. Do you want to see the sunrise from your breakfast bar? Or your bed? Do you want your outdoor living to face the sun? Or escape the wind? A short driveway is cheaper but then your house is near the road where you can hear cars. Should the vegetable garden be near the trees for shelter? Might the tree roots take up all the water and nutrients? If I started, but made a wrong choice, I'd have to begin again. Beginning again wastes time and effort – mistakes massacre efficiency. That's what my father would say.

Dad was a manager in a freezing works where the overriding goal was to kill as many cows as possible in the least amount of time. Every minute counted, and mistakes wasted product, so Dad didn't like mistakes. He didn't like me making mistakes either. When I made mistakes he would point them out in front of whoever was around. That's enough to put you off making mistakes. And when you get belted if you make a big mistake, you *really* don't want to make mistakes. I have become excellent at not making mistakes by thinking through every detail. The only time I'm confident I won't make mistakes is when I create and play music.

I started playing guitar at high school with a group of friends. We wanted to form a band. Mum encouraged me and helped me buy my first guitar. Dad said I'd better not think music was a profession. Musicians are a bunch of long-haired layabouts who are mostly broke. I kept my music away from Dad and practised in my room with headphones. I never told him when our band played. I studied software engineering at uni because I knew Dad was right. I wasn't good enough or confident enough to become a professional musician. I never stopped loving music, though. In music, I feel entire and secure. The rest of the time, I muddle along like everyone else, or worse.

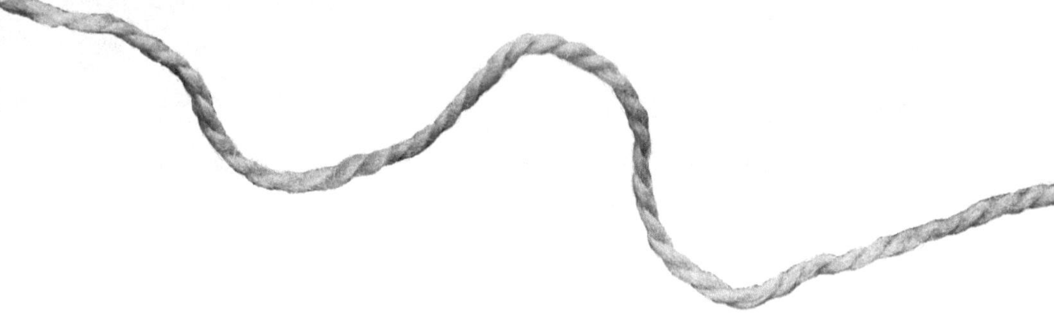

JULIA

21 March 2030

"Kia ora and welcome to our second workshop of Humans with Stories," I say. "Today, Eeman will share a story with us, and I'm looking forward to trying his vegan Christmas biscuits."

Eeman has brought two platefuls of biscuits in a plethora of shapes and sizes. I particularly fancy the monkeys with icing balls for eyes. He also brought carrot sticks with peanut sauce.

"To remind you of our schedule, Humans with Stories will run for ten sessions, meeting once a fortnight. Our intro session was number one. This is the first of eight sessions in which one person will tell their story each week. We'll have a wrap-up session in July. I sent out the speaking order based on our DonkeysRU selections – first Eeman, then Rosemary, me, Victoria, Andrey, Zahra, Lynda and Stephen. All okay so far?"

Heads nod, except for Lynda who is looking out the window. Strange, it's not like her to get distracted and there's nothing visible except a building mass of dark-grey clouds over a sullen grey sea. The forecast for tonight wasn't good. I hope it's not raining by the time we leave.

"Fran, please lead our karakia, then Lynda will explain how today's session will work, following up on our email."

"Tēnā koutou, tēnā koutou, tēnā koutou katoa," says Fran. "Today we'll try our karakia in te reo Māori; I hope you all had time to practise with the recording. However, you don't have to be perfect. The point is to try."

She starts with, "Kua whiti a Tamanui i te rangi!!!"

There's a silence.

"Your turn now," prompts Fran.

I should have practised more. "Ka tīoriori ngā manu, ka oreore ngā ngārara, ka korikori te taiao," I say, accompanied by background burbles.

"He rā hou kua ara mai, e hika mā," Fran responds.

"Ā tēnā, ki te hoe," I say. This time I can hear Lynda.

"Kua tau?" Fran says back.

"E tau ana." Finally, more uptake from the wider group on the easy last sentence.

"Thank you, everyone, a great start," Fran says. "Practise will make it even better!"

Lynda still doesn't seem wholly present but follows on with our planned introduction. "Tēnā kōrua, Fran and Julia. Lovely to see you all again. Please put your phones in airplane mode with sound off, then switch 5G direct comms back on."

Everyone taps on their devices.

"Let's check that the Humans with Stories Warble group chat is working offline. Everyone send a message saying 'Hi' through to the group," Lynda says.

I see my screen fill up with a bunch of 'Hi' messages next to little avatar bubbles. Mine has an oval face, and shoulder-length straight brown hair topped with a bowler hat made out of flowers. Lynda's avatar has a pixie haircut and a cheeky grin and Fran's a wide smile with kind eyes under dark hair. Andrey's is distinguished by a Hercule Poirot moustache under brown eyes. Zahra's dreadlocks cover most of her avatar's face. Victoria's avatar has large round eyes and a red-orange-yellow floral scarf around her neck. Rosemary's avatar has rectangular glasses and curly red hair more contained than Rosemary's actual locks. She tries to tie them into a bun which perpetually unwinds, so curls pop out in a halo around her face. Eeman's avatar has an asymmetrical haircut and an Indonesian flag on one cheek. Stephen's is a pink oval devoid of facial features under bowl-cut brown hair. Weird. Once everyone has sent a message I release them to the group, as Fran and Lynda and I had discussed.

"Tonight Eeman will tell us his story," Lynda continues. "Like with our ball-of-wool intros, when you hear something you relate to, write a brief message on your phone and send it. Then put your cell phone on the front table and Eeman will give you a gift, or koha."

We brainstormed the koha idea when designing the workshops. "Should there be an incentive to bring your phone up, beyond showing you have found a connection?" Fran asked.

"Like what?" Lynda said. "A gold star?"

"Ha, ha," Fran said. "I'm thinking of a small gift – let's call it a koha – in recognition of the connection made."

"That sounds like a lot of work," Lynda said. "Who's going to provide the koha? Us?"

"No, the speaker – connecting them with the group," Fran replied.

"Do you think people will fall for that? They aren't children," Lynda said. "And they've got enough to do preparing their story and bringing kai."

"It isn't about falling for anything. It's about reinforcing good behaviour without being too explicit about it. Everyone enjoys getting a present, even adults. You two can help participants come up with koha ideas, preferably things that are handmade. Once people invest time and effort they're more likely to take the workshops seriously."

I'm always a sucker for anything involving creativity. "I like the idea," I said. "I'm happy to help people create koha."

"Do we need ground rules?" Lynda says. "Like amount of money spent?"

Fran considered this. "Koha should be edible or usable. No ornaments. And mostly, or all, made from materials people already have. We don't want to create extra waste or have people buying anything."

I phoned Eeman as the first speaker because he had less than two weeks to come up with and execute a koha concept. "I don't have much time. Do I have to?" he said.

As we talked it through, Eeman became more enthusiastic. "In Indonesian culture, we take gifts when we visit people," he said. "It is part of Aotearoa culture to bring kai when you eat with someone, and now I am learning it is also Aotearoa culture to give and receive koha. I see why it's a good idea. How about decorated paperweights?"

"Paperweights? Do you think people still use paper?" I had thought they did, but Lynda made me question that belief.

"Teachers do. Our children can't all afford digital devices, so we often do projects on paper. At the beginning of the year, we have an art class where the children each decorate a stone. I make one too. When the children give me work to look at, they give me their stone, so I know whose work I have."

"Decorated stones could work," I say, "as long as they can be useful." Stones are not ideal koha, but we need to cut Eeman some slack as the first participant.

"They can hold tablecloths if you are eating outside. They can be bookends or worry stones. You know, when I was a child I dreamed of being an artist. Now the only art I do is decorating paperweights." Eeman smiles sadly. "I already have some paperweights I've made and a collection of stones I can use; that will be not so hard."

Before the meeting, we put Eeman's paperweights in a covered basket so they will be a surprise. "Eeman, thank you for being our first speaker."

"Hello. Today I'm going to tell you how God brought cycle tourists from Aotearoa to Sulawesi for Christmas and changed my life." Eeman clasps his hands together and speaks faster than usual. I wouldn't have expected a teacher to be nervous talking to a group, but they aren't normally telling their classes personal stories.

"I was on holiday in my village of Guaan, home from teacher training because it was Christmas. I was headed out on my moped to catch up with friends when I saw an arguing trio of *bule*, that's foreigners. There were two hot, sweaty adults beside a teenager with long blonde hair under her sunhat.

"'There's got to be a shop somewhere,' the man said.

"'Have you seen one? I haven't!' the woman replied.

"'I'm super hungry,' the teenager said. 'I'm not cycling any further till I get something to eat.'

"'How about we try left?' the man suggested.

"'We already tried left,' the woman sighed.

"The teenager looked at her phone. 'There's nothing on the map in this village. Why did we come here?'

"'Do you need help?' I asked. 'I'm Eeman.'

"Three faces turned and looked at me like they'd found a well in a desert.

"'You know where we can buy food?' the woman asked.

"I took them to Café Guaan, which triples as a general store, gaming centre and eating place. It's not signposted, but everyone in the village knows where it is. The man had Bali chicken, which lived in the window cabinet all day. Either he was used to Indonesian food, or he'd be vomiting by tonight. The woman and teenager eyed the Bali chicken with suspicion and chose Indomie noodles with boiled eggs. They introduced themselves as Geoff, Iona, and blonde Nicky.

"'Is there a place around here we can stay?' Iona asked.

"'How about the guesthouse on the lake?' I suggested.

"'They weren't helpful when we stopped,' Iona replied. 'We enquired about a room. First, they said the place was full. When we pointed out there were no cars outside, they said things were broken. When we said we only needed a bed, not even power, they said it was extremely expensive. I don't think they want us.'

"'Why don't you come back to my house?' I said, somewhat rashly. I prayed my *ibu* – my mother – would be okay with three extra mouths to feed at Christmas. I hoped she would say at Christmastime we should especially think of others. Mary needed a place to sleep when she was going to have Baby Jesus. There was no room available, but a kind innkeeper let them stay in his stable.

"We did better than straw in a stable – my ibu told my little brother to share my bed so the visitors could sleep in my brother's room. He started to complain, but when he found out he could sit next to a tall blonde teenager from Aotearoa he shut up. He spent their entire visit looking sideways at her; afterwards, he told me she was the most beautiful person he had ever seen in real life."

Andrey goes up to the front of the room, puts his phone on the table, takes the lid off the basket and chooses a stone. I saw the stones beforehand and wonder if he's chosen the most spectacular piece, a panther painted black on white quartz. Lynda also puts her phone at the front. I reckon she'll have picked the koala painted on beach-washed wood because she still has a special soft toy koala her parents gave her. Lynda's walking oddly; I hope she's okay. Next, Rosemary goes up with her phone. It's good people are coming up together. It's less disruptive than if they come up one by one.

"I brought Christmas biscuits for us to eat today because that's what we ate with Geoff, Iona, and Nicky when they arrived. It's a Christmas tradition, baking twenty different types of biscuits and giving them to visitors, including visiting Christmas monkeys. Christmas monkeys make trouble if you don't give them biscuits."

I tap a message into my phone and go up to the front. I like cooking for special occasions. That's what Gran trained me and Johnno to do. I bake elaborate birthday cakes for Lynda and Fran and Robbie, and we get together for an evening of talking, laughing and eating. I select a stone with a delicately painted dragonfly. As I turn to sit down I start, because Stephen has come up behind me and is waiting quietly.

Eeman pauses until we both sit back down, then returns to his story.

"Geoff, Iona, and Nicky only stayed two nights with us, but they changed my horizons. If people could come to Indonesia, why couldn't I go to their country? Air flights were more expensive than anything I had considered possible. But maybe I could do it. Not anymore, of course. With energy quotas, I'll never be able to buy enough extra units for an international flight. I won't be going home …" Eeman looks out at the sea before he continues his narrative.

"I worked hard once I qualified as a teacher. I taught in a local school, gave private lessons in the evenings, worked in a shop in my holidays, and saved up for the flight. I got a special work visa for Aotearoa New Zealand. Finally, I bought a ticket. I was so fixated on leaving our village, I never thought how long it might be before I could return. I didn't think about how my parents would manage their fields, which now makes me ashamed. The weather has become so changeable my family's crops don't grow well. Warmer weather means caterpillars and fungi attack the cabbages and carrots. Big rainstorms wash away the soil. There's often not enough money to send vegetables to the city to sell them. Then my parents give food away in the village, which is the right thing to do. But giving doesn't buy the insulin my nephew needs every day and which the government will not pay for.

"However, that's God's will. You can't argue with God. He sends us trials we must live through to become stronger. My ibu says she is content to hear my voice and know I'm in a good place. I met my wife, Deb, at church here and we are very happy together." Eeman looks at Lynda's stomach. "We hope to have our own children soon."

Zahra and Victoria come to the front with their phones and choose their stones. Have they related to Eeman wanting a child?

"What about Geoff and Iona?" I ask. "Did you see them again when you arrived here?"

"They live in Tāmaki Makarau and I'm in Ōtautahi. I see them on social media. Nicky went overseas to study and now she can't get back from the USA. She comments on my posts and asks how I'm enjoying life in Ōtautahi because it's her favourite place in the world."

Eeman squares his shoulders. "I thank God for giving me the inspiration to come to Aotearoa, where the government helps me if I can't earn money. Where I live near the sea and can see mountains. Where I help children learn English so they can properly belong in this country. Where I have met all of you. I look forward to hearing your stories in the next weeks."

Fran is the last person to take her phone up and collect a paperweight. Then Lynda and I walk to the front of the circle to conclude the session.

"Thanks for your beautiful story, Eeman," I say. "And for the lovely gifts. Now we will enjoy the kai you made us after our karakia."

However, before we can move towards the food Lynda lets out a strangled cry, which is overtopped by the sea siren starting its unholy ascending and descending howl.

STEPHEN

21 March 2030

The siren means it's time for me to hurry towards Scarborough Hill. Damn. I was looking forward to Christmas biscuits. Sirens mean flooding is likely. They were put in after the Canterbury earthquakes to warn people about tsunamis. Then the flooding started, and they got a lot more frequent use. When intermittent whoops begin you are supposed to go home. When there's a continuous howl you're supposed to stay where you are, off roads and away from steep hillsides.

I've put my rain jacket on and pulled my overtrou out of my pack before remembering my cell phone is on the table at the front of the room. Everyone else is also at the front of the room, standing around Lynda. Whatever the problem is, there are enough people helping her. I go to the bench to take a couple of biscuits for my walk and am skirting the edge of the group when Julia's words catch my attention.

"Lynda, what were you thinking?" Julia says. "You came to the workshop after your contractions started? I could have run it on my own! All you needed to do was text me."

"Julia, not now," Fran says. "Lynda, sweetie, how far apart do you think the contractions are? Where's Robbie?"

Lynda breathes hard, sitting on a chair with her hands braced over the lip of the seat. Then she sits up straighter. "Thought it wasn't yet. Three weeks to go. Contractions suddenly stronger. Called Robbie before coming. He's surfing. Magnet. Planned for ages. Pooled energy quotas. Driving back now."

Victoria moves to Lynda's side and puts her hand on her shoulder. "Lynda, I'm a nurse. What's your birth plan?"

Lynda grimaces. "Christchurch Women's."

"It would be better if you can get to the hospital. Anyone got a car?"

Birthing is definitely not in my expertise set. Or sphere of interest. However, I can't get round the group without them noticing so I wait for a good time to make a break while eating a biscuit. I doubt anyone has come in a car. People don't use their tradeable energy quotas to drive short distances if they even own a car. Lots of people gave up cars, like me, when the climate taxes for fossil-fuel vehicles were introduced. I was trying to economise and figured I could get a car through a share scheme if I needed one. Turned out there was a lot more demand than cars. And electric car supply dried up when every country in the world wanted them. The lucky people were the ones with electric cars already. The smart ones got solar panels as well as electric cars.

It seems like forever we've had tradeable energy quotas – TEQs. Everyone gets a weekly allowance, which reduces each year as the country weans itself off fossil fuels. You can sell energy you don't use. You can buy more if you can afford it. Although no one wants to appear energy wealthy. The Green-led Government who boldly implemented TEQs as a global test case promptly got voted out at the next election. To everyone's surprise, though, the next government didn't repeal TEQs but focused on tax breaks instead.

"I don't want to be a nuisance," Lynda says.

"I'll see if my car share has anything available," Rosemary says.

"Oh, you're a doctor," says Julia. "Surely you can help?"

"I'm a psychiatrist," Rosemary says. "It's been a very long time since I delivered a baby."

Fran is trying to catch Julia's eye. "Julia," she says, "I've got to go. Holly's home and she's not well. I can't get caught in Sumner and leave her alone overnight."

"Of course, you go," Julia says, turning back towards Lynda.

Fran puts her jacket on and rushes out the door into the car park. Where's this weather coming from? Usually, bad weather comes from the south but the sky to the north, over the sea, is nearly black. Is that a funnel shape forming below the clouds? Is the siren sounding a tornado warning rather than a storm warning? That would explain why it's wailing when there was no storm in the weather forecast. Should I warn people? However, it might not be a tornado. I've never seen one in real life because we don't have tornadoes here. How can I be sure?

Rosemary's looking at her phone. "There's no reception," she says.

Cell reception often goes out these days. Particularly when the weather is bad. I really need to say something about the clouds. The funnel shape is getting more obvious.

"Er, excuse me, there might be a tornado forming over the sea."

Everyone looks out the front window then back at each other, while Lynda's panting fills the room.

"What can we do?" Julia says.

"I have my cargo trailer," Andrey offers.

"Meaning what?" Julia asks.

"I could take Lynda to the hospital in it."

"You can't be serious."

"You have a better idea?" Andrey says.

"Let's do it," Lynda breaks in. "The longer we wait, the worse everything'll get." She goes to the door, supported by Victoria on one side and Julia on the other. Andrey throws wood and tools from the trailer onto the deck in the rising wind and Zahra carries them into the Surf Club. Lynda collapses into the trailer. It's just long enough for her to lie down with her knees bent.

"Does this make sense?" Julia says. I silently wonder with her.

"Let's get on with it," Lynda replies, and pulls the zipper on the translucent cargo cover closed.

"We're off," says Andrey and powers into action on his e-bike, tucking his head down against the wind swirling around the car park.

As cyclist and trailer disappear into blowing sea spray, the siren becomes a continuous stream of noise. Julia, Victoria, Zahra, Rosemary and I look at each other, then out to sea. The black funnel is moving closer, together with the waves. Who thought it was a good idea to hold workshops so near the beach?

"We should move somewhere safer," Zahra says. "Not this room with glass windows."

"Upstairs away from the sea?" Victoria asks.

"Upstairs isn't good in strong winds," Zahra says.

Julia is wringing her hands. Where's Eeman? The last time I saw him was when he finished telling his story. Has he left?

Rosemary calls out, "There's enough space in the storage room back here and it has no external windows. Oh, Eeman, you're here." I catch a glimpse of Eeman kneeling in the back room. As if any God is going to help us.

It's a tight squeeze in the mouldy-smelling room. Victoria has brought the biscuits in, so we eat our way through monkeys, palm trees, and volcanoes with icing lava streams. The silver balls make the monkey eyes crunch. Then the lights go out and hearing people breathing makes me think of sardines dying in a can.

"What do we do now?" Eeman says in a wobbly voice.

I know what to do to forget where I am, but other people might not like singing. Cynthia says, *Just suggest it, Stephen. If they don't want to sing, they won't.* "We could sing?"

"Sing?" Zahra doesn't sound keen.

"Singing is a great idea," says Victoria.

"We could sing a hymn," Eeman says.

I'm not going to sing a hymn. I search through songs downloaded on my phone. I have a wide range of music to help write songs for dying people because everyone likes different music. Of course, let's start with Creedence Clearwater Revival's 'Have you Ever Seen the Rain?' I put my phone into karaoke mode, enlarge the words, and we form a tight circle around the glowing screen. Next, we sing 'Here Comes the Rain Again' by the Eurythmics, then 'Thunder' by Imagine Dragons. This is my sort of praying.

"How about 'Amazing Grace?'" Eeman asks. It's a bit more hymn-like than I'd prefer but it's good for harmonising. Then we sing 'Riders on the Storm' by the Doors and belt out a torrent of noise that rises above any storm waves or tornadoes.

STEPHEN

21–22 March 2030

When we finish 'Riders on the Storm' it takes us all a moment to realise the siren is no longer sounding. Julia opens the storeroom door, and we can hear the sea, but there's no water in the main room. The streetlights are out so it's hard to tell how bad the weather is.

Zahra opens the car park door and looks out. The wind blows rain across the threshold. "Tornado's gone. Or never happened," she says.

I notice there are still carrot sticks and peanut sauce on the bench; we forgot to take them into the storeroom.

"Still no reception on Twinkle," Rosemary says. "Maybe the tornado took the tower out. Anyone got a signal?"

I join in the chorus of "No."

"I wish we could know how Lynda and Andrey are," says Julia. "We were all in too much of a panic to think clearly. They should have stayed here, with us."

"For all we know, the tornado never touched down," Zahra says. "We didn't hear anything."

"I need to go home," Eeman says. "I need to find out how Deb is."

People pull out rain jackets. I'm still wearing mine. Eeman walks rapidly towards the main part of Sumner. Zahra and Victoria pick up their bikes which had fallen on the deck, then follow him. Rosemary cycles west, towards the city.

"You live on Scarborough, right?" Julia says to me. "I'm walking that way. Best to go through the village, I think, even though the sirens have stopped. It's too dark to see the trip hazards on the Esplanade. It used to be such a nice place to walk and now it's a wreck."

"Okay," I say. I suddenly feel exhausted and wish I was already home, not having to walk up a big hill.

"Hang on," Julia says. "Eeman forgot his plates. I'd better put them in my bag."

She shuts and locks the Surf Club door then we walk past Coffee Culture, the shops, and the Sumner Library in misty rain. There's no flooding, nor any sign of damage beyond a few broken branches on the road. However, as we turn the corner onto Nayland Street, there's debris strewn across the pavement and the further we walk the worse it gets.

"What will have happened to my house? It's not far away. Do you think your house is okay?" Julia says.

"It's not likely the tornado reached my place. New Zealand tornadoes aren't that big." I very much hope the tornado stuck to the valley because nothing will hold a caravan to the ground in a tornado, although, of course, I've guyed it down.

As we walk east, towards Julia's house and Scarborough Hill, there's roofing iron twisted around power poles, entire trees lying across the pavement with their roots exposed and an overturned trampoline in the road. Clumps of people are sheltering under the remaining trees in front of damaged houses, looking at glowing screens. House contents blow past us. I pick up a knitted monster toy with one large, staring eye and the other eye patched over. No one needs a toy monster tonight.

A knot of elderly people shiver outside their fake-stone-clad retirement units. "They'll get exposure!" Julia says and turns towards them. I follow. It's not like anyone is waiting for me at home. Although surely the people's families or the police or someone else will be here soon to help them.

"Let's get inside. You can't stay out here," Julia says to the group.

"What if it comes back?" a man says, leaning on a walking stick.

"It won't," Julia says definitely.

"I can't go in my unit," says a woman sitting on her walker, clutching her cardigan around her shoulders. "It's got bits of roof missing."

"We'll help. Stephen, you look in that row of units and I'll check this one."

We each find a unit with no holes in the roof, walls, or windows.

Julia says, "I should have introduced myself earlier. I'm Julia, and this is Stephen. Who lives in units three and six?" After she raises her voice, two residents raise shaking hands.

"I'm Grant," and "I'm Pauline," the unit owners say.

"Grant and Pauline, nice to meet you. How about a slumber party tonight in your units?" Julia says.

The two look surprised but nod.

"Once everyone's inside, Stephen and I will make sure you're warm and have what you need. By tomorrow, I'm sure there'll be more help. Do either of you have a gas cooker?"

"I do," Pauline says.

"Excellent," says Julia. "Pauline, I'll come with you, and we'll make everyone a nice cup of tea. Stephen, you help people find what they need to sleep tonight and bring it to Grant or Pauline's."

Hang on, who is going to which house? Do I need to decide? It might be some people don't like each other. And how will elderly people sleep on the floor? Can they get down to floor level? Can they get up once they are that low down? Will there be enough room for mattresses? How will they cope with a single toilet? What if someone trips over someone else and gets hurt? Will that be our fault? I shuffle my feet and look at the bricks scattered on the lawn. Julia is already in Pauline's unit.

Unexpectedly, Grant comes to my rescue, pushing himself upright on his stick. "Tuesday night poker crew, you come to my house, and I will explore my capacious cupboards for a spot of whisky to liven up our tea." He leads five men into his unit and the remaining five women shuffle towards Pauline's door.

In multiple iterations, I organise mattresses, find clothes, locate glasses and medicine then take mugs to Pauline's unit to get tea. After their initial confusion, the group seem less upset than I expect. "We may be old," Pauline says, "but we've lots of experience of things not working properly. I grew up in post-war London with rationing and half the city littered with bomb craters. Most of us lived in these units during the Canterbury earthquakes. What a shame. All that repair and now our homes are damaged again."

By the time Julia and I leave the units it's long past midnight and there are still no streetlights. Emergency services are knocking on doors. A cheery rotund man in a St John's uniform asks if we are okay. "We're fine, thanks," Julia says. "And we helped the people in the retirement units get sorted. They're likely in bed by now."

As we go along Nayland Street, the destruction gets worse. The tornado has ripped a path through the centre of suburban Sumner. Julia is walking faster and faster, tripping on bricks and branches. However, as we walk another block and the damage reduces in scale, her pace slows again.

"It was my gran's house," she says. "She left it to me when she died."

"Oh, I'm sorry," I say. "When did she die?" That's a stupid question because I'm guessing Julia's about my age and, if you are around sixty, your grandparents are likely long dead.

"Years ago. I was only in my twenties. I looked after her when she was ill, and she died in her house, like she wanted. I've always thought I'd be the same, you know. Live in my house till I die. Gran's parents built the house. It's the only place she ever lived and the only place I've ever belonged. It's not just my house, it's my home. How do people sell and buy houses so easily?"

I understand being attached to a place. I haven't moved from the section Cynthia and I bought nearly thirty years ago as our forever home. Once there was only me forever lost its significance, but there was nowhere else I wanted to be.

We turn into Head Street. "Nearly there," Julia says. "Here's my garden gate; my front door is round the corner in Wiggins Street." She pulls up short, frowning and squinting into the dark. There's a little light in the sky now, from a new moon dodging between clouds. "What's happened to the big kōwhai tree?" She reaches through a hole in the fence to unlatch something and then pushes at the gate. It only opens a little way. "The tree must have fallen and blocked the gate."

Julia half-runs around the corner. She thrusts her hands in all her jacket pockets, then throws her jacket on the ground to check cardigan pockets until she finds her key, shoves it in the lock, pushes the door open and disappears from view.

I pick up her jacket, then hesitate. Perhaps I should go home and not bother her. I don't like to enter houses uninvited. Then I hear a wail erupt from inside the house. I debate what the right thing to do is until I find my feet taking me in the door and along the hallway towards Julia's cry. I find her staring at the branches of a large tree that have broken through a door and are taking up a lot of a small living room.

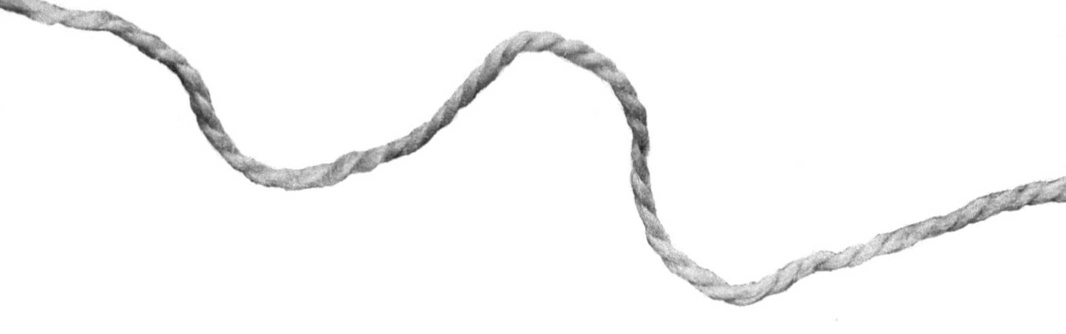

JULIA

22 March 2030

Could an evening be worse than this one? Of course, I always know the answer to that because there will never be a day worse than the day my baby daughter Amanda died in the earthquake. I'll survive this night, but it feels pretty bad right now. My best friend has been rushed to hospital in a bike trailer and I have no idea how she is because the phones aren't working. Sumner is damaged and I don't know how it will be fixed, given the current state of disrepair of everything. My home is damaged, and my kōwhai tree is gone. Actually, it's worse than gone because its branches poke through the French doors into my house with desperate, grasping fingers.

I'm not surprised the tree is down. I've known there's something wrong with my garden for the last two or three years but have been doing my best to ignore it. The kōwhai leaves were as much yellow as green. I used to grow vegetables by accident, with bean and pumpkin vines overwhelming the flowers if I didn't control them and potatoes popping up from tubers I'd missed. Now I'm lucky to get more than a few pumpkins in a season. I've read it's probably from salt water coming up through the soil so plants can't absorb nutrients. And, with the water table rising, roots stay wet and can't breathe. Building raised beds is one option. I could put plastic underneath to stop salt water getting to the surface. However, I like the random layout in my garden, with paths winding through plants rather than square edges on wooden boxes. Curved raised beds would be hard to build.

My grandparents, Ma and Pa Stout, planted the kōwhai tree now intruding into my living room. A part of my past and my home is irretrievably broken.

For decades, I have believed in the name of my business, Broken is Beautiful. I believed one can mend and repair and create golden roses in the cracks of broken gold filigree cups so they're more beautiful than before they broke. However, the world is closing in. Now, once something breaks, there's little future to imagine and no past to retreat to.

Stephen is standing behind me, like a piece of grit in my shoe when I'm walking on the beach. You know the grit's there, but it's not yet sufficiently annoying to bother taking your shoe off to get it out. To be fair, the singing he led tonight was great. He took us out of the terrible moment to a place we could cope. It was nice to walk home with someone and he helped a lot at the retirement units, even if he wasn't good at making decisions. He carried cups of tea and shifted mattresses I couldn't lift on my own. However, I've had my day's quota of other people and I desperately need to be on my own.

As I turn to tell Stephen it's time for him to leave – that it's one in the morning is a reasonable excuse – he asks, "Should we make a cup of tea?" There are few questions that could make me rethink the need for his imminent departure, but the proposition of a cup of tea always raises my spirits. I was so busy making tea for everyone else with Pauline I forgot to drink one. My mouth is parched.

I take a deep breath, let it out, and say, "Why don't you come through to the sitting room where there isn't a tree poking through the window?" I direct Stephen to my favourite armchair. Its red-flowered fabric looks worn these days, but still brightens the space beautifully. Aren't we all getting frayed around the edges?

I shiver involuntarily and, not for the first time, regret agreeing to the removal of my fireplace and installation of a heat pump. No power means no heat. A fire would have been nice right now. Tea will have to do.

I perform my tea ritual, boiling water in my red kettle on the gas stove, putting my brown Temuka teapot on the Indian tray, adding the Boris Johnson Toby milk jug. It's definitely a Kenya Bold sort of night; I need strong black tea to bolster me. I choose a mug for Stephen on which Leunig notes the importance of the cup and how cups have never been celebrated the way they deserve to be. It's the sort of funny message a serious person like Stephen might enjoy. I use the mug Fran gave me as a birthday present. It has a picture of three witches with bats flying over their heads, and 'Lynda', 'Julia' and 'Fran' written underneath. I am about to carry everything to the sitting room when it occurs to me Stephen may want sugar. None of my regular visitors take sugar. Robbie used to, but Lynda broke him of the habit, saying, "You're sweet enough and I don't want you to get diabetes." Sometimes I see Robbie sneak sugar into his coffee at our Broken is Beautiful Ferrymead repair premises, but I don't tell Lynda.

I put sugar in a handle-less mug my Dolls with Stories child, Aroha, gave me. Handle-less mugs aren't so useful because they get too hot to hold, but I never throw any of Aroha's presents away. We have a special bond because she has my Amanda doll, the first ever Dolls with Stories doll, and we wrote an Amanda storybook together. Aroha is no longer a child – she's a teenager with bells on. However, we still get together and grow the Amanda narrative.

Aroha often tells me stories about what Amanda might do to gauge my reaction. "I think Amanda is going to get a tattoo on her wrist," she said last time we met. "Probably of a bee, because honey bees are so good at building communities and Amanda likes it when people get along well."

"A tattoo on her wrist?" I replied. "Wrists are a painful place for a tattoo because of all the bones near the skin. What about on her upper arm instead?"

Aroha rubbed her hand along her wrist. "It could be a very little bee."

A spiral of people decorates my handle-less mug, displaying a range of skin colours and hair styles. Some are upside down, one is in a wheelchair, and one hooks her feet on a trapeze. Nothing stops them holding hands with each other to form a closed loop; the highest person has a ribbon wrapped round her leg and is reaching down to the hand of the lowest person.

When I reach the sitting room with my tray, Stephen is dozing in my red chair. It's surprisingly nice to see someone sleeping in my house. I quietly put a tartan blanket over him. He stirs but doesn't wake. I tiptoe back to the kitchen because I might as well drink my cup of tea.

I check my phone. Still no reception. I do my best to tamp down rising panic about what could have gone wrong for Lynda and her baby. There's no reason anything will have gone wrong. Lots of people have babies with no problem. However, Lynda is forty. On the other hand, lots of forty-year-olds have babies with no problems. Lynda was fine during pregnancy, and she's fit and healthy. Lynda is always a force to be reckoned with. Her baby probably knows that already so did the right thing during its birth.

Did we act precipitately, sending Lynda off with Andrey? Lynda could have given birth at the Surf Club – home births are now the preferred option, with our understaffed medical system struggling to provide proper care, even in hospitals. However, Victoria thought Lynda should go to hospital and she's a nurse.

As I flick between screens, hoping for a signal, or a message received in a brief window of connection, I remember our Humans with Stories Warble group and the messages sent tonight. I'm still wide awake. I'll drink Stephen's cup of tea and see what people said.

> **Andrey**: I have a younger brother too. He needed telling what to do because he never got around to making decisions for himself.

Blunt, but to the point. I'd forgotten Eeman mentioning his brother. Did Andrey's brother actually not make decisions? Or did he not make them at the speed Andrey thought he should? Because Johnno and I are twins and Mum mostly absent, I never experienced a family hierarchy; it must be very different to having a twin.

> **Lynda**: Cycling is in my blood, so I relate to people being cycle tourists. I like you (Eeman) being kind to cycle tourists.

> **Rosemary**: As a doctor, I think caring for people is the best way to improve our world. It was great that your whānau took the cycle tourists in. I'm sad the NZers didn't keep in touch.

The guys are having a hard time being positive in their connections, based on Andrey's and Stephen's messages. At the next workshop, I will reiterate that messages should emphasise commonality and avoid negative statements.

I tap the 'Approve' button so everyone else can see the messages when reception returns. Might there be a circumstance in which I don't want to approve what people say? Lynda and I should discuss that scenario, but I'm too tired to think about it now. We also need somewhere new to meet because no one will want a repeat of the tornado evening. I'm too tired to think about that either.

As I take off my clothes, my hand closes around something in my cardigan pocket. The dragonfly paperweight. Dragonflies experience brief lives filled with eating, drinking, and making merry around ponds. I know this because Aroha did a school project on dragonflies and drew beautiful pictures of their life cycle with endearingly misspelled words. Dragonflies don't worry about the state of the world or the community, or whether they should do anything about either. That mode of life seems appealing right now.

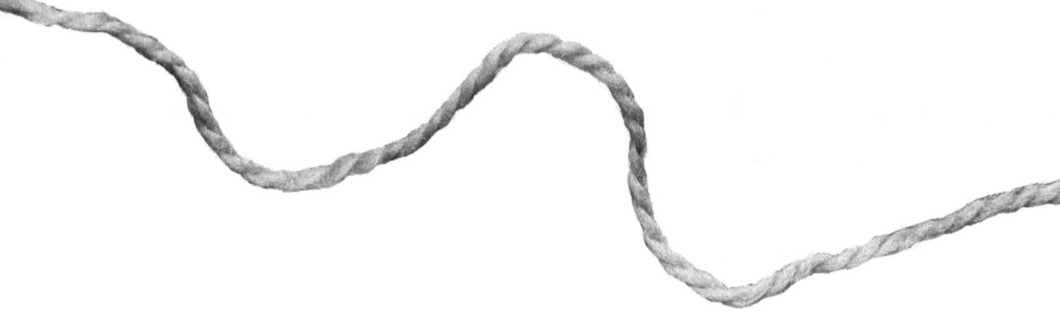

STEPHEN

22 March 2030

I wake with a crick in my neck and a feeling of disorientation. I'm in a small room with white-painted walls. There are two brightly covered armchairs opposite the chair in which I'm sitting under a tartan blanket. This is weird. There are no armchairs in my caravan. Oh, now I remember. I'm in Julia's house. There was a tornado. We walked here after helping elderly people in damaged retirement units. We were going to have a cup of tea.

There's light in the sky and birds are chirping; it must be morning, but I can't hear Julia making any noise. What should I do? Stay until she gets up so I can say thank you and goodbye? Or go now, before she wakes up, so I don't disturb her? Will she think I'm rude if I don't say goodbye? I don't want to upset her. However, she might not be pleased to find me here. Last night I wasn't sure she wanted me in her house. The best thing is to text and say goodbye after I've left.

I creep out as quietly as possible along creaky floorboards. I'm most of the way to the base of Scarborough Hill when I notice the lack of my rain jacket. Damn. I need it but I can't go back now I've left. Way too embarrassing if Julia has got up. I'll ask her to bring my jacket to the next workshop. Although it might rain in the next two weeks. Or I could drop in to collect it. It might be nice to chat over a cup of tea I actually get to drink. Julia might need help chopping up the kōwhai tree. I'll offer in my text.

There's an autumn chill in the morning air as I head up the walkway on Scarborough. I look out over the valley. The path of the tornado up the centre is obvious. Lots of people and a small number of vehicles are moving around the damage. Should I have gone back into Sumner to help? No, I need to check my caravan. I turn my head away from the valley. On the northern zigs of the path, I watch big swells rolling in from the ocean. On the southern zags, I look at the tussock-covered hillsides. The hills used to have sheep on them, but the council has stopped leasing land to farmers to reduce greenhouse gas emissions. Everyone's still hoping for the silver bullet that will stop cows and sheep burping and farting methane. More likely a lead bullet is the best solution – the only ruminant not emitting methane is a dead one.

I try not to avoid thinking about the planet overheating because I can't do much about it. I stick to immediate problems, which I find hard enough to solve. However, I can't completely avoid climate news because it's all over the internet, where I spend a lot of time.

Writing songs for dying people doesn't earn much money. How I actually earn money is online trading. I wasn't straight about that in the first workshop. I don't like telling people about my trading. It's not because I think it's wrong. Although a lot of people don't understand about cryptocurrency – they think crypto is like a black market, when it's just another type of money. However, not telling the whole truth is my long-term habit. I avoid telling people much at all. But, if they ask, I don't want to sound like a lonely loser in a caravan trading on the internet. So I tell them the story I prefer.

I started trading online when Cynthia was first being treated for breast cancer. She would sleep restlessly, waking me up. Looking at the internet was a good way to use up the night time. And I'd quit work to look after Cynthia – I needed some way to keep earning an income. We had enough reserves for three years, but we wanted to spend that money on building a house.

"How's our money going?" Cynthia would ask when she was well enough to worry about the future.

"We're fine, love," I told her. "I'm doing a small contract for Food Solutions that pays the bills." Actually, Food Solutions hadn't been flexible about my leaving. I didn't want to worry Cynthia by telling her I was trading our savings online until I was making money. By the time I was making money, I didn't want to admit I hadn't told the truth. Later still, Cynthia was no longer thinking about the bigger picture.

When I worked at Food Solutions we'd eat our sandwiches and talk about good shares to buy. Everyone joined in because everyone was trading – shop floor, engineering and management teams, the lot. The stock market was an elevator to financial success. Fixed-term deposits were for nervous Nellies. I was nervous, though. Our family didn't risk money. "A sure thing is a good thing," Dad would say. However, after Cynthia got cancer nothing seemed sure.

I started trading cautiously. I invested a little money across a wide range of shares to see how it all worked. I defined and kept to a narrow set of criteria on which to choose shares. I started making money, the one light in the dark time of Cynthia's second round of chemotherapy, after her mastectomy. As I gained confidence I invested more money. My trading was going well but Cynthia was a lot sicker. We kept hoping she'd start getting better, but she didn't. Unbelievably, she died just after her fortieth birthday. Since we got together, I'd never imagined life without her.

I lost interest in trading after Cynthia's death. I walked the hills in good weather and bad, day and night. I didn't sleep much. There was nothing I wanted to do. While shopping for essential food I ran into Felicity, a nurse who cared for Cynthia in the hospice. I'd have avoided her if I could, but the aisles were too narrow.

"Stephen how are you doing?" she asked.

"Fine," I said, looking at the boxes of crackers.

"Stephen, really, how are things going?"

I went to move on, but Felicity put her hand on my arm. "Cynthia was a special person, Stephen. You must miss her dreadfully."

"I miss her every day," I croaked.

"Of course. Are you back at work?"

"Not yet. I'm doing a bit of this and that."

"Would you have time to help me out?"

"Help you out? I'm not a nurse."

"That's not the sort of help I need." Felicity smiled directly at me. "I loved the song you wrote with Cynthia when she was sick and sang at her memorial. Could you write a song with someone else who is dying?"

"How?" I said. "I wouldn't know the person."

"Of course you don't know her yet, but you could find out about her. Suzanne has terminal breast cancer, like Cynthia. She's dying and she has no partner. Now, don't think I'm trying to pair you up. Definitely not – Suzanne only has a few weeks to live. But I think you could help make those last weeks better by spending time with her to write her song."

"I'll think about it," I said.

"I'll call you tomorrow for a chat," Felicity said.

She called the next day. And the following day. And the day after. By the end of the week, I'd agreed to visit Suzanne.

"I'll do it the once," I said. "In memory of your care for Cynthia. One rule. No discussions about Cynthia dying. It'll be easier for me to work closely with Suzanne if she thinks I have a partner."

"If that's what you want, Stephen," Felicity said. "No need to discuss Cynthia with Suzanne."

Suzanne enjoyed country music, which isn't my favourite genre, but I can mimic almost anything. We collaboratively created 'Suzanne Let Your Hair Down'.

"That's perfect, seeing as I don't have hair anymore," Suzanne said.

Suzanne asked that I sing the song at her memorial service. The audience softly joined in the chorus. "Suzanne loved her song so much," Felicity said over the post-memorial croissants Suzanne had specified.

"Who actually likes club sandwiches with egg and ham in them?" she said. "I want croissants, chocolate cake with real chocolate icing, and excellent red wine at my memorial. Send my estate the bill!"

"I'm glad Suzanne found the song right for her," I said to Felicity.

"It wasn't only Suzanne who liked it," Felicity said. "Lots of people said how nice it was to join together singing something special about Suzanne."

"Well, that's good," I said, jaw clenched to keep the tears behind my eyes.

"Could you help other people? There are so many people at our hospice who love music and need to feel special at the end of their lives."

I looked across the room at people eating cake. Saying I was too busy wasn't credible. I could hear Cynthia, *Making music's what you love, Stephen. Why wouldn't you help other people?*

"I did say just the once ..."

"Just one at a time, Stephen. You can stop whenever you like."

"Okay, one at a time. You need to choose people I'll get on with. And we still keep Cynthia's death out of it."

"Done," Felicity said.

Felicity and I have collaborated on 'Your Song' ever since.

'Your Song' started off as live performance only. I would play the song for the person who was dying, and for their friends and family if that was what the dying person wanted. However, relatives asked for recordings. The person dying didn't care how long their song would be around, but everyone else did. I wasn't going to use a recording studio – too much money and dying people don't want to go to studios. There had to be a way to record cost-effectively on my own – and my timing was perfect because it turned out recording music on the computer was a growing field I hadn't noticed. I'd let my music slide with everything else while Cynthia was ill. I recorded tracks in the hospice or rest home, then mastered them in my caravan. Once I got the hang of the software, it was easy.

I'd stopped checking my shares after Cynthia's death, too. However, while I played with song tracks on the screen, I went back to checking my share portfolio. Just a couple of clicks of the mouse to look at a graph. Friendly lines were trending upwards; the stock market was still booming. I started trading again, enjoying the buzz of making the right picks and satisfaction I was no longer dipping into the precious capital Cynthia and I had put aside. One day I would build our house, just not yet. However, trading online was boring. I had to sit and watch stock prices rise and fall to pick the right moment to buy or sell. There had to be a better way.

I developed mathematical equations – algorithms – to pick shares and the best times to buy and sell them. I returned to my old practice of testing my solutions with small amounts of money. Once I was confident they worked, I scaled my investments up. I'm still improving my approaches, but now this activity is called 'machine learning' and everyone does it. The best thing is the value of my portfolio ticks upwards and I don't need to lift a finger because now I've trained my algorithms to train themselves.

When I reach my caravan, the first thing I do is turn my computer on and log in. I need my reading glasses to see the type on the screen so pat myself down. Not in my breast pocket, not in my jeans pocket. Bugger, they must be in my jacket pocket and my jacket's at Julia's. I go to find my spare glasses in the labelled 'Spares' box in the container next to my caravan. There's not much room at my place for duplicates, but glasses are too important. As is organisation when you live in a tiny space.

Although my algorithms manage themselves, checking my portfolio has become a reflex action. It makes me feel good. Will the internet be back now after the storm? Yes.

I stay anonymous whenever I go online. I use multiple levels of protection to hide my identity; a virtual private network, an encrypted browser and secure email. I never use my real name or any details related to me. I accept no cookies, stay away from social media, use FastRabbit as a search engine and *never* use the AI tools available for 'free', where 'free' means 'thank you for giving us all your information to train our model'. For trading, I use only anonymous cryptocurrency. I believe I'm as invisible on the web as it is possible to be. I check regularly and I never appear in any searches I can make up.

I flick through my summary screens. Everything's good. Should I go watch what's happening in the Rappit channels? That's another habit; I check my investments, then do some channel watching. I don't participate; I suppose you could call me a stalker, though I don't think I fit that word. Stalker implies that, at some point, you are going to act. You are hunting prey to bring it down. I watch online to experience the world without directly interacting with people.

Before I open Rappit, I see a notification on Warble. That's right, we sent messages to the workshop group while Eeman was talking. The workshop seems days ago, though it was only yesterday. I scan the Warble avatars; mine looks half-baked. I need to give my avatar facial features but don't know what to choose. Should it be like me? Or like someone I want to be? Or be someone completely invented? I made the avatar for my general online interactions to give nothing away. However, it doesn't look right for a group where you're sharing stories. I'll do something about it soon, once I've worked out what. For now, I'll read the messages.

Andrey has a younger brother. I'm sibling-free; it might have been nice to grow up with someone else who Dad could have disapproved of. Lynda loves cycling and I don't. She went to hospital in Andrey's trailer – I hope she and the baby are okay. Rosemary wrote about her role as a doctor. Julia liked the monkey biscuits.

What will Eeman think of my negative comment about God? No one else wrote anything negative. But religion makes me so angry I react without thinking things through properly. After Cynthia died people said things like, "She's in a better place," or "One day you will be together again." Such rubbish. I will never see Cynthia again because she is dead. Dead, dead, dead. She's nowhere better, she's nowhere at all. She's only kept alive by my talking about her like she's still here. And by her advice inside my head. I don't always take her advice, of course, because you'd be mad taking advice from a dead person.

Victoria and Fran wrote about immigration and communities. I've never been overseas. Cynthia and I planned to travel overseas once we built our house. I've never lived outside Christchurch either; so much risk in going someplace new and not knowing if you will like it or not. I always thought I'd want a trial period if I lived somewhere new. Then I could see if things worked out before I committed.

When I finished my engineering degree the New Zealand economy was a mess. Everything was turned on its head in the 1980s and wasn't any better by the early 1990s. My classmates said there were better places to be and left the country. I thought about applying for jobs in Auckland. However, Cynthia and I had been together for nearly two years, and she got a job at a Christchurch accounting firm. Staying in Christchurch meant Cynthia could keep quilting and sewing and knitting with her groups of women at the Arts Centre. That was far more important to her than accounting, or jobs. We could have done the long-distance relationship thing, but that seemed a huge risk. So I stayed, and we stayed together, and time marched on and Cynthia got cancer. 'And then one day you find ten years have got behind you. No one told you when to run, you missed the starting gun.' *Dark Side of the Moon*, what a classic album that remains.

Zahra wrote about climate change. That's topical – climate change and TEQs have solved any 'where to go' problems because most people don't go far anymore. Everyone can be like me, stuck in place.

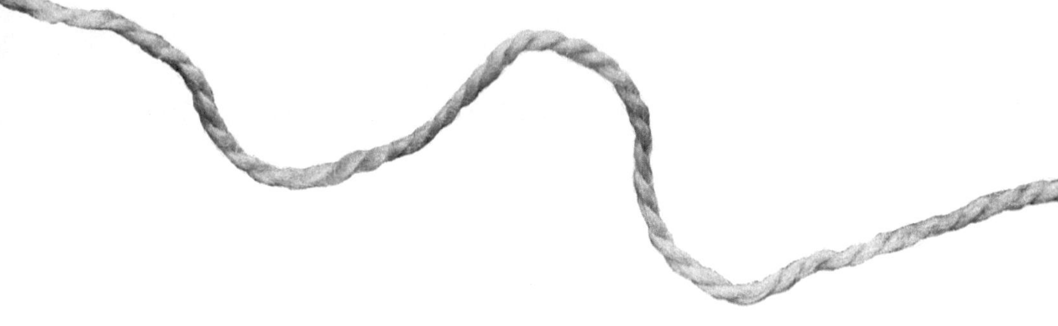

JULIA

22 March–4 April 2030

On the morning after the tornado-terminated workshop, I wake to bright sunlight and a sense of dread. As I surface, I remember two bad things from yesterday: Lynda starting to give birth at our workshop, and the tree in my sitting room. Do I need to put either or both in my brain box? My brain box helps me cope when I'm overwhelmed.

Before OA, my only coping strategy was ignoring problems. Life got much better once Fran, Lynda and I created Dolls with Stories and supported each other, but it's never roses all the way. My creative repair business took off, which was great, but Dolls with Stories was growing fast and needing my time. Then Mum got ill, and I was stressed about whether to go and help her in Takaka. Immersed in the myriad of conflicting demands I skipped talking with the girls.

Finally, Fran called me.

"Julia, how are things? I haven't heard from you for a while."

"I'm okay. A bit too much happening."

"Anything you can talk about?"

I told Fran about the multiplicity of matters on my mind – so many I was avoiding taking action on any of them. "How do you manage, Fran? You have your work and Holly and Dolls with Stories. Don't you ever feel like you're submerging under all the problems coming at you?"

"Of course I do. That's why I have strategies to help me cope."

"Like what?"

"Well, first I talk with people. The worse things are, the more important it is to talk."

"Point taken," I said. "I know I can talk with you. And I can talk to Johnno too – he's turned into a great listener."

"Another strategy is my brain box collection," Fran said. "When I have several difficult things to deal with, I put some of them in my brain box and close the lid. But – and it's a big 'but' – I create a reminder for when to open my brain box and take things out again. I can't leave them in there indefinitely."

"Where do you put the reminder?"

"In my calendar, where I put all my reminders," Fran said.

I liked the idea and have used it ever since. My brain box allows me to not think about everything hard at the same time while preventing me from ignoring difficult problems. Of course, I could cheat and keep delaying the opening date, but so far I've kept myself honest.

Today I decide I don't need my brain box. I can deal with two problems. The tree I have to sort, and I want to talk with Lynda. When I check my phone, the Warble icon has a red dot. Great, communication's restored. I open up the list of groups to see a dot on Lynda's, Fran's and my private group, which we run separately from our Dolls with Stories work conversations. Lynda and Fran were chatting while I was asleep – what a relief! Lynda is okay enough to communicate. What have I missed out on?

L: Hi girls, all good with me, Hermione, and Robbie.

Hermione? Did she name her baby after Hermione Granger in *Harry Potter*? We'd talked about baby names and Lynda had been cagey, saying Robbie had strong opinions about names and she didn't want to upset him. That sounded unlikely. Robbie's a pushover when it comes to Lynda and will do anything to make her happy. Sometimes I roll my eyes at the number of times he says he loves her.

L: Anyone out there? Am I talking to a void?

Lynda sent her message at 4am. I don't know why she expected a reply. At 5am, Fran answered.

F: Great news. Glad all OK. Is she beautiful?

L: Of course. ♡♡♡♡♡

I wish I'd been the first to read about Hermione and respond. I type quickly.

J: Wonderful news. Can't wait 2 c Hermione.

Wavering dots tell me Lynda is typing.

L: Home tonight. Hospital no fun. 😫
Bed in corridor if we stay. No need.

J: You get settled @ home.
Visit tomorrow am? ♡😇♡

L: Gr8. C u 2morrow. ♡😀

I shift to our Humans with Stories Warble group and type a message to the group.

J: Hope you, your families and houses are OK after the wild evening. Just letting you know Lynda & baby Hermione are all good.

A string of love hearts and smiling emojis appears on my screen and brightens my mood in the face of my next task – the kōwhai. That's going to take the rest of the day and some. It hurts my heart to see the kōwhai – a fallen kaitiaki and a forewarning of worse to come. Hah, that's a Māori word I know. Kaitiaki means guardian. Perhaps I have absorbed enough te reo by accident to not need classes?

As I contemplate the kōwhai branches, my phone gurgles. I chose a gurgle as a ring tone as it gradually draws your attention, rather than making you jump. However, with all my water problems, a gurgle sounds sinister rather than friendly. I might change it.

> **S**: Hi Julia. I'm glad Lynda & baby are well. I left my jacket at your place. Could I pick it up? & help with your kōwhai tree?

Nice of Stephen to offer but I want to get on with the tree rather than making awkward conversation. And should I meet workshop participants outside sessions? Last night was a special exception; hopefully, tornadoes won't be a regular event. I remember what happened with Fran when she was running OA and got too involved with one of the participants, Matthew. The particularly bad part was that Matthew was already in a relationship with another woman in the OA group. It all got messy, and Fran needed help to extricate herself. I have no intention of developing a relationship with anyone in our workshop, including Stephen. Sometimes I would like a person in my life for companionship, but they simply wouldn't fit. My house is too small, and I have no practice at compromising how I live.

I realise my imagination is running away with me. Stephen wants his jacket, not a relationship.

> **J**: Thanks for the offer but it's a 1 person job. House too small. I'll leave jacket in mailbox in case I'm out.

> **S**: I'll pick it up tomorrow.

Hopefully I'll be at Lynda's when Stephen collects the jacket so I can avoid him without guilt. The jacket also reminds me I need to message Eeman about his plates. I can put them in the letter box too.

Messaging complete, I head to the living room to cut off the branches poking into my house. But to do that I need to get the saw from the shed and

I can't open the doors to the garden or get in the gate. I climb out my bedroom window, clamber over branches to the shed, get the saw and cut my way back towards the house. Once I've cleared branches from around the doors I find a tarpaulin in the shed and fasten it onto the weatherboards around the door frames. Then I saw my way to the gate. By the time I get there, my arm is wearing out and there are still some big branches and the trunk left. I have enough of a path, so I'll deal with them later.

When I go back inside, my living room is dark and the hallway gloomy. I call Glazed Glass in Ferrymead to order new panes. It's ages since I fixed any glass – I'll go to Mitre 10 en route to Glazed because my putty will be dried up like a walnut. Hopefully, putty will be on the shelves. There are often more gaps than products on store shelves because of supply chain breakdowns.

The next morning, I consider cycling to Lynda and Robbie's to keep my hill-legs in practice, but it's a pain dragging my bike up the steps to their house. I walk briskly up Scarborough Hill and marvel, as always, at their stunning view and how beautifully they have done up the old house perched on an excavated platform high above the road. Robbie's handiness with repair and his early building training, together with Lynda's competence with fabrics and design, have melded perfectly. I don't know how Lynda has found time to do everything in the house, run Dolls with Stories and marathons. She has energy for two humans; however, she now has a second human to use up some of that energy. As I reach the front door, Lynda calls out, "Come in and see our beautiful daughter."

Lynda and Robbie are sitting in armchairs opposite the picture window from which they can look at the street below and across Pegasus Bay to the Kaikoura mountain ranges. Robbie is holding Hermione in an unusually untidy room – there are blankets and clothing on furniture and scattered baby paraphernalia. "Would you like a turn?" Robbie asks. Hermione is bundled up in a purple possum wool blanket.

I take the gift of Hermione and breathe in her smell of milk and wet nappies, evoking infant Amanda. I remind myself to think happy thoughts of how I enjoyed Amanda's babyhood. "She's gorgeous." Hermione has little tufts of bright red hair, the same colour as her dad's, and his stunning blue eyes. I hold her, staring at the miracle of tiny eyelashes and rosebud mouth, until that mouth starts to pucker.

"Lynda, it'll be you and food she's wanting." I gently pass Hermione to her mother, who gets on with the serious business of feeding.

Looking out over Sumner valley, the path of the tornado draws my eye – a track up the centre of the valley with flattened and twisted houses along its route. Numerous workers and a few vehicles are loading debris. "What'll happen to the people from all those houses? They'll need somewhere to live."

"Yes," Robbie says, "repairs will take forever and who knows how long new builds might be. The black market is already running hot for supplies."

I shuffle my chair away from the window to look at the peaceful view of suckling Hermione and doting Lynda.

It's workshop day and I'm at our new venue – the Sumner Fire Station. I'm sad we can't meet at the Surf Club anymore because it's an important part of my history. I had trouble finding a place in Sumner because the commercial centre floods so often. Why didn't anyone think about sea-level rise when Sumner's buildings were reconstructed in the 2010s after the Canterbury earthquakes, one block back from the beach? I finally found this room in the station, several blocks inland and not prone to inundation … yet. Even better, their meeting room is upstairs – a long way from water and, I'm hoping, with sufficient fall for sewage to flow smoothly away.

I'm leading the meeting on my own tonight, although Fran said she would CryptoCast in. "I'm sorry, Julia, but I can't take the risk of being stuck in Sumner for the night if Holly isn't well," she said. "Last time was awful, cycling and wondering if I'd get through. Thinking she might be having another panic attack and gasping for breath on her own. She's not at all well – she needs a replacement heart valve. The waiting list is over two years and private surgery is way too expensive."

"Fran, I'm so sorry to hear that. Is Holly still working?"

"She's doing some hairdressing because she enjoys it, and we need the income. But I have to watch she doesn't wear herself out."

I talked with Lynda last night; obviously, she wasn't coming to a workshop a week after having a baby.

"Hermione and I are great, Julia," she said, "but we need time to develop good sleep and feeding routines. I'm planning to come to the workshop after this one. I want to know about people's stories! I'll do my best to Cast in to keep connected." Then she yawned loudly.

"If you're sure, Lynda. You sound tired."

"Tired is normal with a baby."

"I'll be fine on my own," I said.

"Absolutely, Julia. I have total faith in you."

The fire station meeting room has practical metal-framed chairs with wooden seats around a large table that might be good for old-fashioned board meetings, but not for our workshops. I move chairs out of the way and am about to push the table against the wall when Stephen arrives twenty minutes early.

"Hi, Stephen, nice to see you.

"Thanks for leaving my jacket. I knocked but you weren't in."

"I must have been visiting Lynda. Come by another time and I'll make you a cup of tea."

Why did I just say that when I'd decided meeting workshop participants outside the workshop is a bad idea? I can't immediately take it back.

"That would be nice. Can I help you move the table?" Stephen asks.

"Sure. How good are you with iPads?"

"Anything tech, just ask me."

"Excellent. You can be in charge of connecting Fran and Lynda on CryptoCast."

Rosemary arrives next. She's this week's speaker, having picked the donkey with the second-shortest tail. I rang Rosemary a week ago to remind her about the koha and kai. "I'm not the handicrafts type and my work is overwhelming," she had said. "Can I be an exception and buy something?"

"Exceptions don't work well," I'd said. "Next thing, everyone wants to be an exception. What about mugs with messages as a compromise? You buy the mugs, then add the messages."

"How will I write messages on mugs that won't wash off?"

"Easy," I said. "Glass paint sticks to ceramic. I'll loan you some."

In the meeting room, we put Rosemary's snacks on the bench and her mugs in the wicker basket. She has brought sesame seed crackers to dip in cashew hummus, and gluten-free carrot cake with coconut yoghurt; I like coconut yoghurt but it's a shame there's nothing vegan that's as good as cream cheese icing.

"Let's cover the mugs up. I want the messages to be a surprise for people when they choose," she says.

Like Eeman, Rosemary has become more enthused about the koha process. Maybe our ideas are actually working?

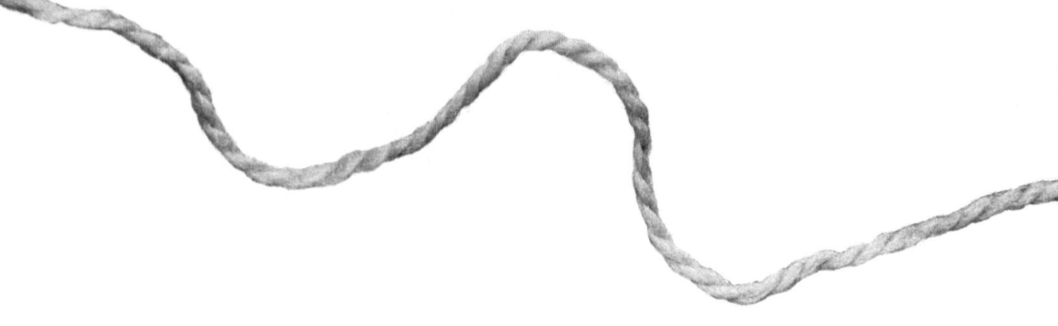

JULIA

4 April 2030

The room is ready and three of the four remaining participants turn up. Andrey swerves into the parking lot down below on his bicycle with trailer behind, then pounds energetically up the stairs.

"Thanks so much for taking Lynda to the hospital, Andrey. Quite the evening to remember, wasn't it? Did you get your tools and stuff back? Sorry, I completely forgot about them."

"It's lucky Lynda is lighter than building materials. I've never cycled to outrun a tornado before. Yes, I got my things back. Robbie helped me get in touch with the Surf Club people."

"Do you happen to have a chainsaw? The wind flattened my kōwhai tree and the trunk's too big for me to cut up."

"I can very much help you cut the tree."

"Thank you. Let's talk about a time at the end of the workshop."

I see Stephen's mouth tighten as Zahra says from behind me, "I also can help with your tree. I'm an arborist."

I'd forgotten Stephen had offered to help with the tree and I'd turned him down. Who'd have thought everyone would be so keen to help cut up a tree trunk?

"Thanks for your offer, Zahra, but my tree is past saving – it's only good for firewood."

"Did it come down in the tornado?" she asks.

"Yes, although it hasn't been healthy for a while. I think it's salt water coming up. Let's make a time for you and Victoria to visit. Also, thank you for helping Lynda at the last workshop; it's such a relief she and Hermione are fine."

"Yes, baby Hermione, such a feminine name," Zahra says.

"It's a beautiful name," says Victoria. "I'm hoping Lynda will send us pictures."

"You can ask her yourself," I said. "Lynda's going to join in via CryptoCast."

At 6.30pm we're waiting for Eeman. Fran and Lynda have half a screen each on CryptoCast and are digitally sitting on the board table against the wall, facing the chairs. They're chatting with each other, mostly about Hermione and how much she is eating and excreting. Lynda holds Hermione up to the screen and Fran coos at her.

Victoria comes over beside me. "Hi, Lynda, hello, Hermione. Aren't you beautiful."

"Me or Hermione?" laughs Lynda.

Robbie comes up to Lynda and holds out his arms. "Time for Hermie's bath," he says. "You concentrate on your workshop."

"Bye, Hermione." Fran and Holly, who's appeared behind Fran, wave vigorously from their screen. "We'll come visit you at the weekend if the weather is good."

Victoria continues to chat with Lynda about things baby while I turn back to the room. Zahra and Andrey are comparing notes about the tornado's aftermath.

"We're at the back of Sumner valley," Zahra says. "There was lots of damage biking home. Houses with no roofing and gardens destroyed. Old trees torn up. So much work for me. Some people injured, but not too badly. Victoria helped them."

"I live in Redcliffs, so not near the tornado," Andrey says. "But now I am worried by the chance of a tornado. I build a tiny home in a tiny house community. Council allows tiny houses for a small rent because the land is red-zoned – too much flood and liquefaction risk. No fixing down of houses – they must be able to move. Our houses can blow away!"

I look at my watch. It's 6.40pm and Eeman still isn't here. Should we start? That's what Lynda would say if she wasn't trapped in a screen. On the other hand, Fran would want to be inclusive and wait for everyone to arrive.

I attempt a middle ground. "Hi, workshoppers, great to see you. We're waiting on Eeman so keep chatting while we give him a few more minutes."

I hope Eeman wasn't put off by our last meeting. Should I have asked Stephen to edit his comment about God? I sent out a reminder about the next workshop, but Lynda and I agreed at the beginning we don't want to chase people to attend. These workshops must be something people want to come to, not have to come to.

Eeman walks in at 6.45pm as I am asking everyone to sit down. "*Apa kabar*, Julia, are we starting already?"

"Yes, the workshop starts at 6.30pm."

"I'm very sorry. In Indonesia, our meetings are not so strict. *Jam Karet*, rubber time. I will remember to come on time in future."

I welcome the group, and everyone says hi to tiny Fran and Lynda on the screen.

"Julia, should we use the digital projector next time?" Zahra points to the ceiling.

"That's a good idea." Why hadn't I thought of that? Why didn't Stephen suggest it when he was setting up the iPad?

"Let's start with our karakia." I hadn't expected to lead the karakia in te reo so soon. Fran had said, "It doesn't make sense for me to lead anything from a screen. Of course you can do it, Julia. Remember, it's about improvement, not perfection." She's right and there are more voices audible this week, together with more enthusiasm in the call and response.

"Today we welcome Rosemary to tell us her story," I say. "Turn your phones to airplane mode and, once you've identified a connection and sent your message, bring your phone up to the front table and find out what Rosemary has made us this week. But first … Lynda, you have something you want to say?"

Lynda agreed to be 'bad cop' today. It's easier to be tough at a remove and Lynda finds being tough easier than most.

"Thank you all for helping me last workshop. Hermione, Robbie, and I are extremely grateful," Lynda says. "I hope to be back with you in person in a fortnight."

"With Hermione?" Victoria asks.

"Hermione's behaviour isn't yet up to workshops. We'll see how her sleep patterns go. Maybe she can drop by at the beginning with Robbie to say thank you in person.

"Now, down to business. It was great to read about your connections last week. This week let's work on writing a little more and ensuring they're positive connections. Of course, we may differ in our opinions or beliefs, but this group is about finding constructive commonalities. It is all too easy to find dissimilarities and issues with other people, right?"

Everyone nods assent, but I see Stephen's face crease.

"Rosemary, what story do you have for us today?" I ask, and Rosemary comes to the front of the room.

"Hello, fellow attendees. Today I'm going to tell you about my being a doctor, more specifically a psychiatrist."

That's right. Rosemary told us she's a psychiatrist at the tornado workshop. Funny, don't psychiatrists have their own support networks? Why would she need this group?

"When I came to Aotearoa to finish my medical training I thought I'd become a GP since that was the only sort of doctor I knew about before I studied medicine. While I was studying I barely considered specialisation, because medical training is so intense it leaves you little mental headroom. In fact, I was working so hard I wondered whether I wanted to do medicine after all. How could I have a decent life if I was on varying rosters, doing night shifts, and sometimes working forty-eight hours in a row? I thought about pathology – dissecting dead people is a great option if you don't want after-hours work – but I went into medicine because people are interesting, and dead people are not nearly as interesting as live ones. And I'm always interested in the stories people tell – that's what finally pushed me towards psychiatry. There's lots of demand for psychiatrists, they are better paid than GPs and they don't have to do night shifts."

Today, Andrey is the first person to come up with his phone, put it on the table and choose a mug out of the basket. He smiles as he picks it up, then hides it in his hands.

"I enjoy the close contact with my patients, many of whom I see over a long period of time. I work in with psychologists to discuss the best way to help a particular individual; will medicine, or talking therapies, or other lifestyle interventions make the most difference? My dilemma, however, is that I believe less and less in the medical approach to many illnesses we say need psychiatric care. How we live, rather than the medicine we take, is what's critical to us being mentally well, or ill. What I mean is, I don't know whether much of the medicine I prescribe is helping. For some extreme illnesses, definitely. But for a lot of the mental health problems I see, not really.

"My first wake-up call was when I worked on a project investigating how nutrients help children with autism and ADHD. We looked at what the effect of taking particular vitamins was compared with our standard prescriptions. What we found was, specific vitamins helped children more than drugs. Could a lot of what we prescribe be doing no good? Worse, could it be harming people?"

Zahra brings her phone up. I glimpse 'I run on coffee and chaos' on the side of her mug. I wouldn't have picked Zahra as someone who likes chaos given her well-thought-through clothing and no-nonsense manner. I'm not surprised she likes coffee; she radiates a constant energy burn. So does Lynda, but in a more sparkly way. Zahra is more intense; if you get too close, you might shrivel up.

Stephen follows on from Zahra. He considers the mugs then takes one saying, 'Never do tomorrow what you can do today'. Is that how he is? Or how he would like to be?

"After we found out drugs might not help autism or ADHD, research was published showing antidepressants don't help many people long term. How could this be right? We've been prescribing antidepressants for decades and more now than ever before. They don't work? And it wasn't drug manufacturers who found this out – it was independent researchers. This made me think pharmaceutical companies want us to keep believing in their drugs, even when the companies suspect or know they aren't effective; like when cigarette companies knew nicotine caused cancer and still kept selling their products.

"I'm also totally overloaded with patients, like all my colleagues. There are far more people needing help with their mental health than there are psychiatrists, or psychologists, or counsellors. Mental health fell off the edge of a cliff after the COVID-19 lockdowns and continued on down through the 2020s."

Victoria comes up. Not surprising, seeing she's in the health workforce. She carries a mug away with a picture of a soap bubble forming in a ring and a trail of bubbles flying up into the sky. The bubbles have words written on them, including 'money' and 'climate change'. I suggested this idea to Rosemary. When I was browsing for an arrival present for Hermione I saw a children's book called *Blowing Bubbles* with the by-line, 'Put your worry in a bubble and let it fly away.'

There's a notification on my screen announcing Fran sent a connection message.

Rosemary continues: "I've spent the years since COVID-19 becoming ever more disillusioned and working with people who believe better nutrition, together with community support of mental health, is the best approach. Now I'm not sure I believe in my profession enough to keep practising. It's damaging to my mental health to do work I no longer believe in.

I get another notification. Lynda has sent her message in.

"I imagine many of you are wondering why I'm here. Why does a psychiatrist need to come to a community mental well-being course? Don't they have support groups of their own? Yes, we do, but it's hard to get support when you are challenging the foundation of your profession. Also, I want more practical ways to help people right now. I particularly like storytelling as a path to better mental health and I think you guys are on the right track, emphasising how interpersonal connections are fundamental to well-being. So I wanted to see how your approach is working while helping myself.

"Saying all this out loud makes me realise I should have let the organisers know my intentions before signing up. I've no right to treat you all as an experiment. Even when I am participating. Perhaps you should take over at this point, Julia?"

I'd been focusing on identifying a connection and not expecting Rosemary to close off her story. Neither Eeman nor I have commented yet.

"Right, yes, thank you, Rosemary. Just give me a second. I was writing my message. Eeman, I think you were too? Everyone, please talk amongst yourselves."

I scurry to corral my thoughts and write something coherent. I also need to talk with Fran and Lynda between workshops about what to do if people don't send a connectivity message.

As I get up, Eeman sits down with a mug saying 'Happy' in a rainbow. I take the last three mugs to divvy up with Lynda and Fran then turn to Rosemary.

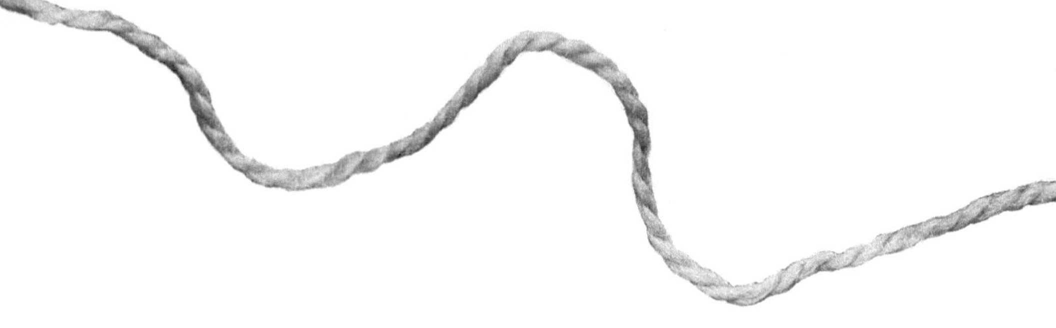

JULIA

4 April 2030

"Rosemary, do you mind taking a break so we can test everyone's comfort levels?"

"Of course," she says.

A voice burbles from the iPad; this is not so functional. I go to the iPad then relay to the group, "Fran says, 'Why doesn't Rosemary take a short walk so we can have a discussion?' Rosemary, I'll text you when we've finished."

"Great idea," says Rosemary. "I need some air."

Once Rosemary has gone I hear the iPad talking again.

Zahra says, "Turn the volume up, Julia."

I push the buttons on the side of the iPad but it's already full volume. "Can everyone move closer to the front of the room?"

They scrape their chairs forward and Lynda fills the screen. "Let's go round the circle then I can summarise. Julia, you start off?"

"I wish Rosemary had talked with us when she signed up," I say. "She'll know it's much harder to get someone to leave a group than never include them. However, if she's genuine about participating in our workshops, I'm happy for her to take that knowledge and use it to help other people. That's how we've spread our work with children in Dolls with Stories. We've encouraged people to bring friends and whānau in to learn how it works, then they create new groups in wider communities. It would be impossible for Lynda, Fran and I to run programmes all over the country. We can only provide a central hub for advice."

Andrey frowns. "I don't like the idea of someone studying us and telling other people what we talk about here. We're telling our stories to the people in the room only. Knowing Rosemary is a psychiatrist makes me uncomfortable. Is she assessing us?"

Zahra nods. "It's obvious the health system isn't helping everyone who needs it, but we don't want the authorities butting into what the people are doing for themselves."

Victoria says, "I'm part of the health system too. None of us has spare time to think about what's going on outside our own jobs. The health bureaucracy won't be interested in this group, for better or worse. Rosemary said she wants to learn and then use that generally to help people. She doesn't want to spread personal information. We just need to ask she keeps all specifics confidential; as a psychiatrist, she'll know to do that anyhow."

"I agree Rosemary should have told us more up front," Fran says. "But it could be an honest mistake. She didn't consider the implications, and now she has, she's telling us."

Eeman and Stephen haven't yet spoken and are looking at each other, shifting in their seats.

"I'm fine with Rosemary," Eeman says quickly. "For me, the most important thing is everyone is happy with each other and kind to one another."

Stephen says, "I'm the same. I mean, Rosemary being here is okay."

I turn back to the iPad. "Fran, how about you?"

"These are the first Humans with Stories workshops. They're a trial – we're all figuring out the best way to form connections through stories. This is a great discussion to help clarify what is okay and what's not okay. I don't see a problem with Rosemary staying in the group. Her background will give her, and us, a lot of insight."

"Lynda, your summary?" I ask.

"First, my opinion," says Lynda. "Rosemary's involvement will likely do more good than harm. I hear everyone is generally okay with Rosemary participating. But we need to make it clear the stories we tell here are for this group, and this group alone. This isn't just a rule for Rosemary. No one's stories are to be discussed outside workshops. Everyone good with that? We should have said this at the beginning but, like Fran said, we're all learning. Anyone got more to say?"

There's a general chorus of "No", but then Zahra says, "It's weird and complicated sending comments to the Warble group. Two weeks later we've forgotten what we said. Why not make our connections during the workshop? Like with the wool?"

"Good point, Zahra," Lynda says. "Fran, Julia, and I did talk this through. We thought it might be difficult for speakers to be interrupted multiple times. However, maybe we should reconsider. Julia and I will message everyone to get opinions."

"Why not discuss it now? Everyone can say what they want. We just talked about Rosemary, which was a lot more difficult," Zahra says, flicking her dreadlocks over her shoulder. "People come to the front of the room, put their phones down and collect their koha – that's disruptive. How would it be worse if they spoke?"

"Fair enough," Lynda says. "Other thoughts?"

"It's not just about the speaker," says Victoria. "It's also about whether people feel comfortable making their comments to the whole group."

"But we're all going to see the comments later, anyhow," Andrey says. "What's the difference?"

Eeman and Stephen are looking at each other again. I've run out of energy. If they don't want to speak up, I won't make them.

"I'm telling my story at the next workshop," I say. "So I'll give it a try; people saying their connections during the meeting. We can all see how that goes."

The group is looking at the floor or the food, they're as done as I am. "Let's go eat. Sorry, Fran and Lynda. We'll think of you while eating carrot cake. Hang in there so I can chat with the two of you once Rosemary comes back."

I send Rosemary a text and join the group to find everyone drinking out of their new mugs – my koha concept was a winner. I'm having my tea out of 'Write your own story', in multicoloured letters. Andrey's mug says, 'I hate mugs with quotes on them'. Maybe Rosemary got tired of making up pithy quotes by the end.

"I like this mug," Eeman says. "We don't have many mugs."

"Would you like another?" Stephen says. "Cynthia likes mugs to be matching."

Eeman reads out, "'Never do tomorrow what you can do today'. Western people are always rushing, aren't they? It's something I miss about Indonesia – time to talk with people properly. In Aotearoa everyone is in so much of a hurry. These workshops are good, but they are still in a hurry. Start at a set time. End at a set time."

How does Eeman think workshops are going to function if no one knows when to come to them? I would like this workshop to be over now. However, we have eaten all the food and are looking at the clock by the time Rosemary re-enters the room. I take her over to make a cup of tea in one of the extra mugs, which reads 'Life is better with …'. I carry the iPad over, put it between me and Rosemary and let Lynda explain what was discussed.

"I'm fine with that," Rosemary says. "Thanks for letting me stay in the group."

It's nearly 8.30pm. "Time for our closing karakia," I say. "Sorry, we've run over time. When Lynda's back we'll be precise to the minute. Please all join in the karakia because your pronunciation will be as good as mine, or better." I grab the iPad which has the words on it; Fran and Lynda signed off Cast after we finished talking with Rosemary.

I lead into the karakia with, "Kua tō te rā ki rungi i te kaupapa nei."

"Kua ngū ngā manu, kua hū ngā noke, kua tau te taiao." The group stumble through the words, looking at their screens.

"Ko te pō kua tae mai, ehika mā," I call back.

"Ā tēnā, me here te waka," the group says more smoothly.

"Kua tau?"

"E tau ana!" everyone choruses.

People disperse quickly, other than Stephen who is fiddling with his pack. I'm too tired for conversation and I don't want to talk about the workshop anymore tonight. I start packing the room up, hoping he'll get the message.

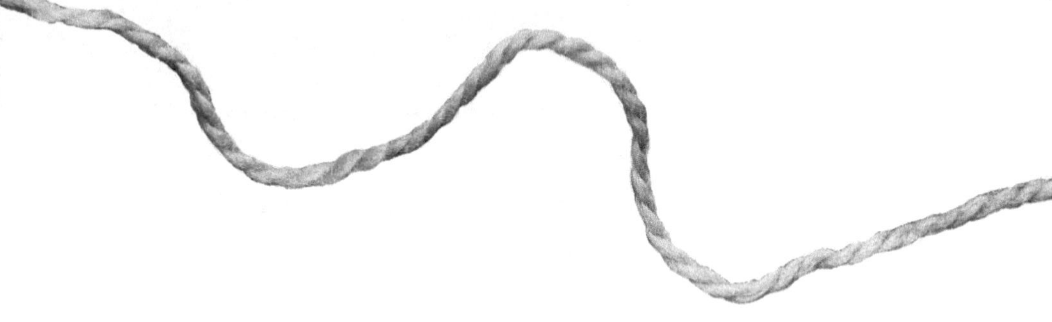

STEPHEN

4 April 2030

"Do you need help packing up?" I ask Julia as everyone else has gone.

"You could put the furniture back," Julia says. "No mugs to wash because people used their new ones. That was nice, wasn't it? Oh, damn, Rosemary forgot her plates, just like Eeman."

We shift the big table to the centre of the room and place the chairs around it. Julia puts three mugs and Rosemary's plates in her pack, together with the iPad.

"I guess we're headed in the same direction," I say in a poor attempt at a joke.

"Yes, we are," Julia replies.

We descend to the ground floor and Julia chats briefly to the firewoman heading the night shift before we exit the building.

We go along Wiggins Street as the most direct route to Julia's house.

"Interesting workshop," I say.

"Yes," says Julia.

We pass jagged outlines of houses partially deconstructed by the tornado.

"Losing my home is one of the worst things I can imagine happening," Julia says. "I almost lost it when I had a loan I couldn't pay back and the bank threatened to sell my house to cover the loan. I'll never take out a loan again. I wonder if these houses are insured so they can build or buy another house. Although another house is never the same. My insurance company sent a letter warning I might not be covered next year. The company is working with council and government to assess risk. I'll get two months' notice before my renewal if I can't be insured. So I can look at other options, but what other options would I have? It's unlikely a different insurance company will take

73

my property on if I've been turned down. Do you have insurance problems on Scarborough?"

"No, I don't," I say. I have no insurance problems because I never felt the need to insure something as small as a caravan containing few possessions.

"Does your wife work?" Julia asks.

"No, she doesn't." I have a well-worn set of phrases loosely based on history covering my wife and her existence but non-appearance. Cynthia is no longer an accountant, to avoid her having a workplace people might know about. "She's allergic to sunlight, so she mostly stays home. She does lots of handcrafts – especially quilting and patchwork. Her quilts are works of art."

"Really?" says Julia. "I'd like to meet her. That's what I love to do too – create new and better things out of remnants. I mostly use three-dimensional materials, like ceramics and wood and glass, but fabric's good too."

Damn. I hadn't thought about the connection between my Cynthia story and Julia. I mostly tell it to clients who aren't interested in meeting new people. Dying people can barely cope with seeing people they already know. Quilting is a soothing occupation to talk about. It was a strange hobby choice for a young person, but Cynthia had a big group of older friends who all loved handcrafts.

Cynthia's stopped making quilts when we moved into the caravan. I bought a container into which we put her many boxes of material, which quilters use as inspiration. We tried setting her sewing machine up in the container, but Cynthia said she couldn't work in a windowless box. Nor could her sewing machine live on the caravan table. "I'll quilt again once we build, Stevie. No problem," Cynthia said. "For now I'll teach classes and make hand-stitched pieces."

I still feel guilty about Cynthia not being able to quilt properly those last years. She made one final pattern when she was ill, stitched by hand in small pieces while she lay in bed. The joining exercise to make the full quilt was hard. I wished I could help. However, when I tried my stitching was beyond ugly. She made it look so easy. "Not to worry, love," she said. "I'm happy doing my quilting and leaving you this piece for memories."

Cynthia's last quilt lives in a box in the container because I can't bear to part with it as much as I can't bear the memories.

I've now got a double dilemma. I need to stop Julia wanting to learn about Cynthia, but I want to learn more about Julia. However, you can't expect someone to share when you won't share back, and my dead wife is preventing me from revealing much.

"We must arrange something for a time Cynthia's feeling well," I say. "Her health goes up and down, you know."

"Sure, I understand," Julia says.

We're nearly at her house, coming out of the tornado zone. Will she ask me in for a cup of tea? How can I make that more likely other than asking myself in?

"Any chance I could use your toilet? Wouldn't want to get caught short on my way up the hill!" I say. Why did I say that?

"Of course. If it's number one, please don't flush the toilet. The sewage system isn't working properly, so I only flush when necessary. Far end of the hall on the left."

The hall is dark – there's a tarpaulin over the broken French doors in the living room cutting out all the light. When I come back, I'm happy to hear Julia in the kitchen. She calls, "Would you like a cup of tea? Or should you get home to your wife?"

"I'd love tea, thanks. Cynthia is self-contained – lots of practice. She knows I'm out on Thursday evenings for these workshops."

"What made you sign up? We're interested to find out people's reasons in case we expand the idea."

Julia's full of tricky questions this evening.

"Cynthia wants me to expand my group of friends. She likes to hear about people I meet. She says that's almost like her getting to meet new people. Not that I'd tell her about our stories, of course."

"She sounds very nice."

Tears well up unexpectedly. Flashes of Cynthia catch me by surprise sometimes. Twenty years on they don't happen so often, but they feel just as bad as when she first died.

"Yes, er, yes." I turn my head away. "Go through to the sitting room, Stephen," Julia says. "I'll bring the tea."

I drink my tea out of a mug that says, 'Lighten up, sunshine – it could always be raining' and has an umbrella emerging from a repaired crack on its side. It reminds me of 'I'm Singing in the Rain' by Frank Sinatra. I forgot that song in our sing-along after the tornado. Julia's drinking out of her new 'Write your own story' mug. This reminds me of the Humans with Stories Warble group and this evening's messages. "Have you released the messages yet?"

"Thanks for reminding me. D'you mind if I quickly check now and then push the button?"

"Go ahead," I say.

Julia scans her phone screen, bites her lip, and then taps the screen. "All done."

"Anything interesting from tonight?" We need a topic to discuss other than Cynthia.

Julia's face tightens. "We shouldn't discuss other people's comments."

"Why not? Isn't that the goal of the workshops? Building connections?"

"Yes, but I don't want us to form cliques and pick on people. We need to keep things positive."

I remember my negative comment from last meeting. "How about if I promise not to say anything negative? If I do, you can stop me, and we talk about something else."

"Okay, let's try. I suppose I could practise for next workshop." Julia unfolds her arms, then crosses her legs.

I pull my reading glasses out of my jacket pocket and open Warble before she changes her mind.

Andrey: Like you, I must direct my own life.
Choose where and how I live and work. Choose
what is important and have the courage to act
on it.

How does this connect with what Rosemary said? Was it about her choosing psychiatry as a speciality?

I flick my eyes down the list to my name.

"Cynthia tried all sorts of diets to prop up her immune system," I say while remembering I was trying to avoid the topic of Cynthia.

"Has she stopped trying?"

Bloody hell, I used the past tense. "Yes, it all got too hard. Now she just tries to eat well. Lots of vegetables and fruit. No sugar. No meat. Nothing special. Although fresh food is pretty special now – it's so expensive."

"I grow vegetables," Julia says. "I used to grow more but the salt water is affecting them. Do you have a vegetable garden? You won't have a saltwater problem."

"Not as such," I say. Not at all. I really should plant a garden, at least vegetables. With everything so uncertain, it would be good to grow my own food. But even if I could decide where to plant vegetables, I don't know how to grow them. Are there easy vegetables to start off with? Could I practise my way up to hard vegetables? When you are a beginner musician, you don't play the hardest pieces at the start. Do I need a vegetable garden tutor? Could Julia be my tutor? I try to read Julia's connection on my phone without losing the thread of our conversation.

> **Julia**: I didn't want to write the obvious, that supporting each other is why we have this session because the mental health profession isn't enough. However, I haven't thought of anything else I want to write more. I had a long time in which I didn't think I needed other people to help me. I didn't want other people interfering in my life. Fran and Lynda helped me adjust my thinking. I still struggle with asking other people for help even while I know it's the only way forward – us all to support each other as much as we can.

She's looking for people to help her. That's an opening. I look at Fran and Lynda's messages.

> **Fran**: I totally sympathise with your feelings of overwhelm. In schools it's exactly the same. I support children who are struggling with their lives. It's real and heart-breaking. There are more children than I can help and no one and nowhere else to send them. We do our bit with Dolls with Stories, but it feels like we're papering over the cracks.

> **Lynda**: When my aunt cared for me, after my parents died, I had a hard time. I was prescribed antidepressants, and today I'm thankful I deliberately forgot to take them because I was a rebellious teenager. Refusing to take the drugs focused my mind on how to make myself better. I found running and cycling, which are still my drugs of choice.

"Do you three enjoy your Dolls with Stories work?" I ask.

"It's been wonderful, so fulfilling. I still have a great relationship with the first child from our programme. Her name is Aroha – meaning love, you know? The whole enterprise has grown beyond belief. It's Lynda's job to manage it. Fran and I are trustees, as is my twin brother, Johnno. We help Lynda make decisions, though she rarely has a problem with that."

"She does seem definite."

"Absolutely. Lynda's great."

I read the last two messages.

Victoria: Everyone's struggling. There are more people than ever talking about anxiety and depression. I'm sure people are finding lives tougher than a decade ago. Perhaps not tougher than when the early settlers arrived in Aotearoa, though. It's all relative, isn't it?

Eeman: In my hometown of Guaan there are no doctors, only two nurses. For a doctor we go to Manado, four hours' bus ride away. We don't talk about needing help for mental health problems. If people have a problem, they go to church to drive out the evil spirits who have taken them over. I know this is not enough. Of course. I'm in this group. But there might be some truth in our Sulawesi thinking. Bad thoughts lodge in people's heads and won't let go. Medicine does not drive the thoughts out.

"Everyone's writing the same things," I say. "How it's hard to cope. How we need new ways to cope. People are looking for help everywhere they can find it, including church. I don't do the Christian or church thing, though. Do you?"

"No," Julia says.

That's a relief.

"I wasn't brought up in a church," she continues. "Sometimes religion seems a nice idea. An omnipotent being who could solve all our problems if we figure out the right way to ask. Pray nicely enough. Mum tried lots of different religions to see which one worked. She didn't stick with any, so I guess none of them did the trick."

"Is your mum still alive?"

"No, she died a few years ago in Golden Bay. We got closer after COVID because she was excited about Dolls with Stories and started the Takaka branch. Johnno lives there now and runs the branch. He moved over from Oz when it got too hot, and people were angry and scared from alternating wildfires and floods. He was an engineering executive but now he's gone all hippy, like Mum when she was young. Grows his own food and trades time and produce for things he needs. Maybe he caught the hippy thing in Golden Bay, or maybe he always had it in him."

"Sorry about your mum. It's always hard to lose someone, even when you expect it. Time for me to go. Thanks for a great cup of tea."

"Thank you for the discussion about the group comments. Now I have an idea how people can talk through connections rather than writing them."

I walk up Scarborough towards my caravan, running our conversation through my head like a warm pebble in my hand, picked up off a sunny beach. Then I wince as the jagged edge of the rock's underside reminds me I cemented Cynthia into a conversation I'd rather have had with Julia alone.

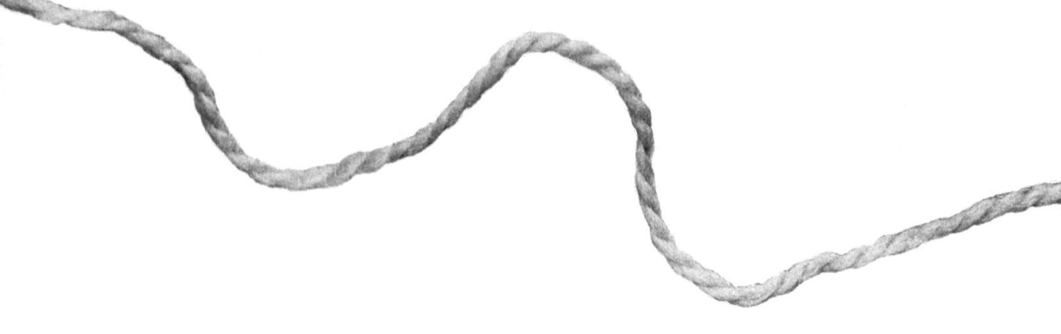

JULIA

5–17 April 2030

I arrange with Fran to meet at Lynda and Robbie's on Saturday. The last workshop could have gone better, and I want to talk about how we'll run the next one. A group chat usually sorts things out. However, first I want cuddle time with Hermione.

I admire an iridescent green micro-scooter parked at the bottom of Lynda's steps. "Like my new ride?" Fran asks as I go in the door. "I've been in the queue for two and a half years and it finally turned up."

"What a glorious colour. Did you choose it?"

"I paid a little extra for custom paint," says Fran. "Holly liked the colour – we're sharing the scooter. She wants to put spots on it and draw beetle wings on the sides. Holly doesn't have the puff to ride a bicycle anymore, even with electric assistance. If we need the scooter at the same time we can play DonkeysRU. She loves that app."

"I could help with the beetle," I say, thinking Holly will always get the scooter.

"Hellooooo," calls Lynda, waving Hermione's hand at us. "Is everyone ignoring me? Am I last month's baby now?"

"Hi, sweetie," I rush over and plant a kiss on Hermione's cheek. "How could I ever think you are less important than a beautiful green scooter? Can I hold her? Hang on, here are the mugs from Rosemary. Who's having which one?"

"I'll take 'Life is better with …' says Lynda, "because I know how to finish the phrase, starting with an 'H'."

"'Coffee is renewable energy …' is good for me," Fran says. "I need all the spare energy I can get."

Lynda passes a well-wrapped Hermione over and Fran and I take turns holding her, looking at the sun sparkling on Pegasus Bay. Robbie brings us all coffee, then takes Hermione away. "Time for you to concentrate and for me to torture my child," he says.

"How'd you find the workshop?" I ask. I'm still wary of Rosemary. However, the group agreed she could stay, and she agreed to follow the group's rules. So I can't go there.

"Rosemary's story was interesting," says Lynda. "You held it together well. Particularly given your history with Rosemary. Not sure I'd want her as my psychiatrist. A doctor who doesn't believe in their profession? The resolution was good. At the beginning of each session, we need to remind people that stories stay in the workshops. Fran?"

"I think you two are managing fine without me needing to provide a view on everything. In fact, so fine I'm handing over these workshops."

"Won't you still Cast in?" I ask.

"You can't just leave," Lynda says.

"I've too much to deal with in my own life, girls. We've got our scheduled Dolls with Stories board meetings, and we can add Humans with Stories as an agenda item. But you need to stand on your own four feet now. Or six feet, if you count Hermione. Never too young to start training for an independent future, right?"

"Anything else you want to tell us about, Fran?" Lynda asks.

"Well," Fran says, "I'm talking with my iwi. It's taking up all the energy and thought I can spare from Holly and my work. I'm considering going up north to meet them."

"Exciting! What have you found out?" Lynda asks.

"Our marae is in Northland, a bit south of Cape Reinga, looking out over the sea. I sent the tribal office the information about my birth mother the Ministry sent through. Then a welcome pack arrived in the mail which had contact details for my aunt Moana, my mother's sister. Moana told me about my whānau. My mother is old and not well, and not yet ready to meet me. Moana hopes it can happen at some point. She says it will be much less confusing for my mother to meet me in person than on the phone or through Cast.

"I'm working on my te reo. I want to be able to talk with my whānau in our language. I did the first three levels at Ara Institute years ago for work. Now I'm improving my conversation and my understanding of the Māori world, te ao Māori. So much to fit in."

I notice again how Fran's skin is crumpling around her mouth and eyes. Her hair is increasingly grey, like mine in which grey strands outnumber the brown. Are we ageing normally, or have the stresses of the earthquakes, then COVID, and now climate change, sped up the ageing process?

"You must focus on your family, Fran," Lynda says. "Like I need to focus on mine." Lynda glances over her shoulder towards the deck where Robbie is talking very seriously with Hermione. "He's so good with her. It's unexpectedly lovely to watch."

Are Fran and Lynda saying I don't have a family, and therefore should be more available? Single women always get the raw end of the deal, like having to care for elderly parents – or grandparent in my case.

Fran reads me easily. "Don't look so huffy, Julia," she says. "Your life is important too. We all need to consider what's most important to us at different times. The two of you can see these Humans with Stories workshops through and then, if it's too much, just stop. It's a trial, not a forever commitment."

"Getting back to business," Lynda says, "What do we think about people interrupting the storyteller to tell their connections? I know I originally suggested that, but now I'm not so sure."

"We'll shift to more of a discussion, less of a monologue," I say. "I think I can make it work. Stephen and I talked about how after the workshop."

"Did you?" Lynda says. "Be careful. We all know what happened when Fran got too close to Matthew at OA."

Fran blushes. It wasn't her proudest moment when she had to ask for help from Lynda and me. Matthew became difficult when she thought she was having a brief liaison and he thought it meant a lot more.

"No problem like that for me," I say. "Stephen has a wife, and I don't do affairs. Sorry, Fran, I didn't mean that the way it sounds."

"Water under the bridge. Although that's not a great saying in times when water doesn't respect bridges, is it?" Fran smiles.

"All sorted then," Lynda says. "Co-designing our workshops with participants is great, isn't it?"

"Will you be able to come next time, Lynda?" I ask. "If not, I'll delegate managing comments to someone else, though I don't know who. I can't tell my story and look for raised hands at the same time."

"I'll come," Lynda says. "I'll feed my little pumpkin. Robbie will bath her and put her to bed. I'll be back for the next feed. Don't expect too much coherent thought from me, though. Lack of sleep is making my brain foggy."

"As long as you keep everyone behaving nicely that's all we need," I say.

I spend the next ten days juggling my various responsibilities, proving to myself I have commitments too. I have a re-creation on the go for a Sumner community charity auction, supporting people de-homed by the tornado. My piece is a human-sized clock created from house debris, including numbers scavenged from broken letter boxes. The hands will point to a thirteenth hour, like in *1984*. We read *1984* in high school and the first sentence about clocks striking thirteen made a lasting impression on me. The world is moving into unprecedented times – my thirteenth-hour rationale. I'm making the clock at the Broken is Beautiful repair centre because it has metalwork tools.

I finish repairing my French doors. I consider a leadlight re-creation, but I'm pushed for time. As a compromise, I make a single leadlight pane commemorating the kōwhai tree. It's great to have sunlight back in my living room and hallway, but I don't want to look at the garden, so the living room remains unappealing. The hole the kōwhai left is like a missing tooth in an elderly person, not a cute child's front gap.

I get Andrey round to chop up the kōwhai trunk. He makes me nervous when he flourishes the chainsaw wildly while talking. He takes the firewood away in trailer-sized increments. The trailer reminds me how brave Lynda was, going to the hospital in the face of a tornado. I didn't ask Zahra to help with the tree – the job wasn't big enough for three and Zahra is rather challenging. However, I must invite Zahra and Victoria round given I said I would.

I call Johnno to tell him about the tornado and its effects. "I don't remember the kōwhai tree," he says. "Must be upsetting, though. I know how much you love Gran's house. How's the garden doing otherwise?"

"Not so good," I say. "Plants aren't growing well. Could be from repeated floods, or salt water."

"Coastal properties up here are in the same boat," Johnno says. "Salt water is killing trees that are decades old. Kannika and I are happy to be in Takaka, well away from the sea." Johnno is in a relationship with one of the Buddhist monks at the yoga centre where Mum worked. He's learnt a lot about Buddhism and is on the way to becoming a monk. My business-focused brother being a monk makes me laugh, but he sounds very happy whenever we talk so it must be the right thing.

"I forgot to mention," I say. "Lynda had her baby the night of the storm. She's called Hermione."

"That's great. Give her my congratulations," Johnno says. "A tornado baby. I'd expect nothing less of Lynda."

I dither about my koha for the workshop. I gave the mug idea to Rosemary. I settle on knitted hats as it's April; trees are turning yellow and orange. Lots of days still in the high twenties Celsius, though. There's no doubt Christchurch is way warmer than when I was a child. I excavate wool from the shed and contemplate interesting hat designs.

I visit Pauline, Grant, and the retirees to see how they are doing – they're doing fine. Everyone who can is tidying up the units, stacking bricks pulled off the exteriors, putting boards over broken glass, and sorting beds in the habitable units rather than just mattresses.

"Lovely to see you, Julia," Pauline says when I arrive. "Shall we have a cup of tea, then you can help us plant some cabbages for winter." No wonder things get done when Pauline is so good at delegating.

My other task is online. I want to find out about Stephen's wife and her quilts. I haven't done much quilting. My creative repair has involved more patchwork – joining together scraps of material rather than layering material and padding. The two processes tend to be confused, with people using patchwork to make bedcovers they call quilts. I didn't ask Stephen his wife's second name, so I type in 'Cynthia, quilting, patchwork, Christchurch'. There are few hits. Unsurprising – many craft people don't publicise their art and not everyone participates in social media. The scale of hate online means lots of people, people who started off keen, now only communicate in secure online spaces and with people they know well. You're never sure whether a 'person' might be a bot. You also never know when your account might be hacked and all your friends sent pictures of mutant three-eyed cats, if you are lucky, or humans doing anatomically impossible things if you are less lucky.

What is surprising in my search results is the top hit – a Cynthia John retrospective exhibition held in 2013 at the Christchurch Art Gallery. Cynthia's patterns are beautiful. They are inspired by New Zealand bush and birds, spanning from realistic to abstract. A lot of her work has a background of greens and browns with a single jewel-like coloured patch drawing the eye. A bright-blue kingfisher darting through lacy emerald leaves. A burst of crimson pohutakawa flowers highlighted by darker green foliage. There's a different piece, dated 2011. It's called 'Catching Time' and is a series of smaller pictures within the larger pattern of the quilt. The pictures are clasped between hands rising out of the subtly patterned background. There's a man's figure, a face, a caravan, two mugs on a table, Sumner Beach seen from above, a small dog, tussocks, a magpie, the sweep of Pegasus Bay. The blurb says, 'The last piece designed and created by Cynthia John before her passing in 2012.'

Could this be a different Cynthia John? It's possible two people of the same name have been quilters in Christchurch. They could both live or have lived on Scarborough, or both have liked the views at this end of the Port Hills. The caravan is a nineteen seventies curved shape with turquoise horizontal panels. The thin face belongs to a man and is framed by curls. He could be a young Stephen, or not.

However, the male figure is holding a guitar.

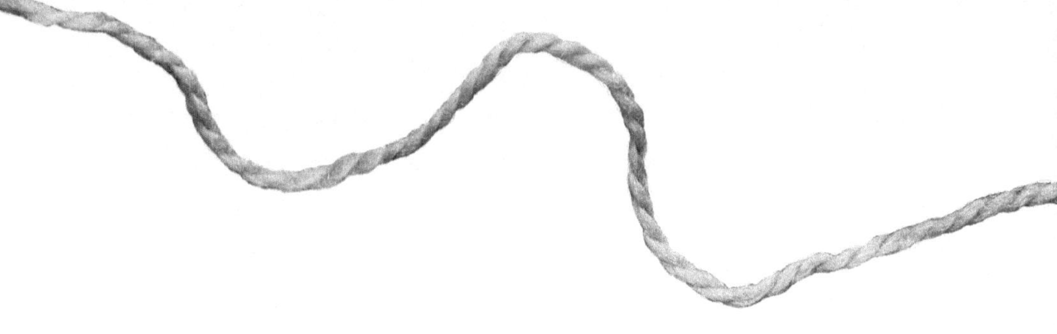

STEPHEN

5–17 April 2030

My untruths about Cynthia are becoming more and more of a problem. Every time I talk with Julia I reinforce them when that's exactly not what I want to do. I went to the workshop to change my story. Why am I making no progress? I only have the same answer to the same question – habit. Programmed words come out of my mouth and I'm struggling to change the code.

I use my routine to avoid thinking about my problem. I check my automated trades. I visit my clients. My oil executive has died. His ex-wife and children are already in the media wrangling over his estate – it will be a long time before my bill is paid. Good thing I have my trading income.

I have a new elderly client who was an opera singer, music teacher and lover of country music. 'Your Song' has taught me how many people love country music. I'd never have guessed. This client wants me to write her a country ballad. She wishes she had tried harder to be the New Zealand Dolly Parton. "Everyone can sing along – country is about people, whereas opera is about performers," she said. "Who doesn't know and love '9 to 5' or 'Coat of Many Colours'? Look at your face, eyebrows raised. Everyone's the same. Opera gets a stupid amount of prestige. Opera paid my bills, so I kept doing it. I should have been braver and done what I wanted."

My client understands living a pretence. I'm tempted to talk with her about Cynthia. However, I'm supposed to be lightening her load through song, not adding to it.

Felicity has asked me to work with a younger client. Felicity's been filling in for some shifts at the public hospital child oncology ward. She's met a child who's had a tough life, much of it in State care, and may die of bone cancer.

"B needs something positive to focus on and adores music, Stephen," Felicity said. "B listens to music every minute of the day. When B's feeling well B's always singing and writing songs in a book that she keeps hidden. B needs to fight for life and needs a reason to take on that fight."

B doesn't fit. I don't work with dying children. And B might not be dying; I work with dying adults. How can I create a meaningful song for B? I don't know what music young girls might like.

Hang on, is B a girl? I don't think Felicity said, which is weird. I'm assuming 'B' is short for Beatrice. This is too difficult and complicated. I need to tell Felicity I can't do it.

It might be fun, Stephen, Cynthia suggests. *Children have so much infectious energy.*

I ignore her.

I check my algorithms are adapting to the changing markets. Yes, all good. I expanded to international shares for a while, but I've retreated to the New Zealand stock market. Exchange rates are all over the place. When a country goes to war, their currency devalues overnight. There are too many wars in too many places. Wars over land. Wars over food. Wars over water.

I go onto Rappit. There's a local scrolling chat channel I like called 'The Republic of Sumner'. Scrolling chat was invented to hook people onto social media – you have to be watching to see the messages and comment on them. They vanish after an hour. I like the impermanence of scrolling chat – messages here now and then gone. You can't even screen shot or photograph them. That's one of the clever parts of the software. I've tried to beat it, but I can't stop the words blurring in the pictures.

Rappit manages to evade authentication laws so it's the right place for people who want to stay incognito. In the early 2020s, there was a big push for online authentication. The Christchurch Call was part of it. Then Prime Minister Jacinda Ardern called for identification of people on social media after a white supremacist gunned down fifty-one Moslems praying in a mosque. The shooter broadcast from a head cam and right-wing groups rapidly shared the video globally.

However, before authentication was enforced the obvious happened – people figured out how to avoid authentication. The web's moles pop up faster than law enforcement can whack them. Rappit requires authentication at sign-up but allows users to select a pseudonym which is dissociated from the authentication. At least the admin info says it is. It might be true – Rappit's claim to fame is that law enforcement has never uncovered one of their users.

I assume 'The Republic of Sumner' started off as a joke – people suggesting Sumner should secede from Christchurch because expensive Sumner houses paid high rates while the city forgot to maintain their infrastructure. Now the city isn't maintaining anyone's infrastructure, so Sumner's nothing special. The seaside and hillside suburbs get flooded or hit by landslides regularly. However, suburbs built in places that used to be swamps, like St Albans and Mairehau, are badly off too.

'The Republic of Sumner' channel started off by suggesting action no one was likely to take, such as cutting off the road to the city to stop weekend tourists. Now it's a cross between realistic action and useful information. Here's a typical post.

RECLAIM THE MATERIALS. 2AM 10 APRIL AT THE CLOCK TOWER

Pekko: Stockpiling? Personal use?

Taiaha: If u need it take & use it. No stockpiling.

Phaedra: What's on offer?

Sophocles: Come n c.

Rhiannon: All comers welcome?

Taiaha: Nau mai haere mai. Everyone's welcome. Leave 0000 for insurance bastards.

What materials might be reclaimed? I assume the Sumner Republicans are 'reclaiming' materials from tornado-struck houses. I could join in; get materials for a shed.

No, I couldn't. How would I carry building materials up Scarborough Hill? And what would I do in a new shed I can't do in my caravan or container? There's a lot of stuff in the storage container I haven't looked at for years. I should probably throw it out. Except, not Cynthia's materials. I don't want to look at those.

And should people be reclaiming materials from broken houses? The owners might need their house parts for repair or to build something else. I wonder whether messages will turn into visible action. I should remember to look at the damaged zone next time I walk to Sumner, likely the next Humans with Stories workshop.

Humans with Stories brings me back to the Julia and Cynthia problem. Julia's interesting. And friendly. Well, more or less friendly. She lives close by. It might be nice to have someone I can visit for a cup of tea. I haven't had a friend for a long time. However, conversations are going to stay awkward if I have to keep my story about a live Cynthia straight and Julia can never meet her.

Could Cynthia become terminally ill and die suddenly? She became terminally ill, only that was twenty years ago. Could I take her through a virtual dying process? It'd be quick because now she'd be unlikely to receive treatment for Stage 4 cancer. I don't know if lack of treatment would have been better, or worse, than what happened to Cynthia. She had a double mastectomy, then chemotherapy, then faded to a shadow before dying. Two years after Cynthia died I had to put Maisie, our Jack Russell down. She was fifteen and had developed widespread cancer. It was a straightforward request to the vet that Maisie be euthanised to avoid pain and suffering. The contrast was too obvious.

I will drop in at Julia's on my way to Humans with Stories next week and we can look at the damaged houses together. She did invite me to drop in for a cup of tea. Except, I can't drop in for a cup of tea just before a meeting. I'll say I was passing and saw her through her window. No, I can't say that because you can't see into her living areas from the street. I will wait on Wiggins Street in sight of her house and watch for her to leave, then catch up with her. Except she has an exit from her garden onto Head Street which she might use. Maybe I'll knock on her door and offer to help her carry things to the fire station. She is talking next meeting, so she'll have food and gifts to carry. Yes, maybe I will.

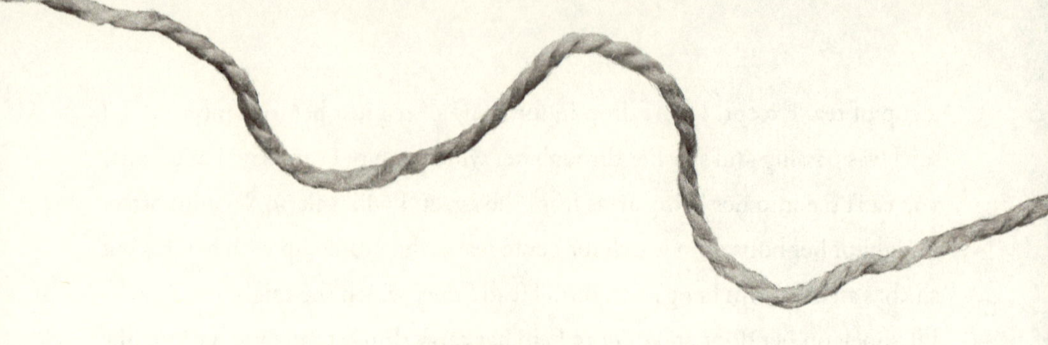

JULIA

18 April 2030

I'm running through what I will say at today's workshop in the shower when I hear a soft knock on my front door. Funny time for someone to drop in. I yank on an old pinafore dress and open the door.

"Hi, I was walking past and thought you'd be heading to the fire station," Stephen says. "Can I help you carry anything?"

I am not ready and wanted to use my walk to put my head into presentation mode. However, I can't think of a polite way to tell Stephen I'd rather walk on my own and he should trot along there by himself. It's nice he thought of helping me. "Give me a couple of minutes to get changed and we can go together. The food is in the kitchen in shopping bags." My knitted hats are in a pack with my iPad in case Lynda decides not to come at the last minute. She's planning to, but anything can happen with a small baby.

Fran definitely isn't coming; nothing Lynda nor I can say is shifting her position. We had a text exchange on Monday.

L: Hi Fran, how's ur week?

F: Busy. Co-teacher sick. Holly sick too.

J: Sounds hard. Will we c u this week? Cd cheer u up?

F: No time. Need 2 focus.

Stephen and I walk along Wiggins Street. I'm trying to rehearse my story in my head.

"Look at what's happening to the houses." Stephen breaks in.

"Happening?" I look at the tornado-struck houses to see they are vanishing piece by piece. Some have partial roofs; on others all the roofing iron is gone. I'm sure they weren't so derelict immediately after the tornado. Windows and doors are missing, and weatherboards are being stripped off. The tornado did not cleanly remove doors and windows.

"You're right," I say. "Something is happening. It's too soon for insurance or the council to be doing anything, even if houses are red-stickered."

We learnt about red-stickering after the Canterbury earthquakes. A red sticker means a house is officially unsafe to live in. However, people are still living in some of the tornado-damaged red-stickered houses, ripping the stickers off the front doors, leaving tell-tale pink strips of dangling paper. There are tents inside buildings that are little more than shells. People are cooking on camp stoves and barbecues. Will Civil Defence, or someone else, come and forcibly evict people from the red-stickered dwellings? Probably not. There's been another massive rain storm event in the north and west of the South Island since the tornado. The Buller River has finally washed away the remains of old Westport on the West Coast. A new town was being built inland; hopefully, it is ready for the people who now need it. The new disaster has sucked resources and focus away from Sumner, so these houses and their occupants likely have a stay of execution. When I look closer, I see occupied houses are not losing their components, only the empty ones.

"Perhaps locals are taking the materials," Stephen says.

"That sounds dodgy. People shouldn't steal bits off other people's houses. I'd be really upset if the outside of my house started disappearing. Wouldn't you? I hope Pauline and Grant's units aren't being pillaged. Although they were fine the last time I visited."

"You saw Pauline and Grant again?" Stephen says.

"Yes," I say. "Haven't you?" I badly want him to stop talking so I can think about my story for this evening.

"No." Stephen speeds up his pace, and we walk in silence the rest of the way.

We're the first to arrive at the fire station. Stephen puts my food offerings on the bench – tomato slices sprinkled with basil on buckwheat, and quinoa crackers and vegan pumpkin pies with smiley faces on them. Mini pumpkin pies are my signature dish because of the number of pumpkins I used to grow before my garden started withering.

Lynda arrives soon after Stephen and me. "Ohhhh, pumpkin pies, my favourite. I love their nutmeg smell. I'll never forget the look on your face, Julia, when we both brought pumpkin pies to OA. You were so upset, and I wanted to cheer you up. Smiley faces on your pies, how cute. Remember the demonic brownies Matthew made?"

Zahra and Victoria arrive together. I hear animated discussion in the stairwell, then the conversation shuts down when they enter the room.

Andrey bounds up the stairs and yells, "Hello, everyone. How are we all today?" He is wearing a bright yellow jacket and purple shorts whose only commonality is the intensity of their colour. Zahra goes over to Andrey while Victoria takes a seat. Rosemary arrives, with a tense pale face, and Lynda greets her. I'm not up to making Rosemary comfortable. Eeman is late, once again, but his arrival at 6.40pm is an improvement on last time.

"Sorry, sorry, sorry, everyone. I was tutoring a student after school and our session ran on. We read the *Blowing Bubbles* book. He wrote down what he was worried about then we blew soap bubbles, named them with the worries and watched as they flew up into the sky and popped. He got his ukulele out and we sang the song from the book together. Turns out, my student is much happier playing his instrument than reading, so we will continue working on his language through song. His family are all very enthusiastic about music. Stephen, perhaps you could join us sometime?"

"Possibly," Stephen says. "I don't play the ukulele, though. The chords are different from guitar."

Lynda walks to the front of the room. "Tēnā koutou, tēnā koutou, tēnā koutou katoa. Great to see you all in person again. Was it only four weeks ago I got in the bicycle trailer? Or a lifetime? It is the lifetime of my new daughter, Hermione. She says thank you to everyone for helping her get born. Or she would if she could talk. So far, she is limiting herself to eating and excreting. She'll get onto talking in due course.

"I was relieved to hear the tornado didn't significantly affect anyone in this group though it has had a major impact on our suburb. If you would like to donate to the cause, there's a Sumner Tornado Give_A_Shit_Then_Give_A_Bit page."

I follow on. "As we talked about last workshop, we agree stories told in this room stay in this room. All good? Ka pai?"

There's a chorus of "Yes."

"And we've changed our format so people will explain their connection with the speaker's story during the meeting. Please try to pick a sensible break in the story – my story tonight – to make your connection. And to keep a record for the group send your comment to the group chat."

"Do we still bring our phones up?" Andrey asks.

"Yes, please come to the front to speak with your phone."

"Do we have to speak?" says Eeman.

"No. If you really don't want to speak, it'll be like before. Put your hand up, bring your phone to the table and receive your koha."

"One last thing," says Lynda, "is no negative comments. We are looking for commonalities, not dissimilarities. I'm excited to see tonight's koha and kai. It's like Christmas every two weeks. Any more questions?"

Everyone shakes their head.

We make our way creditably through the karakia. "Now, please tell us your story, Julia," Lynda says.

I'm on. I remember how stressed I felt when I told the assembled OA participants I was obsessed with collecting broken things. That's no longer my problem. I have a much bigger problem. We all do.

JULIA

18 April 2030

"I'm petrified by climate change and what it means for me and my life," I say. "Climate change threatens my house. Tonight I'll tell you a story about what makes my house my home.

"Once upon a time, early in the twentieth century, Ma and Pa Stout moved to Sumner from Christchurch because rich holidaymakers needed people to work for them. Ma and Pa Stout camped in the sand dunes and marram grass on a piece of land given to them because no one wanted to live on the flat; all the important people lived on the hills, with views. In the valley, winds blew sand into people's eyes and grit into their houses. Rain washed silt down from the hills and flooded the land. However, Ma and Pa Stout couldn't believe their luck. One day they'd have their own house. For the time being, Pa Stout built rich people's houses and Ma Stout cleaned them. In his spare time, Pa Stout started constructing their own house and, piece by piece, he made them a place to live where they brought up my gran.

"Gran raised her daughter in the same house – my mum, Caroline. Then Gran raised my twin brother Johnno and me in it. Twenty-nine Head Street was our haven when we were children, away from the parties my mother regularly threw in the shared houses where she lived. It's the house in which Johnno and I told each other scary stories as we lay in our twin beds. Where Gran made us birthday cakes from the *Australian Women's Weekly* and we competed to be the quickest blowing candles out. It's the house in which we licked sugary cream off the beater and stirred golden syrup into our porridge. Where flannelette sheets in winter kept us warm. Where I cared for my gran as she became older and more frail. The house in which she died. The house she left me."

Stephen has raised his hand. Lynda says, "Stephen, what would you like to contribute?"

Stephen half stands like he's not sure whether to stand or sit.

"Stephen, please come up to the front," Lynda says, but he doesn't move.

"I know what you mean about a place being important, Julia." Stephen pauses and takes a big gulp of air. "Where I, I mean, we live … it's fundamental." His shoulders slump. "On the land my wife and I chose, I love the views in every direction: of Sumner valley, of the sea with shifting patterns of light, of golden hills in summer and green in winter. I couldn't live anywhere else. That's all." He sits back down, propping his chin on his hands.

"Julia," says Lynda, "can you offer Stephen a gift?"

Oh yes, I need to get the basket of gifts. My prompt would have been Stephen putting his phone on the table, but he has forgotten.

I take the hats over to him and he chooses the hat I made like a patchwork blanket, with different shapes and colours crocheted together. The blues and greens and greys of the patchwork go well with the dark-blue Icebreaker hoodie he's wearing.

"Shall I put your phone on the front table, Stephen?" He passes it to me, carefully holding the end out so our fingers don't touch.

It's time for the hardest part. "In the Canterbury earthquakes, someone died in my home. My daughter, Amanda. A mirror fell from the wall in the last big earthquake and crushed her."

I hear sharp intakes of breath. This story still stabs my heart, but nothing like the way it did back when I started going to Obsessives Associated during COVID. At that time, I had told no one about Amanda and had no one in my life left to tell the story to. Telling Fran and Lynda unlocked my future. Now this story has a well-worn track down which I can move foot by careful foot, without tripping when my eyes blur with tears.

"A mural of flowers I painted in Amanda's room before she was born reminds me of her and welcomes guests. My home is the only place she ever slept in her short life."

Rosemary has put her hand up. What could she have to say about Amanda? She got in the way of my telling Robbie about Amanda and getting closer to him when he lived in my house. If I'd had the chance to do that … Don't be ridiculous, Julia, I reprimand myself. You were always way too old for Robbie. Lynda and he are just right.

"Please come up to the front and tell us your connection, Rosemary," says Lynda.

"Julia, I'm so sorry about what happened back at the end of the big COVID lockdown. I shouldn't have come to your house without asking you. It was your place and homes are precious, especially when times are scary, like during COVID and now. My only excuse is I was young and thinking of nothing except how much I fancied Robbie. And how tough my life was because I was working long shifts at the hospital wearing uncomfortable protective gear. I didn't think about you at all and now, hearing about Amanda, I feel terrible and wish I hadn't been so selfish."

"Err … thank you, Rosemary." Can everyone see my face is bright red? This is not what I was expecting. A fulsome apology from Rosemary in front of a room full of people. How can I continue to dislike her now? I hold the basket out for her to look through, forcing myself to look her in the eye and smile over the lump in the back of my throat.

"I'd like this one, please, Julia," Rosemary says. She takes out a bright green frog hat with bulging froggy eyes and surprises me for the second time in the evening. I'd knitted that hat with flamboyant Andrey, or Eeman, in mind. Eeman's eyes are a little bulgy, not that it's nice of me to notice. "I can wear this hat for my clients to brighten up their day," Rosemary says and puts it on her red curls.

I glance down at the prompt cards hidden in my hand to get back on track. Lynda suggested cards would help and she was right, as she usually is.

"The impact of the earthquakes on my home reverberated through my life. Amanda's death never leaves me. And I took out a loan to improve my house when the earthquake damage was being fixed. Gran always warned me about the risks of being in debt, but I chose to learn the hard way. I wasn't paying the interest on my loan and the bank threatened to sell my house to get their money back. My situation looked bleak in every direction. However, from that terrible time came a surprising opportunity. The bank required me to attend a support group and I went to Obsessives Associated, where I met Fran and Lynda."

Lynda comes to the front of the room. It's the obvious point for her to link in. "We have so many connections, Julia," she says. "The stories we keep telling each other about the Canterbury earthquakes. Meeting in COVID times and our friendship as clutter buddies. We learnt how to free our houses and ourselves from the objects we hid behind. And now there's our ongoing connection through Dolls with Stories. You and Fran and I have helped hundreds of children and their mentors to use storytelling to build good, shared lives. I have you to thank for giving Robbie a home in the COVID lockdown. Otherwise he might have left Aotearoa, and I wouldn't have met him. You took him in and became his friend. As a result, he's with me, and we have Hermione. Hermione makes me both happy and scared. What sort of world will there be for her to grow up in? But I'm not sending her back!"

I hold out the basket of hats to Lynda with a smile. I'm sure I know which one she'll take. Yes, she pulls out the hat with a runner on the top. The runner's electric blue hair stands in a vertical ponytail, creating a crowning pom-pom. Lynda puts the hat on and shakes the pom-pom vigorously from side to side as she sits back down.

"Fran and Lynda's friendship helped me stay sane and stay in my home," I say. "I paid back my loan and will never take out another. I thought my life was sorted. It wouldn't always be easy, but I never imagined my home would be at risk again. However, now I have to face the possibility my home is threatened by something I can't fix. On the days I let myself think about what's happening, I don't know how much longer I can live there. When it rains, I can't flush my toilet. Sometimes it takes several days after a downpour before the sewage works again. Should I build a long drop? Would the council care? Might the neighbours complain? Or will they be building one too? But my storm water isn't working properly either, sometimes a lake laps at my doorstep. That might be a problem if I had a long drop.

"My power goes out unexpectedly; I'm sure yours does too. I can still cook on my gas hob. However, Mitre 10 says bottled gas will soon be in short supply. We are phasing out fossil fuel gas by 2035 as part of New Zealand's commitment to the Prague 2026 Emergency Climate Change Summit. But we don't have enough biogas generation. Do I install an old-style wood stove that will heat my house and hot water and cook my food all at the same time? It would be expensive to buy and would make my tiny kitchen hot in summer. What's the best thing to do when I don't know how long I can stay on? And if I can't sell my house because it floods and the sewage doesn't work, how can I afford to live somewhere else?"

Andrey stands up. "Please share your connection with us," says Lynda.

"You are right, Julia," Andrey says. "It is all so difficult to know what's best. So difficult for us little people. The world is dying. For decades, scientists told us climate change would happen. Nearly ten years ago governments admitted we were headed for a catastrophic two degrees Celsius or more of warming. Every year in Aotearoa there are many 'one-in-a-hundred-year' deluges and windstorms. Like our tornado. But the people who make money off raping the planet don't want to stop making money. They continue to destroy our environment by producing things we don't need. They pretend they are good by donating money to help the environment. Better they didn't harm it in the first place. The only good billionaire is billionaire who has given away all their money, I say. Billionaires do not fix things. Governments do not fix things. We, the people, must fix things. We must stand up where the government does not and do what we know is right!"

I'm not sure what connection Andrey is explaining, but righteous fury has overwhelmed him. I offer the hats, hoping to slow his tirade. He shakes his head and blinks, then chooses and dons a red and orange striped jester's hat with bells on. "Wow, listen to me," he says. "Can't I go on!"

"Thanks, Andrey," I say. "I know all these things are happening. The planet is too warm. The sea floods the land. Then I choose not to think about the bad things in order to keep on living. I can't be terrified and unhappy the whole time; who can function when they are perpetually scared? Isn't that why we all ignore what's happening until something smacks us in the face? Like the neighbour's trampoline? We stay in our houses till a tornado blows us out, or a flood washes us away, or we collapse with an undermined cliff. I mend the windows where the kōwhai tree fell into my front room after the tornado. I think about what hats to knit you all, what kai to prepare for our workshop. Small things that keep my brain busy and not thinking about … it's not the elephant in the corner I'm ignoring, it's the tiger in the middle of the room that's already clawing at my life."

Victoria puts her hand up. "Please share your thoughts, Victoria," says Lynda.

"You are describing how my life feels too, Julia. There are so many small things to do every day, there's no time or energy left to think about big things. At the hospital I am working, working, working, every minute of the day. There aren't enough staff. I take on extra shifts. I can't go on holiday because then my exhausted colleagues have to do my work. All these sick people coming into the hospital; sometimes patients are happy to be sick because then they can forget about their lives, at least until they're better. That's a recipe to create a lot of sick people, if being sick is easier than being well!"

I pass the basket of hats to Victoria, and she pulls out my favourite hat. It has an interlocking pattern of people holding each other's hands and feet on a cream background, inspired by my mug from Aroha. Every person connects to four other people as if they are skydiving en masse. Some are falling right way up, some are falling upside down, some are falling like sacks of potatoes and some dance as they fall.

"I remember giving myself up to being sick, Victoria," I say. "It was easier to be sick than well because getting better required too much effort. The way things are now, I no longer know what better is. Better might not be very good. Do we need to accept things won't get fixed? They won't be like before?

"I should do something about big problems, but I can't solve my own tiny problems. Do I really need to help solve climate change? I'm doing my bit. I've never learnt to drive, so I never owned a car. That was lucky for me when energy quotas came in, I didn't have to give much up. I've never flown in a plane. Neither Mum nor Gran could afford airfares when we were children. Then I was too busy looking after Gran. Then I had no money. Then there was COVID. Finally, I had enough money and was planning to exhibit my re-creations internationally. But Air Aotearoa went down the gurgler, along with so many other international airlines."

Zahra has her hand up and Lynda asks her to come forward.

"I resonate with what you're saying, Julia. But I think we need to tackle the big problems, not just the little ones. We need to stop pretending things will be okay if we drive less, stop eating meat, recycle properly. No one collects the recycling bins half the time. And who knows where the recycling goes? But that isn't the point, is it? We have huge problems and the people in power are doing nothing to solve them. Like Andrey said, it's up to us little people to do whatever we can. We must make the change we need to see. We need to be the change!"

I'm not sure being the change is what I was trying to convey, but I proffer the basket of hats and Zahra chooses a plain black beanie with a long wool plait of many colours hanging off it. She perches the hat on her head with its bright tail falling through her dreads, then sits back down.

"The last part of my story is about my garden." I need to wind up before everyone tires of hearing me talk. "My garden is an extension of my home and myself. Ma Stout planted the oldest of my kōwhai trees. Gran left me nasturtiums and Granny's bonnets and daffodils. My dahlias and peonies remind me of my friend Bev, who surfed until she died, aged ninety-two. I have a bird of paradise plant as a memorial to my mum because it's so colourful when it flowers, but random in its flowering. In the middle of my garden is my mosaic sofa with swirling taniwha and fish, created from the remains of Gran's plates and cups I picked up off the floor after the February 2011 earthquake. Then there's my ugly shed, where I remember golden lockdown days with Robbie. When he helped me start sorting the broken objects that were overwhelming me.

"My garden is as much my home as my house is. But it's dying. Nothing grows properly anymore because salt water is coming up into the soil. My oldest kōwhai tree fell down in the tornado. My cabbage tree leaves are yellow. My fruit trees barely grow leaves and had no fruit this year. My garden used to supply food for me that I shared with friends. Pumpkin pie won't be the same with bought pumpkins. And what will the birds eat next spring if there are no kōwhai flowers or fruit blossom?"

Eeman puts his hand up tentatively. "Please, tell us what you'd like to share, Eeman," Lynda says.

"God has put us on this earth to care for it, protecting and enhancing his beautiful work. For me, gardening is the same as praying. When I am in my garden, I am closer to God and his creations. I grow vegetables to remind me of Guaan. When my garden doesn't grow, I am sad. I am sad for you, Julia, that your garden is no longer growing well."

I see Andrey and Zahra exchange a comment and Stephen screw his face up. Eeman's on his own here in his belief in God. However, apart from God, what he believes in doesn't sound so different from what I believe in.

There are two hats left in the basket. I knitted an extra so the last person could choose, rather than being left with the hat no one else wanted. Eeman opts for the hat with red roses erupting from the knitted surface.

"Thank you for the hat, Julia," Eeman says. "In Guaan we always tried to grow roses. Year after year we tried. When the rains came, the flowers would stick shut and the leaves would go black and wither. In Aotearoa, I grow beautiful roses and it makes me quietly happy."

I take the last hat out of the basket and put it on, given everyone else is wearing theirs. One half has sunflowers under a blue sky. The other has a tornado with something disappearing up into its spiral which could be a tree or a person with only their arms visible, reaching desperately towards the ground.

"I'm a workshop co-leader, but we're all the same, aren't we?" I say. "We're galloping down the road wearing blinkers so we don't see the frightening things coming our way. But if we can't see what frightens us, how can we avoid it?"

I stop and take in a big breath. The room is still and seven sets of eyes stare back at me like horses who have swung their heads far enough sideways to glimpse an oncoming double-decker bus.

After a pause, Lynda steps forward. "Julia, those are all hard questions. Should we act? At what scale should we act? Do we try to change the country, save ourselves, or both?

"Right, time for some breathing space. Anyone for kai? Julia makes the best pumpkin pies."

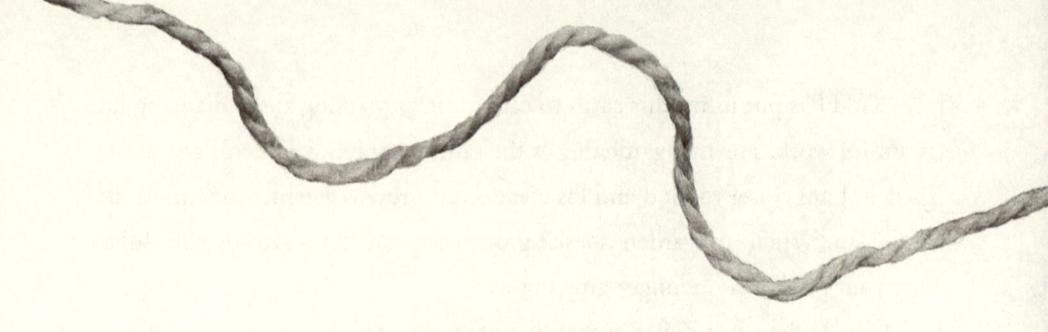

STEPHEN

18 April 2030

Everyone is wearing their hats, so I put my patchwork hat on. I'm glad I didn't end up with a frog on my head. I would prefer to get my drink and food and listen to other people's conversations, but Rosemary comes up beside me as I take a sweet bite of pie.

"Which supplements has your wife tried? Have you seen Julia Rucklidge's *Eating Your Way to a Great Brain*? It covers which micronutrients might be missing from your food."

"Thanks for the suggestion," I say as the pie crumbles in my fingers. "I will tell Cynthia about it. She's tried so many supplements I can't remember them all. Just got to wash my hands. Back in a minute."

When I return, Rosemary is talking with Julia and Lynda, although Julia is edging away.

I follow as Julia goes to the bench for a hot drink. "Oh, bother. I've chosen peppermint," she says, sniffing the tea. "I meant to get feijoa. Peppermint tastes like postage stamps. How they used to taste. Remember postage stamps?"

"Of course," I say. "I've always thought that about peppermint tea, too. Great pumpkin pie. I'd ask for the recipe, but I'm not much of a baker." I wait for Julia to say, "I could make you some." Of course she doesn't. I have a non-dead wife who could make me pumpkin pie in our non-existent kitchen. "There are a lot of songs about tea. Do you know 'Katie's Tea' by Camille?"

"No, but we used to sing 'Tea for Two' with my gran."

I'm about to follow up with another tea song when Lynda interrupts us.

"Well done, Julia. That was great. We need to be able to raise difficult subjects. I try to get Robbie to talk about some of this hard stuff. How the world is falling apart, and we are watching it happen. How Hermione's future may be a scorched earth. He agrees with me, then changes the subject; like how many times Hermione pooed today. Or he pooed today."

"Lynda, we don't need to know how many times a day Robbie poos," Julia says.

"He said sometimes five times a day. I said, 'No way. Are you sick?' He said that's normal for him. How many times a day do you poo? I only go the once unless I do a big run too soon after eating."

"Lynda, were you listening to me? Nobody other than people with babies talks about poo all the time."

"Have I forgotten normality already? Only one month in? Sorry, Julia. Sorry, Stephen."

Hopefully, Lynda won't tax me on how many times a day I poo. Morning and evening? Should I know?

"What did you two think of people making their connections during the story? Did it work for you, Julia? I reckon it made for a better workshop," Lynda says.

"It wasn't as hard as I thought it would be." Julia sips her tea. "It was good to talk for short bursts with breaks. The cards helped when I had to restart, although it was hard not to repeat myself."

"How about Andrey's rant?" Lynda says.

"Andrey's intense. He obviously cares a lot about what's going on, on a big scale."

"Wonder what he'll talk about next workshop when it's his turn?" Lynda says.

I shift my attention to Victoria and Eeman, on my other side. I'd like to talk more with Julia, but not while Lynda's there.

"What vegetables do you find most productive?" Victoria is asking Eeman. "I'm trying to grow vegetables. I'll have more time when our babies are born; Zahra and I will both take a year off work for whānau bonding."

"Lettuces are easy. And sprouting broccoli. When I first met the cycle tourists in my village, I knew nothing about vegetables in other countries.

I took them to our cabbage patch and asked if they knew these vegetables. Geoff said politely, 'I recognise them. Cabbages, right?' I joke about that with Nicky sometimes – how ordinary cabbages are in Aotearoa. She reminds me we introduced her to Pepsi Blue, and she wondered if it would turn her pee blue. She was very disappointed we had a pit toilet so she couldn't see the colour. People here don't know how lucky they are, having electricity and water coming to their houses."

Why is everyone talking about pee and poo today? Did Julia's mention of her sewage problems set the group off? I use a composting toilet. It's a good option where there's no sewage system. Perhaps Julia would like to see it. Except she can't come to see my composting toilet because then she'll see my lack of a house. And lack of a wife.

"Stephen," Eeman says, "could you come visit my local family next time I tutor there? I want to use more music in my teaching, but I have no formal training and do not play an instrument. You led our singing so well in the tornado."

I clear my throat. "I'm quite busy." Eeman is fine but the less I have to do with religion the better.

"That's okay, I wouldn't want to inconvenience you," Eeman says.

I can look rude or say yes. Julia might be listening. "However, next week is less busy than usual. Someone cancelled."

"Next Wednesday afternoon? I will check with the family." Eeman smiles. "Thank you so much for offering, Stephen."

I didn't offer; however, his smile is heart-warming to the point I almost forget he is religious. "Let's talk about which songs to sing."

We exchange phone numbers then I slide away to check the pumpkin pie plate. It's empty. I hear jingling and see Zahra and Andrey on the far side of the room. Andrey is waving his arms, shaking his jester hat. Zahra stands with arms crossed.

Lynda calls the room to attention. "Lovely to hear so many enthusiastic conversations, but it's time to wrap up. Did making connections during the session work?"

"It was fine," says Andrey.

Victoria says, "I was concerned for the speaker, being interrupted, but I liked it as a listener."

"I didn't like the idea before I spoke, but it was okay," Julia says. "Should we ask the people who haven't yet spoken because they will be the most affected?"

"Andrey and Victoria have already told us," Lynda says. "Zahra?"

"No problem," Zahra says.

"Stephen?" Linda says.

Everyone else is happy. "Fine," I say.

"Any other changes people would like? No? I'm sure everyone has plenty to think about after tonight. Thank you, Julia, for being so honest with us. Now our closing karakia and then everyone can go home to enjoy the long Easter weekend."

I'm not sure about this Māori language thing. It's okay for kids in school to learn Māori; it expands their brains and they can all talk together. However, everyone knows it's nearly impossible to learn a language well when you're older, and who wants to speak a language badly? You could be saying something completely different from what you mean. It's hard enough in English. I practised the karakia, using the link Fran sent, but I'm sure I sounded nothing like the orator's beautiful deep voice. However, repeating the words of the karakia with the group is calming and warming at the same time. I gather that feeling to carry home.

STEPHEN

18 April 2030

I hang around to catch Julia, but she stays deep in conversation with Lynda and doesn't notice me. Asking if there's anything she needs carrying home is too pathetic because Lynda goes in the same direction and could help. I leave the room with my new hat on and wave in their direction.

"Mā te wā." Lynda waves back.

Julia's story impressed me. She talked about how scared she is, but she wasn't acting scared. We're all in the same boat with climate change affecting where we live. Although we might be in different boats. Julia's house is already close to going under.

I used to feel superior to people near the sea. Why didn't they think about what might happen? Huge houses were built near the shore. People with too much money and no common sense. They should have built on the hills. I hadn't thought as much about people who'd lived in Sumner for a long time. People who bought ordinary houses because they enjoyed being near the sea when no one was worried about sea levels rising. Those people belong in Sumner. They can't sell their houses so can't buy anywhere else. Will people have enough money to rent if they lose their houses? Will there be enough rentals for them to live in? Could people like Julia end up homeless?

It was surprising how positive the room felt today given Julia's story. Maybe humans bond best when they are facing a common enemy. I wasn't expecting to get a sense of connection out of the workshops. I just wanted a place I could tell my real story and not be judged by anyone who knew me. And I messed that up right from the beginning.

I don't necessarily like all the people in the workshop. I don't like all my clients either, of course. Eeman still irritates me with his tiresome God thing. God put us on this earth to be the rulers of this kingdom and care for it – give me a break. We aren't doing much caring. If human beings vanished off the planet it would be better off. The gods don't make much sense.

I consider my own small kingdom as I walk up the first steep incline on Scarborough, then gently along the top of the hill. How secure is my place in the face of climate disaster? Pretty good, overall. It's near the crest of the hill, with a gradual slope off the western side, so not flood-prone. Big macrocarpa trees on the boundaries protect me from wind. Should I plant additional lines of trees in case the macrocarpas die? I have wondered this often. If I plant new trees, they could harm the macrocarpas. Or the macrocarpas might prevent the new trees from growing, wasting my efforts.

My caravan and container are guyed down with wires, attached to metre-deep concrete piles. I didn't like putting the concrete in, in case it interfered with future pipes or wires. However, after a big nor'wester early on, when the caravan rocked from side to side and Cynthia couldn't sleep all night (nor could I), I did it to stop her worrying.

I'm not connected to city power, water, or sewage; this now seems like an advantage. When we bought the property, it didn't have to have connections. I've avoided having anything to do with authorities because I don't want anyone to notice I've lived in a caravan for years. I collect rainwater from an iron roof I built above the container and store it in a thirty-thousand-litre tank. That's more than enough water given my composting toilet. My 5kW array of solar panels is on frames, built so I can move them to optimise a house site; I bought them when we moved here so they're not producing as well as they once did. They're hooked up to a second-hand lithium battery from an electric car. I'd like another battery for when we have a lot of grey days in a row but there's a queue of at least a year for orders. Perhaps I should go ahead and order. I have waited because there'd be better tech around the corner. However, there'll be an even longer queue for anything better.

My other weak point, like Julia, is gas. I cook and heat water with gas. A wood stove would be better, but stoves don't belong in caravans. I could revisit building a shed in which I could put a stove. Have it as a kitchen and bathroom? Then I'd need to plant trees for firewood. Maybe at the far end of the paddock? But no, I already decided new trees near established trees might not be a good idea. That's enough thinking for tonight; time to check up on my Sumner Republicans.

PREPPERS UNITE. MAKING PLANS. TEXT 030 7703 7733 FOR MTGTIME/PLACE

Sophocles: Interested.

Chey: Me 2.

Taiaha: We need action. Not meetings.

Chey: Need meetings to create action.

EcoWarrior: I'm keen.

Prepping is everywhere, including in Sumner. Planning for collapse is easier than fixing climate problems. But how many bags of flour or dried peas can you store and protect from mice and earwigs? I have an emergency supply in sealed bins in the container. I should check my can dates. I just need to avoid Cynthia's boxes.

Don't be so silly, Stephen, Cynthia says. *It's only a bunch of old fabric getting in the way. You won't forget about me if you get rid of my stuff you don't use. Get on with it.* She might be right, but it can still wait.

I'm back to wondering about growing food again, too. Most people in the workshop are growing vegetables. But there's so much I can't grow, like wheat or sugar. Would it help to be part of a group and share or swap food? Not necessarily, because we can all only grow the same sort of stuff. Not so much grows in winter, either, even if winters are getting warmer. This reminds me of Eeman's family thinking cabbages were special and different. Five decades on, I still remember the smell of boiled cabbage in winter. I'd need to be really hungry to want to eat boiled cabbage again. Maybe I don't need to grow food because if there's no food to buy, things will be so bad I might not want to be around.

I scan down the posts for something more interesting.

Pekko: I'm in. Where? When? How?

ShiningLight: Can you dive?

Pekko: yep.

Phaedra: I can climb. Need to get onto the ship?

ShiningLight: Need more divers.

Taiaha: I've m8s I can ask.

Atka: Me too.

Rhiannon: I can.

ShiningLight: gather troops. Watch for updates.

That's the most interesting post I've ever seen. Sink the ship? A coal ship? Is New Zealand still exporting coal? Didn't coal exports stop in the 2010s when the government coal mining company went broke? Here we are wondering if we can cook dinner and heat our houses when some company is still exporting the worst possible type of fuel in terms of climate change? Who's doing this?

I search online but find nothing current about a New Zealand company exporting coal. The last article is from the early 2020s, when Bathurst Energy was still saying 'It's How We Mine That Matters'. Nice angle, making out the environmental problem is the scars on the landscape, not the changes in the atmosphere. Bathurst still exists on the companies' office website, but all the shareholders are offshore companies – the Taipan Trust in Australia, the Tiger Fund in Singapore, and Crocodile Capital in the Caymans.

When I investigate these offshore companies, I only find a web of companies owning companies and nothing online about the companies. Is it Bathurst that is mining? Is New Zealand allowing a dangerous product to be shipped offshore by a foreign-owned company? How does that make sense, to enforce TEQs and sell coal? The Republic of Sumnerites are onto something – something people should know about.

Not that I'll tell anyone, of course. It's none of my business. I could have it all wrong. The Sumnerites could be playing an online game and chatting about it in a forum. The references to coal and ships may not really be about coal and ships at all, they're code for … something else. I could make a big fuss about something that's nothing and completely embarrass myself. I definitely don't want to do that. However, I'm interested to see what happens.

JULIA

19–20 April 2030

Tomorrow will be my fifty-ninth birthday and would have been Amanda's nineteenth birthday. What would a nineteen-year-old Amanda have been doing? It's a confined world for today's teenagers. There's little opportunity to do the traditional 'overseas experience' which so many young New Zealanders enjoyed for years – if not me. They'd need to find one of the rare berths on freighters and work their passage.

Amanda might have been doing nothing; that's a common option in the current atmosphere of malaise. There's no problem getting a job if you want one. Employers have been perpetually short of staff since the post-pandemic wave of retirements and the government offers a multitude of incentives to encourage people into work. Funny to think how people in the 2010s were terrified robots might take their jobs; now we pray for robots to help us, but our country can't afford to make or buy them.

Nineteen-year-old Amanda might have liked repair and be helping Robbie in Broken is Beautiful, with aspirations of starting her own business. Or she might have been nothing like me, studying medicine at Otago University in Dunedin; we desperately need more doctors. I'd be calling her in the student halls and bursting into a semi-tuneful rendition of 'Happy Birthday' when she answered the phone. Her voice would sound groggy and gravelly, saying, "Mum, I only just got to bed. Why're you ringing me now?"

I pull myself out of Amanda imaginings to the real world in which Hermione is my best chance of a dose of mental sunshine. I give Lynda a call.

"Julia, what's up?"

"How're you placed for offering a caffeine-deprived visitor a coffee today or tomorrow?" I ask.

"The machine had to go to the repair depot. It's a Robbie job. It was blowing steam out of inappropriate parts of its anatomy."

"I'm devastated. I suppose I can make do with seeing Hermione," I say.

"She's blowing stuff out of parts of her anatomy too. I shouldn't have had curry for dinner last night. I was so desperate for something with a bit of spice."

"Seems like our conversations regularly take on a scatological bent these days."

"That's a great word, Julia. I'll teach it to Hermione as soon as she starts talking. Why don't you drop round tomorrow morning? We can discuss the workshops. And talk about our next special doll for Dolls with Stories. I've some ideas to run past you."

The next morning, I walk the two blocks to the sea before heading up Scarborough in sparkling autumn weather. The sea threatens us, but I still get great enjoyment out of its varying colours and energy when it stays in its bed. It's high tide and waves are breaking over the rip-rap boulders onto the walkway. I pass Scarborough Fare Cafe, deserted since a storm swept through the building a couple of years ago. I walk through the children's playground where waves uprooted play equipment in the same event. Seagulls splash and shriek in the remnants of the paddling pool.

As I step onto the deck, Lynda calls out, "Hi, Auntie, Hermione can't wait to see you."

I receive the sleeping bundle. "She's put on weight."

"I hope so. She's eating enough. All day and all night. I'm going to turn into a shadow of myself." Lynda sucks her cheeks in.

"I hope you're looking after yourself, and Robbie is looking after you. You're not the youngest-ever mother."

"Phooey to youey. I'm not that old. Not as old as you, anyhow. And the same age as you when you had Amanda."

There are few people who could say that to me other than Lynda. I bite my lip and nod.

"There are more babies born to women over forty than under twenty now. Good thing – us older women know how special babies are. However,

I'm borrowing Hermione's special powers till she needs them to help me out. I could really do with being in two places at one time."

"Shall I take that as a call to talk business?" I say. "However, I'm not handing Hermione back, at least not till she wriggles. She can learn how to mix business with pleasure at an early age."

"First, Dolls with Stories," Lynda says. "Which collectible next? What about an eco-activist, based on your story last workshop? Greta Thunberg with her trademark plaits? Though I'm not sure we could give her accessories. Greta wouldn't approve of anything faintly consumerist. Or Leonardo di Caprio? We'd need to make a youthful version. He's rather broad in the face these days. Tina Drylands? She's the girl who threw tomato soup at the Van Gogh, kicking off the Art Activism movement in the early 2020s. She could have a can of soup and a bunch of sunflowers. Or Chlöe Swarbrick, as the first Green Party Prime Minister of New Zealand?"

"Are we still confident we can deliver the doll to whoever buys it?" I ask.

"It is a problem. I'm investigating international transport insurance, but insurance won't replace a doll. Should we limit the auction to New Zealand and Australia? We can build international demand when shipping sorts itself out."

"You think shipping will sort itself out? Does anything sort itself out?" I say.

Lynda looks at her feet, then back at me. "No, I don't, but I need to hope things will get better. Don't you?"

"I need hope, but not that things will get better. Just that things will be okay. That things will be good enough. It's behind what I said on Thursday. I don't think there's much better to be had in our futures, and if we don't face up to the fact we are going to trip over the obstacles we are putting in our own way and fall flat on our future faces. Somehow, we need to hold on to hope and face reality at the same time."

"Julia, our last workshop was great. It got people interacting at a new level. I loved the hats too. I'll wear mine running in winter. However, our workshops aren't aiming to solve climate change. Or to solve people's life problems resulting from climate change. All we can do is help people cope with their lives better. Our goal is to tell stories. Make connections. Increase mental well-being."

"I agree. And I disagree. How do we help people to be mentally healthier if their lives are falling apart while we talk? Talk isn't enough."

"Talk isn't enough, Julia, but it's what this group is for. There are other groups and other forums that deal with practical matters."

I'm not satisfied, but it's hard to argue with Lynda. "Couldn't we do some small practical things, as well as talk?"

"Like what?"

"I'll think about it. Hermione, don't you hate it when your mother is right? Perhaps you don't yet, but you will soon enough."

Hermione opens her eyes, lets out a huge fart, and a pungent smell wafts through the room. "There you go," I say. "Hermione's protesting. We need to be practical."

"You're absolutely right on that one," Lynda says. "Robbie, you need to be practical. Hermie needs changing!"

Robbie comes in and takes Hermione from my arms. "Hey, stinky baby, time for a new nappy? How're you going, Julia? Heard it was a full-on workshop on Thursday. You got everyone fired up about climate change. It must be a worry for you, what's going to happen on the flats in Sumner. Nothing's imminent though, is it?"

"Nothing from council or government so far. However, I have little faith in them holding back the tide," I say. "There's no sign of our sewage or wastewater improving. In 2028 they put pumping stations along Wiggins Street. I don't know if the stations aren't working properly or what, but they made no difference."

"Well, the good news is our repair business is booming. There's literally a queue out the door some days. I'm looking at contracting four of the students we hired part-time over the summer. They can log hours against the professional requirements for their engineering degrees, so it's a win-win. And we're running drop-in Repair Clinics every Wednesday night. Bring your broken item and we'll help you fix it for koha."

"You're doing a fantastic job with repairs, Robbie. I know I haven't been paying proper attention, but it's only because I trust you completely."

"Dinna fash yerself, lassie." Robbie breaks into his broad Scottish accent, which always makes me laugh. He usually sounds more like a Kiwi than a Scotsman these days. "I'll come and ask if there's a problem I can't solve. I know you've plenty on your plate with Humans with Stories and Dolls with Stories."

"Robbie!" Lynda says. "How long are you going to stand there with that baby while poo drips from her blanket?"

Robbie casts a horrified glance downwards since he's holding Hermione almost directly above me.

"Gotcha," Lynda laughs and turns back to me. "Next week's workshop – who's speaking? I've lost track."

"Next is Victoria, then Andrey, Zahra, you, and Stephen is last."

"Oh yes, Stephen. Did he walk you home again after the workshop?"

"No, he didn't. I was too tired to want to make conversation on the way home. He did come by on the way to the workshop and helped me carry the food."

"And...?" Lynda raises her eyebrows.

"And nothing," I say. "Except I thought I found something out about his wife, which can't be right. It appears she's dead."

"That's a major something."

"Yes, it would be if she really were dead. But how can she be? He said he lives in a house on Scarborough with his wife."

"So what were you doing looking her up?" Lynda asks.

"He mentioned she's a quilter and patchworker. I'm always interested in creative arts so I looked her work up. She made beautiful quilts, some of which were displayed in a 2013 retrospective."

"C'mon, Julia. That can't be Stephen's wife, can it? Why would he say she's alive if she died years ago? You know what happened the first time you investigated someone you were interested in. That didn't go so well, did it? Though what a turn-up, Rosemary apologising to you. Did you ever think that would happen?"

I cross my arms and look out the window. I'd like to forget the whole Rosemary-Robbie fiasco; I pretty much had till she turned up at the workshop.

"No, I didn't think Rosemary would apologise. She wasn't really guilty of much. She probably shouldn't have been in my garden, but it wasn't like Robbie and I were in a relationship. He could kiss anyone he wanted to. My throwing him out was an overreaction."

The truth was, I was jealous. Robbie and I'd been having a lovely time working together, and I'd hoped for more. I knew it was unrealistic – Robbie and I are twenty years apart in age. However, being stupid doesn't stop you from feeling hurt.

The worst part of the event, which Lynda has just reminded me about, was my interest in Robbie led me to investigate him online. I discovered he'd accidentally run over and killed a toddler in his hometown of Dingwall while still a teenager. When I demanded Robbie leave, I was so angry I told Rosemary about the accident and how awful I thought Robbie was. Robbie's amazing, though. He has never shown any sign of harbouring a grudge. When he and Lynda started their relationship she tricked me into meeting him again and we have got on well ever since.

"I wish you'd stop insinuating I might fancy Stephen," I say to change the subject.

"Sorry, Julia. I was just teasing. It's a rare opportunity to give you a hard time about men. And online investigations … well, they only show part of the picture, right? There's always another side. You need to get it from the person. Everything leads back to Humans with Stories – making connections and seeing whole people."

"You could be nicer to me on my birthday."

Lynda should know when my birthday is because we celebrated my fiftieth birthday together with a feast of carrot cake covered in cream cheese icing. I remember the lemon peel in the icing and the novelty of having a friend with whom to celebrate my birthday.

"Oh no, I completely forgot. Can we blame it on baby-brain? How about we do something next weekend? Except on Sunday, my ante-natal group is coming here. I'll need to prepare on Saturday. I can't believe how long it takes to do anything when a little monster constantly wants feeding and changing. How about the following weekend?"

"Sure, if it works out. Let's see how busy you are after the next workshop. I'd better be going. Should make the most of the sunny day. Say bye to Hermione and Robbie for me."

I head down the stairs less happily than when I'd ascended. Now Cynthia's back in my brain I might as well continue my investigations. A ghost of a thought flits – it would be nice to have someone to celebrate my birthday with every year. Someone for whom I'd be important enough that they'd remember the date.

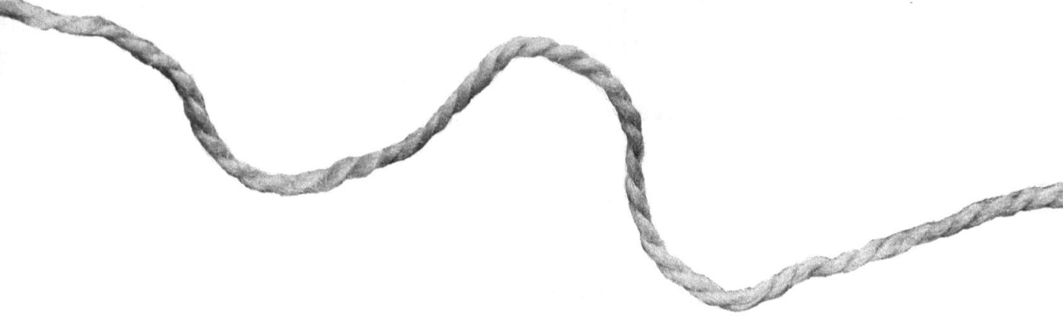

STEPHEN

19 April–1 May 2030

I'm waiting for the next interesting item on The Republic of Sumner channel. I'm now checking regularly in case they post at an odd time and I miss it.

The Republic of Sumnerites don't appear to respect legality. However, blowing up a ship is many steps beyond taking expired food out of dumpsters or even iron from other people's damaged house roofs. Did the message last week really mean what I thought it said? I'm sure I read it, didn't I? I usually like how Rappit scrolling posts disappear. However, now I want to be able to check what that post said.

There's nothing very exciting today.

FOOD FORAGING FRENZY. TEXT 030 773 7733 FOR MTG TIME/ PLACE

Phaedra: legit or pushing boundaries?

Taiaha: I like pushing boundaries.

Pekko: I'm on evening shift. Can it be late?

Chey: dumpster diving too?

Atka: dumpster diving another time.

Buy Nothing Got things you don't need?
Need things you can't buy? Join at localwise.
com/groups/sumnerbuynothing/

SumnerSummerSurplus Got more produce
than you can eat? Join at localwise.com/groups/
sumnersummersurplus to find enthusiastic recipients.

Broken is Beautiful Give your goods their
longest life. Wednesday repair workshops
at Homestead Crescent, Ferrymead.

Keep your TEQs in the community – join the
SortedSumner group on TradeUrTEQs.co.nz

Community tiny home building We'll help you learn
– check us out at localwise.com/groups/Ur4EvaHome

Julia's business is 'Broken is Beautiful'. Could Julia be connected to The Republic of Sumner?

I need to focus on my music so set a one-hour timer for Rappit. My opera singer's country ballad is nearly finished. I've done the piano accompaniment, now I'm checking the two-part harmony. We will sing it at the hospice soon. The opera singer is determined to have a duet, rather than me backing her. She wants two different voices explaining the tension between her love of country music and her duty to opera.

"Which of us is which voice?" I asked. "I'm hardly a trained opera singer. And how can I pretend to be you? My voice is an octave deeper!"

"Let's not worry about reality," she said. "I'm past concerns about proper and real. Let's just sing. I'm going to be the country voice because I'm dying, so I get to say. I no longer sound like an opera diva anyway. You will imagine yourself an opera diva, a word that has never gained much traction. Opera is one of the few roads where women have an easier route to fame than men."

This is a busy week. As well as a practice with the opera singer I have two other appointments. Felicity wore me down and I've agreed to meet the young person with cancer. At least that won't require any preparation. I'm also going to meet Eeman's ukulele player and their family.

Eeman texted me.

E: Wed still OK? Family say yes. Thank you Stephen.

Why is he thanking me before I have agreed to come?

S: Wed fine. When? Where?

E: 30 Campbell St 4pm. Thank you.

S: Song ideas?

E: Hoping you have ideas. Thank you.

S: Age? English level?

E: 7 years. Intermediate. Also some other children will sing. Thank you.

S: C u Wed

What's with all these 'thank yous'? How many other children are there? What ages are they? I need to find a song a seven-year-old child can sing who is learning English. I know simple songs we sang at school many years ago, like 'Old MacDonald Had a Farm', or 'Ten Green Bottles', or 'The Cat Came Back' in which a cat lives out nine lives while children and adults die in horrific accidents. Will those interest children now? I search online for more recent songs. I find 'One Day a Taniwha', where a taniwha tries to lure a child into the sea. I find 'Bite' about fleas and nits and lice biting people. I find 'The Mangaweka Monster', in which a monster forms a team with a dog who wants to eat baked beans, while the monster wants to eat the cans. I settle on 'There Ain't No Brakes on Roller Skates' because it has a catchy chorus and lots of repeated lyrics.

I walk down Scarborough Hill on Wednesday afternoon with my guitar on my back and turn left, towards the upper end of the valley. Eeman's family live on the edge of the tornado's path. The low, pink, fake stone garden wall looks like a monster took chomping bites out of its top. There are large patches of bare earth where trees must have stood. However, the pink house doesn't have any obvious damage outside. Through the window, I see a living room full of children chasing one another like cats chasing their tails.

As I walk up the path, Eeman comes to the front door with a short smiling woman with thick dark hair cut close around her face and heavy-framed red glasses matching a red streak running from the top of her head to the centre of her fringe. "I'm Rosa. Welcome to our home," she says. "Thank you so much for coming to sing with the boys. They are very excited about you coming."

I go into the living room where the chaos has been organised into three rows of dark-haired boys with bony knees holding ukuleles. The ukulele is a funny little instrument which sounds like a hyperactive bumblebee. However, it's a lot better than no instrument.

"Boys, this is Mr Stephen," Eeman says. "Stephen, meet Matthew, Mark and Luke, Coco, Antonio and Rico, Sonny, Buddy, Prince and Rudolph."

Rudolph? The unusual name lodges in my brain and I forget all the other names. Which is the original boy Eeman was talking about helping?

"Hello, Mr Stephen," the boys chorus. They are dressed in T-shirts with patches, overlarge or too-tight shorts and bare feet. Boys are giggling and elbowing other boys. Do they all live in this house? Are they from one family?

"Do you all play ukulele together?" I ask.

"Yes." "No." "Sometimes." Someone farts loudly and the troupe eye each other and giggle.

"Can you play me a song?" I ask. "Using the ukuleles, rather than farts."

The boys snigger and two fart more loudly.

"Boys," Eeman says, "enough playing around. We're here to play music. Let's sing 'Amazing Grace'."

The boys dutifully strum and sing 'Amazing Grace', but it's more suited to a funeral – or scared people in a storeroom – than a hive of little boys.

"Do you have a song you like even more than 'Amazing Grace'?" I ask.

More giggling and poking and prodding. The tallest boy says, "'Happy'. But we need our goggles."

They need goggles to sing a song? Eeman explains, "The song is from the latest *Minions* movie – *GranPa Gru*."

Minions?

The boys tumble out of the room to return with cut-out cardboard goggles. Some goggles are single with a large eye drawn in the centre and some are double, encircling their real eyes. The tallest boy counts down to 'Happy'. I know the song, it's by Pharrell Williams. Maybe I knew it was in a movie then forgot. Ruby appears and claps in time together with Eeman.

None of the boys has any obvious trouble singing in English. I'm not sure what Eeman wants me to do. We can just sing. "Boys, that was fantastic," I say. "First, can you tell me about Minions? Then we'll sing 'There Ain't No Brakes on Roller Skates'." I realise 'ain't' might not be the best English to teach the boys. Too late now.

"What are roller skates?" asks a smaller boy.

"Stupid. They're shoes with wheels," says an older boy.

"We don't call each other stupid," Eeman says. The older boy looks down at his ukulele and mumbles something sounding like, "*Be wakuf.*"

"*Poka.*" The small boy shrugs.

"So Minions are?" I ask.

Eeman helps out. "They're from animated movies. Minions are little banana-coloured people. They wear denim overalls and goggles and have their own language. They like to have fun and trick people and each other. The movies are old but the boys like them a lot and *GranPa Gru* was just released. Gru is the main character. He's a reformed criminal and has a team of Minions who help him, together with his three daughters adopted from an orphanage."

"Bee do bee do bee do bee do bee do," the boys chorus.

I teach the boys the chords and the chorus of 'There Ain't No Brakes on Roller Skates'. I ask Eeman to speak the words of the verses and Ruby to be the voice of the mother, telling her son to go slow on his skates.

Three well-muscled, dark-haired men in high-vis work shirts arrive and sit in chairs on the lawn, drinking beer and watching through the living room window. An even smaller boy appears in the living room. Has the music woken him from a nap? He acts like an out-of-control roller skater egged on by the ukulele players to climb, then jump, off the furniture. We perform for the men on the lawn. Everyone's now shouting the chorus and neighbours are leaning over broken fences, joining in, and applauding loudly at the end. "Encore, encore," they shout.

"The boys need to have dinner, but we have to do this again," says Eeman. "Would you like to stay for dinner?"

"Thank you, but I need to be getting home. Maybe another time."

"Yes, please come back. In two weeks? The boys had so much fun, didn't you, boys?"

"Yes!"

I'm surprised by how good that 'yes' makes me feel. Dying people are easier to manage than small boys but they don't reach high pitches of excitement. I'd never thought singing with children could be a type of medicine.

I go on the bus to the Christchurch Public Hospital to meet B. I can't imagine this will work. Why would a very ill teenager want to talk with an old man? When I was a teenager, everyone older than twenty-something was in the 'fossil' category. I go through a maze of identical cream and brown hospital corridors, finally reaching the oncology ward after several dead ends and two lift journeys in the wrong direction. Felicity welcomes me at the nurses' station and takes me to B's room.

"B, here's the songwriter I told you was coming. B, meet Stephen, Stephen, meet B."

I can't see much of B. A black hoodie hides most of B's head and B's face is turned sideways into the fabric. Black sweatpants, black socks and black trainers complete B's outfit.

"Hello, B, nice to meet you," I say.

"Yep," B replies.

"Felicity didn't tell me how to spell your name. Just wanted to check."

"B," B says.

"So how is that spelt? B-e-a, or B-e-e?"

"B," B says.

"Sorry, Stephen, did I not explain? B's name is the letter B. B also doesn't use pronouns."

I look sideways at Felicity. I don't think she forgot to explain anything. She was reeling me in, leaving out the tricky bits.

"B," Felicity says, "I've been telling Stephen how much you love music and how I'd like the two of you to write a song together. Stephen's sung songs with lots of people I know."

"Mmphh," comes from the hood.

"What sort of music do you like, B?" I ask.

"Ariana Doo Doo. Flo Milli. Class Act King. Farqya. Know them?"

"Not yet, but I'm always interested in finding out about different musicians and music. Have you got a playlist you can share with me?"

B pulls a phone out of the hoodie pocket, revealing a minimum amount of skin by keeping thumbs firmly in the loops at the sleeves' ends.

"Do you like B's fingernails?" Felicity says. "We did them together. B painted the gold bees. They contrast well with the black, don't you think?"

Fingernails aren't something I notice.

"Do you like bees?" I ask.

"Doh, that's my name." B pushes the phone at me, far too close for me to see anything; I jerk my head back. A rap song is playing with sounds coming out of the rapper's mouth faster than I can pull the words apart. Is it English?

"That's Farqya," B says as the song ends.

Another song starts which is just as hard to hear. We watch five song videos and B sways to the beat behind the clothing wall. All the singers are young, black and of indeterminate sex. The images leave me as confused as the words I can only understand intermittently. Young black people gyrate, lick the necks of other young black people, lick other parts of other people's anatomies. Sometimes they lick parts of their own anatomies with a flexibility I should probably admire because I couldn't do those things myself.

Some of the dancers wear costumes so tiny and see-through you wonder if they'll rip apart. Other dancers are cloaked like B. Fabric touches, merges, draws apart. Bright colours alternate with black. There's an air of sex and tension and danger. B lives in a world about which I know nothing.

"Your music is very interesting, B," I say. "I mean … well, I mean you know a lot about music I don't know very well."

"Too old, huh?" B says with a shrug of black cloth.

"No, not at all." I almost start going on about no one ever being too old to learn. Luckily, Felicity breaks in.

"What's the best next step, Stephen?"

"I need to go home and educate myself. Then let's meet again in a fortnight. B, please drop your list to my phone." I pull it out of my pocket and fumble with the screen.

B sweeps my phone from my hand and manipulates a screen in each hand. "It's in Streamify." The olive hand with black nails is briefly revealed as B returns my phone.

"Thanks so much, Stephen," Felicity says. "We'll see you when you are more educated. Looking forward to it, aren't we, B?"

B turns away as I wave goodbye. Felicity gives me a half hug. She knows I don't like close contact. "You can do it, Stephen," she says in my ear. "B needs your help."

I walk along the river to the bus station. Autumn leaves drift out of plane and oak trees and pile on the river banks under the still, blue sky. Across the river is the Canterbury Earthquake Memorial *Oi Manawa*, naming the 185 people who died in the February 2011 quake. Human beings are strange. We publicly remember each individual killed by an earthquake but if B dies the city will flow on, unseeing.

I imagine kicking piles of leaves in the air. *Do it,* Cynthia says. Yellow, orange, and brown leaves lift, spiral and fall back to earth around my feet. I drive my foot through the pile again, ignoring stares from an older couple sitting on the bench. I think they're older than me, although I make that mistake more and more often. Falling leaves cover my shoes. I enjoy the kicking and rustling, and dry scent of the end of summer mixed with the start of decay.

I reach down and throw leaves up and into the river. As they cascade out of my hands I see young Stephen who jumped in puddles, ran through piles of leaves, and tasted the smell of ozone before rain – when being alive was enough and everything.

JULIA

2 May 2030

I should be working on my clock sculpture but I'm on the computer, investigating Cynthia and Stephen. Lynda be damned. I want to know where the truth lies. On Stephen, I draw a spectacular blank. He has no social media accounts I can find. I try Friendbook, Instashot, Mammoth, Tiktak and Gabber – nothing. A general Chatterificous search for 'Stephen John' – nothing. There are two Stephen Johns in Auckland; a surf lifesaver with broad sporting interests and a gynaecologist struck off for professional misconduct. There's a retired forester in Rangiora. It's impressive how low a profile Stephen has kept – challenging in the online era.

I cross-check my previous searches for Cynthia to see whether I was mistaken about her death. I conclude Cynthia is definitively dead. She still has a Friendbook profile, but it hasn't been active since it was transferred from Facebook. Her pictures are of quilts and patchwork and smiling women gathered around quilts-in-the-making and colourful piles of material. Only two photos show Cynthia – one on Sumner Beach and another on the Port Hills above Sumner. On Sumner Beach, there's a man behind Cynthia who looks very much like Stephen. He's crouching down to let a terrier off the leash. The Port Hills photo shows the back of a walking Cynthia with the terrier running out in front. There is indisputable evidence of Cynthia's death embalmed in Friendbook – lots of posts in 2012 with pictures of candles and praying hands and comments about how people will miss her warm smile and her passion for material arts.

So what to think about Stephen? He doesn't post on social media. I can hardly fault that – nor do I. He says he is married to a woman who is long

"

dead. That's an obvious problem. What other lies might he have told? Does he live on Scarborough? He could walk in that direction, then turn around and go somewhere else. He could have a different name. He and Cynthia mightn't have been married. He could be someone who didn't know Cynthia but stole information about her from social media.

However, why would someone come to our workshops pretending to be someone else? In the same vein, though, why come to workshops and pretend you are still married? Should I tell Lynda? Or Fran? Or everyone at Humans with Stories? Not Fran. When we have our Dolls with Stories meetings she looks too tired and distracted to be burdened with someone else's worries and she's been clear that Humans with Stories is for Lynda and me to run. After my conversation with Lynda about Stephen I'm not rushing back to tell her I've found out more online. There's no one to tell. And the status of Stephen's wife is not anyone else's business, except that our workshops are about creating connections. Connections shouldn't be based on deceit. Is Stephen's deceit his own problem to solve? Or mine to expose?

I head for the kitchen and walk past Amanda's room with its colourful mural. The room I kept locked for many years after Amanda's death while I kept Amanda a secret from everyone. That's only one step different from Stephen – I hid both Amanda's life and her death. I should give Johnno a call, see what he thinks.

At that moment someone knocks on the door, so I shelve talking with Johnno. It's Stephen on his way to the workshop, smiling broadly when I open the door. "Just a minute, I'll get my jacket," I say, as the cool air reminds me it's autumn.

We walk briskly towards the fire station along the shortest route, given we're late. That route includes Tornado Alley which I try to avoid. Potholed, stone-strewn tarmac beside the waves is preferable to ruined buildings beside the street.

In houses where people are camping, repairs are happening. Damaged roofs have replacement iron, and some broken windows have fresh glass, while others are boarded over. Many of the uninhabited houses are reduced to framing and beams.

"Do you think materials from damaged houses are being used to repair other houses?" I say.

"Yes, it's local people doing the stripping," Stephen says.

"How do you know?"

"People talk about reclaiming the materials on a local Rappit channel."

Stephen does engage with the internet. I've heard of Rappit. It's a dodgy communication app.

"A local channel for deconstructing houses?"

Stephen looks straight ahead and speeds up. "Not deconstructing houses, as such. It's called The Republic of Sumner. It's about lots of local things. I found them when I was looking for … umm … for someone local who does repairs."

"If you need repairs done, Robbie can help at Broken is Beautiful. Go to Homestead Crescent in Ferrymead. There's a big sign outside – I used broken objects to make the lettering. Robbie has a team of people and heaps of tools. There are Wednesday drop-in clinics from noon till 9pm, or I can put you in touch with Robbie directly. We're co-owners of the repair part of the business."

"I fixed the thing myself in the end. However, I keep reading the group's posts because they're interesting. They mentioned Broken is Beautiful."

"Robbie's always looking for ways to get the word out. Are the posts mostly about businesses?"

"There are lots of different posts. Business and individuals. Some are about taking action like we talked about last workshop," Stephen says.

"What sort of action?" I ask, walking faster to look him in the face.

"Oh … errr … like food foraging, dumpster diving, that sort of thing,"

"When I think of dumpster diving, I imagine a dumpster with a pair of legs waving out of the top and a muffled voice coming from the bottom, yelling, 'Help me!'"

"It wouldn't make sense to climb in head first," Stephen says. "I think you climb over the lip and crouch on whatever is inside. Look around to see if there are useful items and pass them to people on the outside who keep the lid open."

"That's very literal, Stephen."

"Oh, yes. Silly me. Sorry."

"That's okay. Are you as literal with your music?" I ask.

"In my music? I don't know how I am. I'm just me," he says. "I don't think about what I'm like making music because music is the same as breathing. It's what I am."

"I'm the same with my re-creations," I say. "I don't need to question whether I'm doing them correctly – I know. I see them in my head, then they flow from my brain to my fingertips."

"Yes, yes, exactly," Stephen says.

We continue the last block to the fire station in companionable silence.

JULIA

2 May 2030

When Stephen and I go up the stairs to the fire station meeting room everyone else is there, Eeman included. The wall clock reads 6.35pm. Lynda raises an eyebrow at me, and I ignore it.

"Hi, Julia and Stephen," Lynda says. "Let's get started with our karakia." Afterwards, Lynda welcomes Victoria to the front of the room.

"My story is about the people for whom I care," Victoria says. "And I have an emotional gift for you, rather than a physical one. My koha is a hug."

I flinch internally. I hug Fran and Lynda and, occasionally Robbie. I hug Hermione though she's still too small to hug back. That's the list. I was never a huggy person. We were not a huggy family. Years of living on my own haven't inclined me towards random physical contact with strangers. What do other people think? Rosemary is nodding, as are Lynda and Andrey. Eeman has his arms crossed. Stephen's face is rigid, and his legs are so far crossed his foot has wound round behind his ankle.

"I studied nursing because I wanted to help people and be employable. Healthcare sounded interesting, but being a doctor was way too long a process. When I went to uni I had no idea what nursing meant. It means you help everybody. Whether you like them or not. Every sort of person can turn up at the hospital. Some patients are nice, some are mean, and some are desperate. In our ward at the moment there's a lawyer, a sheikh, a rapist, a gang member, a teenage snowboard champion, a P addict, a mum with five children and no partner, and a dad who cares for his son half time. Some are on the dole, some in the top few per cent of earners. Being wealthy doesn't make you immune to illness or accident, though money, it helps a lot if you are sick because it pays for private medical care and home help."

Zahra comes up to the front and gives Victoria a hug. "I will have one hug first and then another later. I love how my beautiful partner cares for all the people she works with. I do not love how some patients treat her. I do not love how tired she is every day when she comes home. When we have babies to look after, I am not sure nursing is a job she can keep doing."

Victoria goes to speak but Zahra hugs her again, putting her arms around Victoria's neck, which is easy for Zahra as she is a head taller than Victoria.

When Zahra releases her, Victoria says, "I get to know my patients extremely well because I work in spinal care – my patients are in for the long haul. People ask how I can bear to be with gang members, drug addicts or rapists. Aren't I scared of my patients? And why should the medical system treat criminals when so many good people aren't being treated promptly?

"I'm not scared. Some of my gang members are lovely to deal with. The sheikh, not so much. How about the rapist? Do I worry he'll attack me? No, I don't, because his spinal cord damage means he won't be raping anyone in the future. I could consider his injury divine justice – if I believed in a God. Sorry, Eeman. I don't believe in deities because, if there are deities, they are pathologically unempathetic. Why would you torture people to test their devotion to you? Though plenty of people torture their pets or family. Maybe there are deities who are as fickle and thoughtless as humans, but I won't be worshipping them!"

Stephen goes up to the front. "Given what's happened in my life, if there's a deity in charge I don't like them either," he says. "However, I believe we're on our own in this universe. There's the same amount of evidence that aliens exist as deities – none."

Lynda and I look at each other. We've asked everyone to stay positive in their connections. Should we intervene?

Victoria says, "I'm sorry for the tough times in your life, Stephen," and rests her hand gently on his shoulder. He turns to face her, then goes back to his seat, looking less agitated than when he stood up. Nicely done by Victoria. Though it might have been good for Stephen to be hugged.

I raise my hand. Stephen got the hugging thing over and done with. I might as well too.

"Julia, please tell us your connection," Lynda says.

"You mentioned people waiting for treatment. The state of our health system scares me. The thought of getting ill and not being treated worries me more and more. I've never been able to afford health insurance and now I'm older the premiums are more out of reach than ever. So far I've been healthy, but who knows when that will end? I might find a lump in my breast, or blood in my poo, then wait months to get diagnosed, to find out it's too late to do anything. Will I be cared for while I die? Or will all the hospice beds be full of other people who didn't get diagnosed in time?"

"Yes, it's terrifying, isn't it?" Victoria says. "So many scary things taking away our ability to enjoy our lives. Would you like me to give you a hug?"

Victoria's question disarms me, and I step forward. Her round stomach presses against me and grief washes through me as I remember my baby who didn't live to be an adult. I hug Victoria back and the sadness settles as I return to my seat.

Victoria continues, "There's a young woman on our ward who is a gang member – the gang's her whānau. Her partner is a gang member; she loves him, and she is terrified of him. She was driving the getaway car for a burglary and crashed into a power pole. The other gang members in the car died; she escaped with a broken spine. Does she worry about climate change? Or her house being flooded? No, because she doesn't own a house. She worries about who is looking after her girls aged three, five and seven and her eighteen-month-old twins."

Lynda goes to the front of the room and stands beside Victoria.

"I never knew what it was like to worry before I had Hermione," Lynda says. "People ask me if it was scary travelling to countries like Colombia or running long distances in the mountains on my own. I've always said, 'No. I can manage whatever happens.' Except, with Hermione, I'm no longer in control. I have ridiculous thoughts about what I'll do if someone breaks into the house and attacks her. So unlikely. But I still worry. I'm her protector, but I can't guarantee to protect her."

"Thank you, Lynda," Victoria says. "Our babies aren't born yet but I can already feel the love and the worry." She looks at Zahra's stomach, which Zahra rubs her hand over. "The best antidote is expressing our concerns so we can check whether our fears are real, do something about them if they are, and shelve them if they are not. Would you like a hug?" Lynda moves without hesitation into Victoria's embrace and hugs her firmly back.

"How can we protect our children fully?" Victoria says. "We can't. However much we'd like to."

I know that. I live that. I will never escape feeling I should have prevented Amanda's death.

"My paralysed patient will never protect her children again," Victoria says. "Her sister, who broke away from the gang and has gone to live with whānau in the East Cape, would take care of them. My patient would like her children to go to her sister; she would rather they were safe than near her. However, the children's father says he will track his children down to the ends of the earth and bring them home rather than lose mana through someone else caring for them.

"As well as fearing for her children, my patient is terrified of what will happen when she goes home. She'll always be in a wheelchair and of little use to her husband or the other gang members. She won't be able to care for herself. Will they care for her? Or will they leave her to starve? She can't think beyond the immediate future."

Eeman stands and Victoria pauses.

"My people in Guaan have the same problem, needing all their energy to survive. There's no room to think about the big picture. What's important is feeding your children when the crops die. Mending your house when water pours in during a thunderstorm. Deciding whether children can go to school or must stay home and work in the fields. In Guaan, they know the seasons are not the same as in the past, but there's no time to think about why." He breaks off, then continues.

"And I don't need other people to believe in my God. For me and my God, it is enough I believe in him, and he is there for me. He keeps me strong and helps me be happy and enjoy every day of this life."

"Thank you, Eeman," Victoria says. "Would you like a hug?"

"Where I come from, it is not normal for people who do not know each other to hug," Eeman says. "Particularly, it is not normal for unfamiliar men and women to be in physical contact. However, I now live in Aotearoa where physical contact between people is much more casual. So it is okay."

Victoria smiles and gives Eeman a quick hug.

I'm impressed by how Eeman vocalised what he is feeling.

"The next patient I would like to tell you about is a young world-class freestyle snowboarder who broke his neck practising a Switch Backside Double Cork 1260. His optimism, determination and good humour are contagious. He encourages other patients in our gym and chats with all the staff. We have watched countless YouTube videos of snowboarding during my lunch break. He educates me about trick names, like Stale Fish, Weddle Stiffy and Beef Carpaccio. The Beef Carpaccio combines a Roast Beef with a Chicken Salad."

Andrey leaps to his feet.

"Andrey, what's your connection?" Lynda asks.

"My connection is mountain biking," Andrey says. "Slopestyle mountain biking also has trick names. We have the Superman, the Windshield Wiper and the Truckdriver. Nothing as good as Beef Carpaccio. In Russia, men hug men, not so much women they don't know. But in this case, I make an exception because you are a beautiful person and I now know you." He gives Victoria a bear hug and she hugs him back.

Victoria goes on with her story. "My lawyer's an interesting case. She says she's almost happy about a drunk driver T-boning her car because now she's seeing life in a whole new way. Before her accident, she worked ten or more hours a day. When she came home to her partner and young children, she was exhausted and struggled to pay attention to them. Her marriage was on shaky ground, as her partner repeatedly pointed out how they were more like flatmates living in the same house than lovers. Now, when her whānau visits at the hospital, she is as much there for them as they are for her. 'I won't go back to corporate law,' she says. 'I'm done with the rat race. I want to be present with the people who are important in my life.'"

Rosemary comes up to the front. "I totally empathise with that story. I need to get out of the rat race. Everyone needs to get out because we've lost sight of the point of living. Introduction of the TEQs created a glimmer of hope when we stopped travelling out of Ōtautahi for work and used Cast instead.

Travel used to take me away from my whānau all the time. It was a wonderful relief to be home more, have time to exercise, more time just to be. Then the hospital figured out we could have more appointments if we worked from home. But having seen the possibility, I want it back for me and my patients."

Victoria gives Rosemary a tight squeeze, then she returns to her seat.

Lynda puts her hand up as Rosemary sits down. "I relate to that need to slow down. Hermione has made it very clear, though Robbie has been trying to get through to me for years. And I have had Julia's example to follow, but I've never seen it properly."

What is Lynda saying? That I sit around doing nothing? My life has always been perfectly full enough, at least since Lynda and Fran have been part of it.

"Julia pays attention to what she is doing. She focuses on her creations. She focuses on her house and garden. She makes what she touches beautiful. She takes time. I've always rushed from activity to activity. Tried to cram everything in. From meeting to meeting as a CEO and from place to place to support Dolls with Stories branches. Training for races. Running marathons. Travelling overseas to run marathons. Running, running, running. The crashing end of air travel and TEQs still didn't bring me to my senses. I was annoyed I couldn't live like I had before. However, since I became pregnant with Hermione, and even more since she was born, I see slowing down is an answer, not a problem. Julia, thank you for being right all these years."

I hope my red face isn't obvious to everyone in the room. I'd never thought I was someone Lynda would aspire to be like. I have always aspired to be like her – more direct and robust, and better dressed.

"Lynda, what a lovely connection," Victoria says. "I'll give you a hug." Victoria and Lynda hug warmly and, before they finish, I get up and hug them both so no one can see me crying.

The three of us disentangle and Lynda and I retake our seats, smiling at each other.

"So that's my story," Victoria says. "It doesn't have a proper end because there is no end to the people who need care, or the money needed to pay for care, or the staff required to care for the people. But there are bright moments in the day, like this one, when everything seems worthwhile."

"Thank you so much, Victoria," says Lynda. "Let's all enjoy our kai. What are we looking forward to eating?"

"I have brought traditional Pakeha kai – vegan cheese rolls and lamingtons; raspberry and chocolate."

"Yum," Lynda says. "Who is a raspberry lamington person and who is a chocolate lamington person? Everyone who is chocolate stand up."

Lynda is joined by Zahra, Andrey, and Rosemary.

"Excellent, we have the same number on either side of the lamington debate. There will be plenty of lamingtons of each colour."

I move between the groups that form and reform. Lynda and I meet over the lamingtons.

"Going well, isn't it?" Lynda says.

"Yes. Victoria's hug koha was a stroke of genius for breaking down barriers, even if I didn't think so when she announced it."

"You need to come and hug Hermione more often."

"I can't get enough Hermione hugs, that's for sure. We could hug more often too."

After our karakia, I go over to Stephen. Why not walk back home with him? I know there's no wife on the scene and we have quite a bit in common. Like Lynda said, the best way to find out about someone is in person.

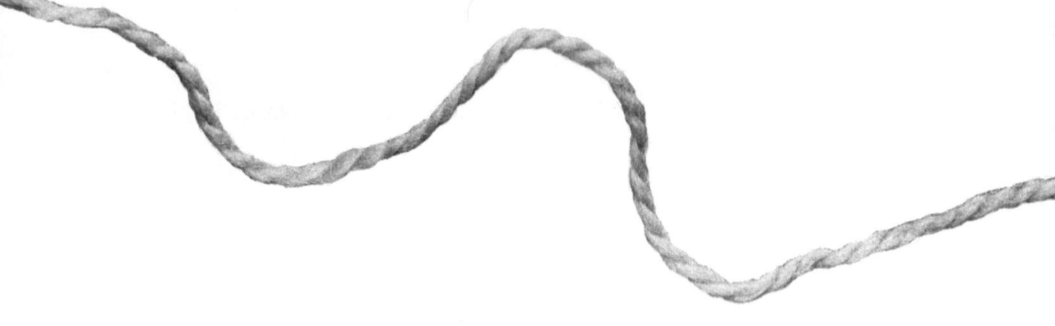

STEPHEN

2 May 2030

Julia comes over to me at the end of the workshop. "Would you like to walk back through Sumner?" she says.

How nice. I enjoyed our chat on the way to the meeting. Although, what do I think of someone wanting to be friends with a married man? *Oh, Stephen,* Cynthia says. *Women and men can be friends. Being friends doesn't mean you want to have sex with someone!* Of course it doesn't. Although, it has been a long time since I had sex with anyone.

I've learnt you can get as practised at not doing something as doing something. Sex fell out of my life when Cynthia became very ill. In the eighteen months through which she was diagnosed, tortured by medical treatments, and then died I was more an automaton than a human being. I did all the things I had to, but I couldn't believe I was living the life I was in. A life where the partner I intended to grow old with was going to die before we'd built our perfect house on our perfect section. Before we'd really lived at all. Was that when I started lying? When I started telling people about the life I wanted, hoping the telling would make my story come true?

I became well-practised at not having sex and not telling the truth. I didn't tell people about Cynthia's diagnosis or illness. We didn't have many joint friends. We were content with our lives as they were, just the two of us. Except, that was only true for me. Cynthia had plenty of friends. She saw them at quilting bees and handcraft classes. I didn't feel the need for anyone other than Cynthia. My colleagues were fine — we talked at work — but I didn't want to have them round for dinner. *Maybe when we're in our house,* I thought. *There's no room for dinner in a caravan.*

Once I left my job, my social interactions became even more limited, to brief interchanges in the supermarket. Checkout operators weren't wanting to hear about my wife's cancer diagnosis, or death, when they asked, "How's your day been?" What would their reply have been if I'd said, "Absolutely awful. This morning I sat with my wife while she told me having IV chemo was like having acid poured into her veins. Then I took her home to our caravan where she spent the afternoon vomiting. I changed and washed her sheets twice." Lucky for them I didn't want to talk about it.

There's no longer any pressure to be honest with supermarket checkout operators because checkouts are all automated. If the checkout mis-scans, it's a nightmare because there's no one to come and reboot it. I just go back in the queue and wait for another booth to come free. Some things don't change. If your computer isn't working, switch it off. Wouldn't it be good if you could do the same for humans who aren't working properly? Switch them off, then switch them back on so they fire up all fixed. Could I have a reboot and then stop talking about my wife in our lovely house on Scarborough?

I am getting a long way ahead of myself in thinking about sex and truth when Julia has only asked if I'd like to walk back from a meeting with her. Except I'm not ahead. I'm behind because I've been thinking rather than replying. Julia is turning away. "Yes. I'd love to hear more about your re-creations," I say.

"Let's go along Nayland St – see what's happening in the retirement units," Julia says. "Pauline and Grant would like to see you again."

Lynda comes over to Julia. "I'll catch up with you at the weekend. We need to celebrate your birthday, like we talked about."

"It's no big deal," Julia says.

"Of course it's a big deal, Julia. We'll have carrot cake with cream cheese icing, to remember the first time we celebrated your birthday together. Stephen, would you like to come? Your wife is welcome too? Two pm Saturday."

Julia says, "That's fine with me. When does Hermione sleep? I don't want to miss her."

"I'll make sure she's fed and down for a nap by noon, then she'll be ready to greet guests at two pm," Lynda says.

I say, "Errr … umm … Saturday. I need to check. Cynthia's quilting group might meet in the afternoon. However, I'd love to join you. Anything I can bring?"

"Absolutely," Lynda says. "If we are re-enacting Julia's fiftieth birthday, we need Lindt chocolate and Lindauer sparkling wine. I doubt there's imported chocolate in the supermarket but see what you can find. I still shouldn't drink alcohol so how about sparkling grape juice? I'll invite Fran and Holly, of course. Looking forward to seeing you guys. Now I must dash because Robbie has to go to Ferrymead tonight to catch up with his repair queue."

Julia and I descend the stairs. "When's your birthday?" I ask. I actually know because I overheard Julia and Lynda's conversation at the last workshop.

"Two weeks ago, but Lynda forgot. Now she's feeling guilty and trying to make it up to me. You don't need to come if you don't want to."

"I'd like to come."

"Your wife won't mind you going to the birthday party of a woman she doesn't know?"

"No, Cynthia's never been the jealous type." Can we get off the Cynthia topic so I can enjoy this walk?

When we reach the retirement units everything is tidier than I expected. A row of LED lights shine on the street side of the houses. There are rows of vegetables in the garden. The fake stone cladding that fell off is stacked neatly. Broken windows are covered with plywood. "Do you think we should bother them?" I ask Julia. "It looks like they're getting on fine. Will they even remember who I am? Perhaps they'll be asleep?"

"I want to talk to Pauline. I'm not sure 'fine' is a great description of how elderly people crammed into damaged flats are getting on." She walks up to Pauline's front door, and I hear a buzz of voices inside. It takes a few knocks until Pauline opens the door. "How nice to see you, Julia and …"

"Stephen."

"Hello again, Stephen. My nephew is called Stephen, don't know how I forgot that name. Come in, have a cup of tea."

"Only if it's no trouble. I know it's late, but we were walking home after a meeting," Julia says.

"It's not too late for elderly night owls, love," says Pauline. "We have a drink and a biscuit before bed. It's decaffeinated tea, hope you don't mind. It doesn't taste like real tea. Trying to minimise the number of times I need to pee in the night."

The room is filled with elderly women on chairs. The walkers between the furniture leave little space to manoeuvre. Pauline goes to her tiny kitchen then passes out tea in smoky grey Arcoroc mugs through a hatch between kitchen and living room.

"These mugs survived the earthquakes, and they'll outlast me," she says. "One day there'll be no humans. Some other animal will wonder who made such ugly drinking vessels, and why they made so many of them." As she says this, the lights flicker and go out. "Candles, girls," Pauline says.

The women light candles in more Arcoroc mugs on side tables.

"Did you think us old coots might wither and die without normal creature comforts?" Pauline responds to my look of surprise.

"No, not at all," I say. "I'm impressed by your organisation, like I was on the night of the tornado."

"We didn't grow up pampered. We shared bedrooms – one for the boys and one for the girls. Not one each and a bathroom. One light and one power point per room. We swapped vegetables with neighbours over the fence. Too many marrows, that's what I remember. Stuffed marrow, curried marrow, marrow soup, marrow cake. But we know how to get along with what we have and that's what we're doing. My Granny in the country, she lived her whole life with a dunny outside and a wood stove. She chopped wood for her stove until she was over eighty. The same age I am now. I don't feel eighty. I feel like a thirty-year-old trapped in a failing body I'd like to upgrade."

"What's happening with the other units? Are they being fixed? Will you all be able to stay here?" Julia asks.

"Yes, they're being fixed. We're sorting the fixing; Grant and Bob are leading it. Judith's grandson brought his student friends round to help. If we held our breaths waiting for anyone else to do the fixing we'd all be blue, and you wouldn't be getting a cup of tea. Maybe that's what the government hopes. We'll turn blue and stop being an expensive problem they can't solve.

Some people left. Nicola and Annette went to their children – they couldn't cope with the stress. That's helped. Fewer of us to fit in the non-leaky rooms. The tornado almost did us a favour – we are much better friends than before. Can't fall out when you share a bedroom, can you?"

"Is there anything we can do to help?" Julia asks.

"How good are you at roofing, love?" Pauline says. "That's the most urgent job and none of us should climb on roofs. I see Grant up there, wobbling around, and I'm waiting for him to tumble, plop, into the garden."

"I haven't done much roofing, but I know someone who is extremely practical. Andrey can do most building. What d'you think, Stephen?"

I don't think anything. Would Andrey like to help these people he doesn't know? Does he have time to help them? Does he enjoy helping old people? "You could ask him," I say.

"I'm sure he'd like to help. I'll send him a text and suggest he cycle by." She taps on her phone. "Reception's out again. The message will go through later. Andrey's larger than life, but well-meaning. He likes black tea and IPA."

"What's IPA, dear?"

"India Pale Ale. It's a type of beer."

"How interesting. Never drunk that myself. White Russians are more my thing. That's what we should do, girls. Have a cocktail night. We're cheap drunks these days, Julia. One drink will set everyone up nicely."

Heads nod over teacups and biscuits as one of the party says, "I've got some coffee liqueur in my cupboard. It's been there for years, but I'm sure it's still good."

"Funny, Andrey is a Russian," Julia says.

"We won't hold it against him if he can stop the leaks in our roofs. Horrible man, Putin. Killing all those Ukrainian people because he wanted their country. Can't believe he's still running Russia. We're almost exactly the same age, Putin and I. Here I am living in a little unit damaged by tornadoes and he's living like a king in his palaces. Ah well, I wouldn't want to be him – always scared someone might poison me to get a chance at power. Any of you girls thinking of poisoning me to get my unit?"

A chorus of, "No, Pauline," rises from the tea drinkers, some of whose cups tip at precarious angles as their eyes close.

"Of course they'd say that, wouldn't they?" Pauline laughs. "No point telling someone you're planning to poison them."

"Thanks so much for the tea, Pauline," Julia says. "Stephen and I should head home, and I'll come by again soon. Next time I'll drop in on Grant and the boys too."

"There'll always be a cup of tea for you here, or a whisky if you go see Grant. I'll tell the boys you asked after them."

"You're very at home with elderly people," I say to Julia as we walk towards her house.

"Yes, I've had some practice," Julia says. "Caring for my gran, then spending time with my friend Bev the surfer and her husband, Bill. But you must meet elderly people in your work, singing their songs?"

"Yes, sometimes. Not all my clients are old. Funny, now you mention it, I think of my clients as dying people rather than thinking about their ages."

"Exactly," Julia says as we arrive at her red front door. "No need to think about ages, they're all people."

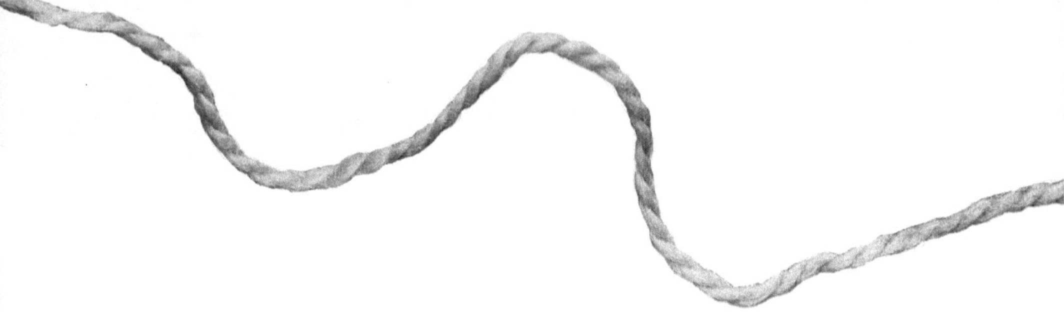

JULIA

4 May 2030

I'm on my way to Lynda and Robbie's for my birthday party carrying my trademark pumpkin pies. Then I catch my toe in a pothole and dump the pies on the ground. "Shit, damn, bother." Gran told us off for swearing and my language remains restrained. Johnno wasn't similarly affected. I asked him if he remembered Gran stopping us swearing. "Did she, Julia? I don't remember that at all." It's always unsettling when your memory of an event is different from someone else's memory. Whose is correct? I salvage what I can of the pies and return them to my basket, then trudge up the steps to the house.

Robbie greets me with a hug on the deck. "We're nearly ready but Hermie didn't sleep well last night, so we didn't either. Lynda's putting the icing on the cake. It's a lot fancier than the cake I made you. Was that a whole ten years ago? Seems so long and so short."

"I loved the overgrown scone you made me. I can still taste the raspberry jam and cream filling. Do you remember how we started sorting my boxes that day?"

"You had impressive stacks of boxes. Do you remember how you'd get caught up looking at the contents of each box?"

"You were so patient. You spent a lot of time on your phone, waiting for me to progress."

"Yes," Robbie says, looking out the window. "I was trying to get in touch with someone. A girl I'd hiked with, Sandy Walker."

I remember that name. In my doomed investigation of Robbie on the internet, I'd found a plethora of pictures of Robbie and Sandy hiking the Te Araroa trail. "Did you get in touch?"

"No. I wanted to contact her because we were hiking buddies, but I never got to say goodbye when she'd ended up in hospital. She was swept away in a river, and I felt like it was my fault. Her parents flew in from America and stopped me from seeing her again. I gave up looking for her years ago, though."

"Is my Auntie Julia out there chatting and not paying attention to me?" emanates from the house, together with the smell of cinnamon. "Robbie, sweetheart, can you take Hermione and I'll finish the icing. I'm not concentrating well this morning."

When she's with Hermione, Lynda's edges are rounded off. I wouldn't mind if they rounded off some more when she's in CEO mode. Hopefully, Hermione will infect Lynda's entire life over time.

"No rush on the icing," I say. "We can always eat it out of the bowl. You know how much I love cream cheese icing."

"Hi, Fran, just getting Hermie," Robbie calls out as he heads towards the kitchen. I look down to see Fran and Stephen coming up. Fran's parked her beetle-green scooter at the bottom; you can't miss the bright splotch beside the road.

"Hi, Julia," Fran pants, and rapidly sits down on a chair as she reaches the deck. "I found a lost visitor searching for the right flight of steps."

"Hi, Stephen, nice to see you," I say. "Cynthia had something on, did she?" What am I playing at? I'd like him to own up that Cynthia's dead, but he isn't suddenly going to change his story in public.

"Yes," Stephen says. "I forgot she leads the Saturday afternoon quilting group."

"Have you thought about expanding the Humans with Stories connections?" says Fran, still seated. "You girls could organise a get-together for everyone's families. Only people who wanted to come, of course. What do you think, Stephen?"

Stephen looks at his hands. "Cynthia is so busy with her friends and groups – that's why she thought it would be good for me to attend the workshops. I've always found it harder to make new friends."

"Let's put it to the group next meeting," Lynda says as she comes outside. "I'd like to meet everyone's families. You could meet Rosemary again, Robbie."

"Rosemary?" Robbie asks.

"You know, from lockdown," I reply. "Your friend Rosemary."

"You mean Rosemary the surfer? She was a great outdoors girl – climber, diver, cyclist. It was her idea I try mountain biking. Where I met my darling wife."

"She turned up at our workshops. How weird is that?"

"Typical Kiwi two degrees of separation, or less," Robbie says.

"In our workshop, Rosemary said she was sorry for coming to my house without asking. We were all so jittery then, immediately after lockdown."

"Aye, guess we were," Robbie says. "I'd completely forgotten I stayed at her flat for a few days after being at yours. Then I moved into a surf house. Hermie, do you want to go to Auntie Fran, seeing as she's sitting down?"

This is another recollection glitch. My eviction of Robbie and Rosemary from my mosaic bench when I found them kissing, remains seared into my neurons. For Robbie, it's apparently not a memory at all.

Fran holds out her arms. "You're smiling for Auntie Fran, Hermie!"

"Robbie thinks she's burping because she takes after him," Lynda says. "I'm sure she's smiling."

"Here's what I brought." Stephen fumbles a box of chocolates and a bottle of sparkling grape juice out of his pack.

"Thanks, Stephen. Come and help me with the glasses." Lynda says.

We sit outside in the afternoon sun, watching the rolling swells arriving on Sumner Beach and eating large slices of carrot cake washed down with the grape juice. Fran doesn't eat much of her carrot cake; she pushes the plate under her chair.

"How's your connection with your Northland whānau going, Fran?" Lynda asks.

Fran looks at the distant Kaikoura Ranges before replying. "Great. Holly and I Cast with them every weekend and the aunties are extremely keen to meet her. I'd like Holly to have more family. It'll be a long way to go."

"Could we help by saving up TEQ units and transferring them to you so you could afford a flight?" I ask.

"That's so kind, Julia" Fran glances at Stephen, then says, "I'll think about it."

Hermione, who has done a complete circuit of everyone's lap other than Stephen's, squawks then yawns. "Come to Mum, Hermie-bundle. Is it nap-time?" Lynda holds her arms out.

"I should be going," says Stephen. "Thank you. It's been a lovely afternoon."

"Nice to meet you again, Stephen," Fran says. "I won't join you on your return trip down the stairs because I have some business to discuss with the girls. See you another time."

"Bye, Stephen," we chorus and wave as he heads back down to the road.

"Shall I put Hermie to bed, love?" Robbie says. "I'll warm up some milk for her."

Fran, Lynda, and I create a familiar circle with our chairs. What business might Fran want to discuss with us? It's normally Lynda leading the conversations these days.

"Girls, I have some tough news," Fran says. "I'm leaving."

Lynda and I turn shocked faces towards one another, then back to Fran.

"Leaving?" Lynda says. "What's wrong? What's happening?"

Fran presses her lips together. "I'm not well. And Holly needs whānau."

"But you have us – she has us," I say. "You can't leave us. We're whānau too. What sort of not well? Why didn't you tell us?"

Fran sighs. "This isn't easy, girls. For any of us. I'm not just unwell. I'm dying."

A bomb blast has gone off and sucked all the oxygen out of the air and the light out of the sky.

We stutter half sentences.

"But can't you …"

"Surely they …"

"Isn't there …"

"What about …"

"Here are the facts. I have inoperable colon cancer. Ten years ago I might have fought to get treatment and a few more months to live. But now there are long queues of relatively well people waiting for operations – there's no time or money to treat the dying. I need to settle Holly somewhere she'll have support; her life expectancy isn't great either. Looking after Holly isn't something I can ask you two to do. Lynda and Robbie need to focus on Hermione."

I don't want to admit Fran is right. As much as Fran is my whānau, I can't take Holly into my house because I don't know how much longer I'll have a house. And there's only one of me; there's no resilience in one.

Fran reaches out and takes my hand and Lynda's. I reach out to Lynda, and we sit as a circle of falling tears because what else can one do?

STEPHEN

5–15 May 2030

My enjoyment of Julia's birthday party stays with me for several days. It makes me feel better when I think about singing with my opera diva, who I will miss. We are ready to sing her song; she is nearly ready to die. She falls asleep in the middle of our conversations. When she is awake, her interest in the world is fading.

I will also meet with both B and the ukulele orchestra this week. I have a plan involving B and the orchestra that I need to suggest to both. I work into the early hours of multiple mornings on a rap song called 'Shitkickin' Life' that a young black person might sing.

I've got my shitkickin' boots on to kick the shit out of life
Shitkickin' boots kick the shit out of life
Shitkickin' shitkickers, shitkickin' shitkickers
Kick shit kicking shit shitkickers shitkickin'

I'll get the ukulele boys to do backing music and vocals while B will be the star. What small boy doesn't like being allowed to swear? Hopefully, a Christian household will cope with swearing. And a thirteen-year-old with cancer will want to sing with a band of small-boy ukulele players. I will have to use my best reframing of the truth for this to succeed.

While working on 'Shitkickin' Life' I watch The Republic of Sumner Rappit channel on a second screen. I'm pretty sure the Sink the Ship post said they'd post again within a week. Finally, something comes through, scrolling between messages asking me to join community groups.

Shining Light: We need a vehicle and a driver.

Rhiannon: I'll find a vehicle.

Phaedra: I can drive.

Pekko: It is on?

Shining Light: All go once the vehicle is secured. Txt NO2COAL for more deets.

Taiaha: Who's in?

Shining Light: The less you know, the less you can tell.

I'm about to turn the computer off and go to bed when I realise I haven't checked my algorithms in several days. *Screw that,* an unexpected voice says in my head. *We're self-learning algorithms. You trained us and now we're grown-ups. Leave the worrying to us and you sleep.* I obey the algorithms. Then I worry I'm going mad if I'm doing what algorithms tell me to do.

I head down the hill to sing with the ukulele boys. I must learn their names. I'm stuck at Rudolph and Buddy. When I arrive, the boys are leaping around the living room. "Be do be do be do be do," blasts me as I come through the door.

"Settle down," Eeman says through the din. "Nice to see you, Stephen. You will stay for dinner with us tonight, yes?"

I can't turn down Eeman's offer again. Especially when the boys yell, "Be do be do be do be do be do," at volume.

"Yes please to dinner. I have a new song for you, boys." How will we practise the shitkicking song without upsetting anyone given this is a small house and Eeman is in the room? "However, first you sing me another song you like. Then Eeman can have some of his own time while we learn the new song together."

"*Kampai*," the boys chorus.

"What will you sing me today?"

"'Y.M.C.A.'!"

'Y.M.C.A.'? A song about a Christian association, hijacked by the gay community. Eeman isn't likely to know that history and the boys are even less likely. They shove each other into line and start the ukulele hum. Completely off-key. The covert grins of some smaller boys suggest they may have deliberately detuned their ukuleles.

"Boys, your ukuleles are out of tune. Your enthusiasm is fantastic, but it will be much better if everyone is playing the same notes."

The group calms down as they focus on tuning.

"That's kinder on my ears. Can you tell me your names again? I'm older than you, so my memory needs help. Let's go row by row. If you stand in the same order each time that would help my poor brain."

The boys reel through their names. I'm still struggling to find identifying features I'll remember when they move. Antonio and Rico are twins with similarly wicked smiles. They'll have to make do with their names being interchangeable.

The boys play 'Y.M.C.A.' with gusto and I join in the chorus with Eeman. The tiny roller skater from our last get-together turns up with three even smaller friends. Sonny gets them to put their arms in the shapes of Y, M, C and A.

"Great job," I say. "Now for the new song. Eeman, do you have homework to mark?"

"Always things to do. Sing out if you need help, Mr Stephen."

Once he's gone, I tell the boys, "This song is called 'Shitkickin' Life'."

Eyes go round and boys poke other boys as they whisper, "shit", "shit", "shit" to each other.

"Yes, you can say 'shit' because it's part of the song. That doesn't mean you can say 'shit' other times, though." Is that a reasonable rule small boys will follow?

"For now, this song is our special song, and we won't be singing it to anyone else until it is ready. We will perform it with a beautiful person who is the star."

"Oooohhhh," Matthew says. "A boy or a girl?"

"Next time I'll bring a photo of B to show you," I say.

We practise the chords. Then I teach the boys the words. We practise the words as a spoken thrum that will be the rhythm under the verses. Preventing the boys from raising their voices in a crescendo will be a major challenge. Perhaps I'll use the crescendo to build from verse to chorus, rather than fighting it. I get the tiny children to act out kicking at the front which works well until they kick each other.

Eeman comes to say dinner is ready. The boys and I look disappointed as we're in a shitkickin' flow.

"Dinner now, more practice in two weeks," I say. "One last thing. What's your band called?"

Boys look at each other.

"You come up with a name and tell me next practice," I say.

"This way, Mr Stephen," Eeman points to the kitchen.

I lead a file of boys into a space devoid of furniture other than kitchen units. Ruby and another smiling woman dish rice and vegetable stew from huge saucepans onto our plates and Eeman points me to the floor. Sit on the floor? What will I do with my legs? As I dither, the boys all sit down neatly cross-legged with plates in their laps and bowed heads.

I haven't sat on the floor with my legs crossed since I was at primary school, and when I try it's not happening. I sit with one leg tucked in and one outstretched, trying not to drop my food on my legs or kick Rudolph, who is opposite me. Eeman says a prayer of gratitude for dinner and then an eating frenzy ensues in which no one notices outstretched legs.

I go into B's room feeling more nervous than is reasonable, given I'm a sixty-year-old man helping a teenager. Could it be I want B to like me? Why would

I care if a monosyllabic, androgynous teenager likes me or not? It must be because I want to please Felicity, in return for her care of Cynthia.

"Lovely to see you, Stephen," says Felicity from her chair by the window, where she's talking with a middle-aged woman wearing John Lennon glasses, a denim shirt and jeans. "Stephen, meet Miranda. Miranda, this is Stephen, the songwriter. Miranda is B's carer. B stays at Miranda's house when she's out of hospital. What have you got for us today, Stephen?"

B is as sheathed in clothing as on my last visit.

"Hi, B," I try to copy Felicity's upbeat tone. "I worked on a chorus as a start of a song for which you can write the verses. I'm thinking you could sing it with a band. It would be more fun for you to sing with other young people." Fun sounds like an old word. What's the current slang for 'fun'?

"Okay, boomer," B says.

"B ..." Felicity says.

"So who's the band?"

"They're a ... a surprise," I say. "My plan is you play together next meeting, or the one after. When we've worked on the song."

"A surprise," B says with arms firmly crossed.

"Yes," I say. "Let's see what you think of this chorus."

I sing the 'Shitkickin' Life' chorus, watching for a reaction. An eyebrow rises under the hood.

"Shit's the slackest word you got?"

"We need to think about our audience – if there are children in it," I say.

"Huh," B says. "It's no GOAT but it'll do for now."

That's the longest sentence I've heard B say. I'll take it as a positive. What does 'GOAT' mean? I'm guessing it's not a ruminant with horns.

"B, I want you to come up with verses for our next meeting. We'll keep the shitkickin' chorus running in the background with your voice over the top. I want to hear what you have to say."

"What I have to say?" The hood turns sharply in my direction.

"Of course. That's why we're doing this, B. To hear what you have to say."

"Yeah. Right. I'm tired now."

"No problem. See you in a fortnight."

"Thanks so much, Stephen," Felicity says as we go out the door. "So good. B was more excited than I've ever seen."

"B's one cool dude if that's what excitement looks like."

"Funny, Stephen. If you're seeing B in two weeks from now, she'll be at Miranda's on a break from chemo. Perfect timing for songwriting. I can't wait to see the performance. I know this will be great."

I'm glad Felicity knows this is going to be great. I'm yet to introduce B to the band, which could be a showstopper.

JULIA

16 May 2030

It's Thursday, nearly time for me to run the next Humans with Stories workshop and I can't be bothered. My world is off-kilter to a degree beyond self-righting. Fran, Lynda, and I have been a team for ten years. Without their support, I don't know how I will survive. No, that's melodramatic and selfish. I am alive with no specific physical threat on my horizon, while Fran knows she is dying, and soon. As hard as I try, I can't imagine what it's like to be Fran. It's impressive how good we humans are at simultaneously knowing we will die and not fully believing it. But that goes for many things. I know the sea is threatening my house, but I don't believe I'll need to leave. I'm hardly doing anything about it.

Fran, Lynda, and I get together on Cast nearly every day. That's what we agreed on Lynda's deck. We'll make the most of the time Fran has left to give us. Once she goes north in two weeks, she will focus on Holly and her whānau.

I'm minimising my use of energy units for two weeks so I can transfer them to Fran to help get Fran, Holly, and their belongings to the far end of New Zealand. They will catch the train to Picton, the ferry from Picton to Wellington, another train to Auckland, and then a local bus north from Auckland for a whole day. The moving company requires a combined payment in money and TEQs for their belongings. Holly needs every cent Fran can leave her; I can do without power or gas for two weeks. Cold showers remind me of what Fran's going through. I always have spare units anyhow, which are automatically sold on the open market for me. Why did I never think about trading my units with, or giving my units to people who are important to me? I'm changing that, as of now.

"Can I go with you, Fran?" I asked. I haven't ever left the South Island. This could have been my opportunity to branch out, although as I was offering Fran my spare TEQs it wasn't a practical suggestion.

"What a lovely offer, Julia," Fran said. "Thank you, but no. This is a trip Holly and I need to do together. You, Lynda, and I will say goodbye here. No drawn-out farewells. And, for these last two weeks, I need you to help me stay strong. There's so much to organise I can't be the blubbering wreck I'd like to collapse into. When you come to help me sort out the house we'll go through my things, throw a sad party, and then cry as much as we want."

"What's a sad party?" I asked.

"It's a time when we can be sad together. We'll turn the lights down, Lynda will make a sad sound track, and we will cry and yell and break things because what's left in my house will be stuff none of us wants."

"I've never heard of a sad party," Lynda said. "But it makes a weird sort of sense. Celebrate the sadness because it's as significant as happiness. Let's bring black clothes to change into. And out of again."

"I'll bring black food," I said, playing along.

It will be a first, us going to Fran's house. We have always met at Lynda's or my house since we both live in Sumner. How could I have known Fran for a decade, but never gone to her house? I don't even know what the inside looks like because her Zoom background is a green forest. So much about Fran I don't know and now there's no time to find out.

Most things other than Fran and Lynda dropped off my radar this week, including my sculpture for the tornado charity auction. It's getting urgent because the auction is the beginning of May. The clock face is nearly complete; it features a miscellany of objects collected after the tornado welded or glued together. The numbers stand above the clock surface and are highlighted with gold paint. The number thirteen is larger than all the rest. The clock hands are exactly that, metal hands with five fingers, the index finger pointing to the number thirteen. I am including sound in the sculpture – a recording of the tsunami sirens playing at random intervals for random lengths of time. Robbie thinks the recording will be extremely annoying, so has persuaded me to include an audio off switch. I still need to make the stand. The clock takes up a whole repair table which isn't making Robbie happy. Repair Wednesdays are so popular he needs every centimetre of space.

The lion's head knocker on my front door thuds cautiously. It must be Stephen, picking me up on his way to the workshop, although he's very early. I haven't seen or communicated with him since my birthday party at Lynda's – he dropped off my radar too.

"Hi, Stephen." I open the front door with a smile. "Come in while I grab my things."

"I wasn't sure whether to come by when you didn't answer my texts," Stephen says.

"I'm sorry. I got some bad news and haven't been thinking straight."

"Was it about Fran?"

"How did you know that?"

"I guessed, seeing how she wanted to talk with you and Lynda privately after your birthday party. And she wasn't looking well."

"Yes. She's sick. And she's leaving." To my horror, my voice quavers, and my face crumples.

Stephen tentatively puts his hand on my shoulder. "Julia? I'm sorry about Fran, whatever the problem is."

"It's not just a problem," I say. "She's dying."

"Dying. A business I know all too well," Stephen says with a sad smile.

Of course. Stephen sings songs for dying people. Or is it with dying people?

"Do we have time for a quick cuppa before we go to the workshop?" Stephen asks. "Could I make you tea?"

I almost refuse automatically. When did I last let someone else provide for me in my home? Then I think better of it and sit down at the table. "There's a kettle …" I begin.

"I may be an older male, but even I can recognise a kettle when I see one," Stephen says. "However, you can tell me where you keep your tea."

It's definitely a Kenya Bold moment. I point out the cloisonné caddy containing the tea leaf. "One big scoop in the teapot, please."

"A Temuka teapot," Stephen says. "My parents had one of those."

"This was my gran's. Why don't we use her cups, too? I normally use mugs, but if you look at the back of the cupboard, behind the mugs, you'll see two gold filigree teacups."

Stephen pulls the teacups out. "What happened to this one?" he asks, pointing to the cup along whose cracks roses sprout.

"It's a long story," I say. "That cup tells the story of me and Gran, and Amanda, and Robbie, and Fran, and Lynda and my re-creation business."

"That's one important cup," Stephen says. "I wouldn't want to rush your story. Perhaps you can tell it another time when we aren't going to a workshop?"

"Would you like to come round for tea next weekend? No, next weekend Fran and Lynda and I are having a sad party. How about the following weekend? Saturday afternoon?"

"That suits me," Stephen says.

The spectre of Cynthia flits into my thoughts but I brush her off. If good friends can hold sad parties, developing friends can have tea parties in which a ghost does not interfere. And he is quite good-looking.

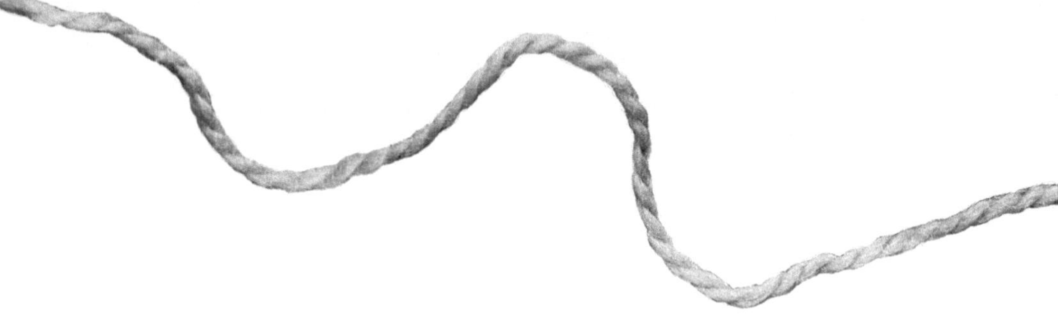

JULIA

16 May 2030

Stephen and I walk to the workshop through Sumner.

"I've a favour to ask," I say. "Not for me, but for Pauline and the retirement unit girls. They're excited by the idea of you singing with them."

"I guess I could," Stephen says.

"I was chatting with Pauline about how we sang at the Surf Club during the tornado. How good it was, everyone singing together. Pauline said she and the girls love singing but none of them play an instrument and it's more fun to sing with accompaniment."

"Did Pauline mention what sort of music she likes?" Stephen asks.

"No, but they're seventy-five to eighty-five, right? What would have been popular when they were young?"

"Hmmm … 1960s to 1980s. Off the top of my head, Beatles, Neil Diamond, Dolly Parton, Simon and Garfunkel. Those are all good to sing along to," Stephen says. "I have a reciprocal favour to ask of you. Could you help me with some costumes?"

"Sure. Lynda's more imaginative than me on the clothing and materials front, but I can sew. Who and what are the costumes for?"

"I'm helping a young client perform a song, together with a band of small boys. B dresses in black, very covered up. We need to talk with B about what B wants. The boys like being Minions."

"What are Minions? Other than someone who is told what to do by someone else?"

"Minions are in a series of movies called *Despicable Me*. They look like a yellow pill, about a metre high, with either two eyes or one eye, round grey goggles and denim overalls."

"What do they do?" I ask.

"I don't know. I'm sounding more knowledgeable than I actually am. I've only just learnt about Minions from the boys Eeman has got me singing with," Stephen says. "I'm turning into your regular sing-along guy. Next, I'll be singing at weddings."

"I'll search online for pictures of Minions. Denim overalls are easy – I could make them out of second-hand jeans. And dye second-hand T-shirts yellow. I'll go to the second-hand clothing warehouse next to our repair workshop. Is B male or female?"

"B doesn't regard B as a boy or a girl."

"Then I definitely need to meet B to create a costume."

"It's a deal," Stephen says. "You come meet B and I'll come to the units."

"Great. Let's go visit Pauline and Grant on our way home," I say.

Stephen and I go up the fire station stairs to find everyone else already there, chatting. Our cup of tea has made us late, again.

"Hey, Julia, Stephen, good of you to turn up," Lynda says.

"Sorry, Lynda." I take her arm and move us slightly aside from the group to speak in a lower voice. "We were having a cup of tea. I told him about Fran and got upset."

"Oh, Julia," Lynda says. "I didn't mean to call you out. All good. Well, things are not all good, of course. But I've got Robbie and Hermione. You need extra people too."

She raises her voice to call the room to attention. "Okay, everyone, let's take our seats to hear Andrey's story. All ready to go, Andrey?"

"Yes." Andrey looks past Lynda with a smile that doesn't reach his eyes.

Why is he so nervous tonight? That's not our normal Andrey.

Once everyone is sitting down, I lead the karakia, then Andrey comes to the front of the room and takes a deep breath.

"Hi, everyone. Here's my story of a boy, a girl, and a dog. Once upon a time, a boy met a girl. The boy lived in Helsinki with his mother. They'd moved to Helsinki from Russia after his father died because his mother fell in love with a Finnish businessman. Finland was a much nicer country to live in than Russia. The cities worked better and the government built houses for everyone who couldn't afford a home. Russia was grim while Finland was more like a fairy-tale, although a fairy-tale in the tropics would have been nicer because Finland was as cold as Russia in winter. To help the boy feel happier about moving, the mother gave the boy a one-eyed dog and he called her Luna."

Rosemary puts her hand up and comes to the front of the room.

"What's your connection, Rosemary?" Lynda says.

"Our whānau has a one-eyed cat called Luna. I wouldn't have got a cat; she adopted us. One day she turned up, walked in the door, and sat on the sofa. We thought she must be someone else's pet, but she never left, so I gave in and bought cat food. My husband doesn't approve of us keeping Luna. He says the best cat is a dead cat, because cats eat so many native birds and skinks. Not to mention the environmental impact of pet food. He's right, in theory. So much environmental theory sounds excellent. But, in practice, once you've taken something in, how can you kill it?"

"Thank you, Rosemary," Andrey says. He gives her a polished piece of wood with an 'R' shape in the centre filled with epoxy glue containing rosemary flowers. "You can use it to put hot plates on."

"Thank you, Andrey, it's beautiful," Rosemary says.

The wooden piece is truly lovely. Andrey must have been working on his gifts for some time if he has made similar shapes for everyone.

As Andrey is about to speak, the lights flicker and go out. Then the sound of a generator kicks in and the lights come back on; a back-up power supply is an unexpected bonus of meeting at the fire station.

"Now I continue my story," Andrey says. "In the apartment next door to the boy and his mother, a girl lived. She was beautiful with a thin, muscular body and long blonde hair, usually tied in a bun on top of her head. The boy and the girl attended the same school, but he was older, so they were in different classes. Every day he saw the girl and hoped she might talk with him, but she never did. Finally, in desperation, he found out she was in the trampoline team. So the boy joined the trampoline club."

"On Thursdays after school, the boy would learn how to do back flips and front flips. He was a terrible trampolinist. He was never sure whether his head was pointing up or down, so he often fell headfirst into the trampoline mat. The girl was a fantastic trampolinist. She flew high in the air and did somersaults and corkscrews and many other manoeuvres the boy didn't know the names of."

Zahra comes forward. "I was a gymnast at high school, not so different from a trampolinist. The boys got to wear loose trousers while the girls had to wear tiny leotards – so unfair. It was my country that changed the competition uniform for women. In the Olympic Games of 2021, the German team wore full-length unitards, protesting against the sexualisation of women in gymnastics. Most teams copied them. I was very proud of my country."

"Thanks, Zahra," Andrey says. "I'd never thought about how the different uniforms weren't fair. To be honest, I was only thinking about how beautiful Anastasia looked in her leotard, or anything else she wore. I wasn't interested in the other girls." He gives Zahra her wooden plate. Her 'Z' has zinnia flowers embedded in it.

"One day after trampoline class the boy's prayers were answered, even though he didn't believe in a God," Andrey continues.

"'Hi, Andrey,' the girl said.

"'You know my name?'

"'Sure, you're my next-door neighbour. And you've been coming to trampoline club because you want to meet me, right? Want to walk home together?'

"There was nothing to say but, 'Yes!'"

Stephen puts his hand up and comes forward. "You have reminded me of when I met my wife Cynthia – at high school. She and her friends ate lunch in the covered area outside the school hall, knitting or sewing. I was fascinated by Cynthia's face, which lit up when she talked with her friends. I wanted to get to know her, to have her light shining on me. It took me forever to speak to her. Approaching a group of girls was worse than offering meat to a great white shark without the protection of a cage.

"I finally summoned up the courage two weeks before our final-year school dance. I picked my time carefully – when Cynthia was sitting on the outside corner of the table. I walked up to her, trying to stand straight and not mumble. 'Would you like …' I said. Cynthia said, 'Are you finally going to ask me to go to the dance with you? Thank goodness. I've been waiting for you to ask forever.' After that, I couldn't imagine life without her."

"You understand, Stephen," Andrey says. "Here's your gift." Stephen's 'S' has jasmine flowers in the epoxy. "Jasmine plants are called *Stephanotis*," Andrey explains.

"It's excellent, Andrey," Stephen says. "We … um … I will find lots of use for it."

"The boy and the girl spent ever more time together," Andrey says. "She helped him study. He helped her fix their family's car. They swam in the lake in summer and ice skated on it in winter. He did his military service and trained as a chef while she studied economics at university. Then, in 2022, Putin invaded Ukraine and the face of northern Europe changed. Where military service had seemed like a different sort of school, now the boy could have to fight another country. The boy and the girl didn't believe in war. They believed in love. They planned. As soon as the boy finished his service they would leave Finland and go somewhere far away from the war.

"When they were ready to leave, the boy told his mother. The girl didn't tell her parents; she only left them a letter because she was scared they would try to stop her. The boy's mother was sad but realistic. 'Go and find your life,' she said. 'Here's some money your grandfather left you. It's the right time for you to have it.'

"The boy and the girl bought a beat-up station wagon and drove south. As Finns, they were EU citizens; they would find an EU country in which they wanted to live. They were careful with the money. They couch-surfed or slept in the station wagon. They picked fruit. The boy freelanced as a chef. The girl helped out in people's houses. They got as far south as Slovenia and liked it. It was not too cold in winter – they'd had enough of snow and ice for a lifetime – and not too hot in summer. There were lakes and rivers to swim in. The earth was good for growing crops. But they couldn't live out of a car forever. What would they do?

"One day, they drove past a For Sale sign on a steep hillside. Trees grew out of a tumbledown farmhouse. Where the land wasn't smothered with blackberry or creepers it was littered with roof tiles, piles of stones and tangles of fencing wire. 'Maybe this land won't cost too much,' the boy said. The girl said nothing because it was too much to hope for.

"But they were lucky. No one else wanted that land or the farmhouse that was hardly a house. It would take almost all the money the mother had given the boy, but that was okay. They could make this work."

Lynda puts her hand up and Andrey pauses. "I know what you mean about the work required to turn a broken-down old house into a beautiful home, Andrey. Although the house Robbie and I have done up doesn't sound nearly as hard work as yours. What an amazing amount of work you and Anastasia must have done."

Andrey looks sad. Of course he would. He and Anastasia don't live in their house in Slovenia anymore. He must miss it like I would miss Gran's house if I wasn't living in it. Andrey hands Lynda her koha.

"Yours was too easy, Lynda," Andrey says, "as 'Lynda' means 'beautiful'." A bird of paradise flower sits in the crook of the 'L', shining orange and purple.

Lynda holds up the 'L'. "Amazing, Andrey," she says, then sits back down.

"Like Lynda says, the boy and the girl worked. They worked, and they worked, and they worked. They cut down vines that curled around their legs. They attacked blackberry that tried to rip their hands and arms. They took the fencing wire to be melted down. They stored the roof tiles for later. They used fallen stones to retain the slopes and make vegetable beds. They repaired the roof and the bats roosting in the rafters had to move into the shed. They put windows in the gaping holes and geckos had to go live under the stones in the garden. The snakes slithered out to find holes under trees instead of under the floor.

The boy and the girl and Luna the dog had a home. They took Luna for walks in the woods, where she chased imaginary animals through the leaf litter. The boy experimented with home-brewed beer. The girl grew beetroot and cucumbers and tomatoes and courgettes and capsicums and potatoes. They ate huge salads and traded potatoes for peaches. They were happy."

Victoria comes up to the front. Today she is wearing a green and blue kaftan with fish swimming through rolling waves. The kaftan swirls around her protruding stomach. Over the kaftan, Victoria has a turquoise cardigan in a light woven fabric that folds and swirls with her movement. Round her neck, she has a deep green scarf shot through with silver, like light on water. She reminds me of my mosaic sofa, where a taniwha plays in green, blue, and silver waves.

"Like I mentioned in another meeting, we have started a vegetable garden at our rental. I love it. I love the peace of being in the garden and the freshness of the produce. Gardening is something several of us have in common, isn't it, Julia and Eeman?"

"Yes, Victoria." Andrey nods. "Gardening connects us with the earth and with each other. Your koha has water lilies in it because Victoria is also the name of a genus of water lilies."

Victoria admires her wooden stand. "That's clever Andrey," she says. "I would like a pond with water lilies in our garden."

"The boy and the girl were happy until the fires started. When they bought their house, no one in the area remembered there ever being a forest fire. However, now it wasn't snowing in the winter anymore, or raining as much as it used to in summer. The rivers and lakes were shallow and tree leaves were becoming brittle. Everyone said, 'This is bad. It's climate change, but what can you do? We need to drive our cars to get to work. We need to fly in planes to see our friends. We need manufacturing to support our economy.'

"The first fire was thirty kilometres away. It burnt a few houses and a lot of forest. The second fire was only two valleys away. In that fire, a whole village went up in flames, but the people all escaped.

"Then everyone talked about what we should do. We should clear gutters out. We should cut down trees close to our houses. We should build water reservoirs. The government should install sirens. The government should employ more firefighters. We did what we could and, when there was no big fire the next summer, we breathed easier again."

I could say something here. About sirens as warnings and how they strike fear in your heart. How floods and earthquakes and fires destroy homes and communities and leave humans unsure what to do next. How there is always another disaster bigger than you can imagine lurking around the corner. How you relax when you peek around the corner and can't see the disaster, because you don't realise it's waiting for you behind your own door. Except Andrey's narrative is transfixing us all, so I'd rather say nothing and remain connected through the attention we are paying to his story.

"The third fire started one morning in spring. A morning when someone was smoking in their car on their way to work and absentmindedly threw their cigarette butt out the window at the bottom of the river valley. The boy was in Italy, working as a chef for a fortnight. The girl and Luna were home. It was a hot day with a strong wind forecast. The air started to fill with smoke and the fire gathered strength. By the time anyone realised how widespread the flames were, there was nowhere to run because the fire was roaring up the valley sides, all the way to the tops of the hills.

"The boy never returned home because he had no home to go to. His heart had been burnt to a tiny cinder. Why not go to the sea and swim towards the horizon until you are so tired you sink beneath the water? But he was still too alive to die. So he got on a plane to the country that seemed the safest in a world of wars and climate change. He flew to Aotearoa.

"Now Aotearoa is where the boy lives. He lost his home, he lost his heart, but he still hopes to make a difference to the planet. He's just figuring out how."

The room is stiller than an unruffled pond awaiting the first raindrop of a thunderstorm.

After a long pause, Lynda gets up and hugs Andrey. "Andrey, I'm so sorry," she says.

One by one, everyone in the room hugs Andrey, then looks expectantly to Lynda and me.

Anything I say is going to sound ridiculously trivial, so I say the truth. "Andrey, I need a cup of tea. Can I make you one too?"

"A cup of tea would be perfect, Julia," Andrey says.

I bring Andrey his tea. "My connection, which I didn't say during your story, is we have both experienced disaster. Earthquakes killed my daughter and damaged my house. I hope living through one disaster might mean I'm better at living through the next one, but I'm not so sure."

"Thank you, Julia. Here's your koha." Andrey says. "Roses for you, although I couldn't find an actual 'Julia's Rose'. I hope when you see it you will remember me. Here is a big piece and a little one."

"Of course I'll remember you, Andrey," I say. "I'm not likely to forget you when we've got workshops every two weeks." I look at the wooden stands. The small one is odd. It has two opposing curves on the outside, like it's intended to fit into something rather than be used on its own. Might Andrey have forgotten to bring the whole item? That seems unlikely. I put them both in my bag to take home.

It's a subdued group drinking tea and eating vegan cheese-filled buckwheat pancakes and Finnish gingerbread biscuits. Snippets of conversation drift past my ears.

"We really should …"

"But what can you …"

"How terrible …"

I am exhausted by the weight of Andrey's story and its reminder that, when a threat is looming, it's time to act. If I had checked the mirror after the first earthquakes then Amanda might … except I don't go there because there's no rewinding time. However, the threat of flooding to Gran's house is here and now. I can't hold back the tide. I realise I will have to leave.

JULIA

16–24 May 2030

I put the room back in order with Stephen, after telling Lynda to head home to her family. "I'm not up to chatting with Pauline and Grant tonight," I say to Stephen. "I'll drop by soon and organise the sing-along. I was also supposed to ask everyone about a separate get-together with families tonight, but by the end of the meeting I didn't feel like that either."

"I know what you mean," Stephen says. "I'm not up for much after hearing Andrey's story. I don't know how you move past something so terrible. You definitely don't get over it. Of course, you know all about that, your daughter having died in the earthquakes."

"Yes and no," I say. "Everyone's losses are unique, aren't they? We're all the same and we're all different. I'm worried about Andrey. He said something strange when I gave him his cup of tea. It sounded like he thought he wouldn't be around much longer."

"Maybe he doesn't need the workshops anymore since he told his story about Slovenia?" Stephen says.

"Maybe. It felt bigger than that."

Walking back to my house requires concentration so we don't talk much. There's no light from the moon and the streetlights are still broken from the tornado. The footpaths are more damaged every rainstorm. When I say goodbye to Stephen at my front door, he surprises me with a kiss on the cheek. *To hell with a non-existent Cynthia and workshop propriety*, I think, and kiss him, briefly, on the lips. He steps back, looking surprised, then smiles broadly.

"Night, Stephen," I say. "Thanks for listening to me earlier. See you Saturday week. And text me about B."

This afternoon Fran, Lynda, and I will hold Fran's sad party. That's bad enough but then my day gets a lot worse. My mistake was forgetting to select 'Do Not Disturb' on my iPad while I read recipes on it. So the notification of an email from the Christchurch City Council pops up in the right-hand corner of my screen; 'URGENT NOTICE'. I try to ignore it, but that is harder than ignoring dancing elephants in my tiny kitchen, so I desert a Black Velvet Cake recipe for my inbox.

URGENT NOTICE 18 May 2030
Christchurch City Council Section Taking Opportunities
for Retreat Management (STORM)

Dear Julia Stout

We are actively managing urban retreat around our coastlines and waterways, as flooding overwhelms infrastructure and houses. We are prioritising retreat in areas already subject to flooding and where flood levels will render houses untenable by or before 2050.

We are delighted to inform you of your eligibility for a Retreat Management payment, calculated at fifty per cent of your Registered Valuation. In your case, this will be a sum of $400,000, based on your most recent valuation of $800,000.

Your options from here are:

1) You can query your valuation through the online
Council Valuation Objection process.

2) You can reply to this email informing us you will
take up our offer.

Once you accept our offer, you have six months in
which to vacate your property. You may remove any and
all structures and plants from your property. However,
removal will be at your own expense. The council will
provide an upfront payment of $100,000 upon acceptance of
this offer to facilitate your move to another location.
The remainder of the payment will be made on the agreed
exit date.

If you have questions, please feel free to contact
the STORM helpline on 0800 STORM (78676) or through the
contact form on our STORM website.

Best regards

Joeline Smithies STORM AREA MANAGER

I do not share the council's delight. Half the value of my home won't buy me
any other property in Sumner, or in much of Christchurch. Will I be forced
to buy a tiny apartment in a satellite suburb far west of the city on the flat and
hot Canterbury Plains? I was coming to terms with having to move, but the
reality of where I might go hadn't yet entered my consciousness. However, reality
won't help me bake black velvet cake with chocolate ganache icing, black sesame
gelato, or black rice sushi rolls. In order not to waste ingredients and run out
of time for baking, I close the email and use my brain box. I create a calendar
entry for 'Council offer' seven days away. It's not like the council is going to
take dire action in the next week. Today, I will think only of Fran and Lynda.

I found something new out about Fran when we were discussing the sad
party menu. She isn't vegan. All these years I've thought she's vegan because
the snacks at Obsessives Associated had to be vegan. I never asked. Just like

I never asked more about her being adopted. Just like I never found out she is Māori or visited her house. It turns out Fran wanted to be as inclusive as possible with the snacks, and we have carried on the tradition in Humans with Stories. Fran is actually partial to cake of any sort. So I am making the best, richest velvet cake anyone ever baked.

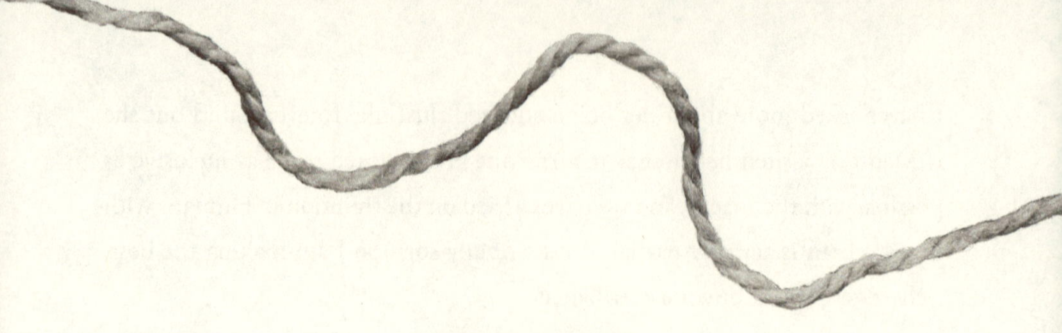

STEPHEN

16–24 May 2030

My footsteps up Scarborough Hill are light after Julia's kiss. When I get home, I check The Republic of Sumner channel. There's nothing about sinking ships. The last message sounded like it would happen soon. They are probably communicating privately now. I was going to tell Julia about The Republic of Sumner messages tonight but first she was upset about Fran and then Andrey's story didn't help. It'll have to wait until we get together Sunday week. It isn't like either she or I will do anything about the messages.

The idea of having someone I can tell random interesting things to is nice. I replay the touch of Julia's lips on mine as I get ready for bed.

When I go to my next rendezvous with Eeman's boys there's an air of tension. Ruby greets me briefly, then heads back into the kitchen. Eeman's smile is thin. Is this about my teaching the boys an inappropriate song? The boys are cavorting around manically. When Eeman calls them, they are slow to come to attention. Buddy has Sonny in a headlock and Sonny is trying to kick him backwards in the balls.

"Boys. Boys!" Eeman's voice becomes sterner, and one by one they stop what they're doing and take up their ukuleles.

"What's up, Eeman?"

"The families must leave this house," Eeman says. "The notice came this morning. Council is no longer maintaining social services housing on the flat in Sumner valley. The notice said they have nowhere else to offer. The families must find somewhere for themselves."

"How long do they have? Where will they go?" I think of my large patch of land with just me living on it. However, there's no space in my caravan for one extra family, let alone an unknown number of families with fourteen children.

"They've got six months' notice, so the boys can finish the year at their school. But the families have no idea where they will go. I have no idea where Deb and I will go, either."

"Eeman, you are losing your house as well? Why has the council done this?"

"Perhaps the tornado was the final straw? Too many problems. Too much money required." Eeman sighs deeply. "So many problems everywhere."

What will this mean for Sumner? Will the council stop providing services to whole suburbs, like after the earthquakes? Will we lose the shops on the flat, which are often flooded?

"Should I give up on playing with the boys today? Given everyone's so upset?"

"No," Eeman says. "They love their music. Although I don't so much like the song you taught them last time."

"The 'Shitkickin' Life' song?"

"Yes, that one."

"I can explain. It's a song for a young person who is very ill – B. B likes angry music. B's had a tough life and may die of cancer soon. I would like the boys to sing with B to make a performance of the song."

"Aha," Eeman says. "The boys love the song and 'shit' has been the most common word in the house for the last two weeks, along with 'butt', which Minions say often. Their parents have not been happy. However, 'shit' seems like the right word since the notice came. Your explanation makes sense, but it would have been helpful if you had told me first."

"Of course. I've a new song today which has 'shit' in it also," I say. "Only once, though. And nothing worse. Is that okay?"

"You are pushing the boundaries, Mr Stephen," Eeman says with a smile.

"Right, boys," I say. I've another song for you to learn today. But first, what's your band name?"

Randolph pipes up, "How 'bout 'The Minions'?"

"That's possible. But there are already bands called 'The Minions'."

I'm losing them. There's shuffling, sly elbow pokes and Sonny is grabbing Buddy's ukulele.

"What about 'The Maximinions'?" I suggest. "There are no bands with that name. You'd be special."

"Be do be do be do be do be do be do," they yell.

"Right Maximinions, let's sing."

We practise 'Shitkickin' Life'. Then I teach them 'Always Look on the Bright Side of Life' to sing to B when they meet.

When we take a break, I hear subdued voices in the kitchen. I go down the hallway and poke my head in. "Come and join us?"

Eeman, Ruby and three other adults look up, faces tense.

"The boys need encouragement," I say.

"I doubt that," Eeman says, "but we can come."

The chorus of 'Always Look on the Bright Side of Life' is irresistible. The room fills with sound. Everyone, from adults to the smallest children, dances around the ukulele players. Ruby finally calls us to attention because dinner is past ready. We share our meal on the kitchen floor, avoiding conversations about houses or moving.

Two days later I'm about to catch the bus with Julia. We're headed to Waltham, between Sumner and Christchurch, where B's caregiver Miranda lives. It seems like forever since I saw Julia, though it was only last week.

"How are you?" I call as I stride up to the stop.

"Fine," she says in a low tone, looking at me, then quickly looking away.

"Are you okay about coming to see B?" I ask.

"Yes. I hope I can help," she says, staring at the other side of the road.

I remember Cynthia acting this way. It was usually because I had forgotten something important. I'm great at thinking through all the ramifications of my plans, but not nearly so good at remembering what other people have going on. What was happening for Julia? Fran's sad party. Last weekend.

"I'm sorry, Julia," I say. "I completely forgot to ask about Fran's party. How was it? Sad, I guess."

"It was as good as a sad party can be," Julia says. "Although that was my first one. We helped finish packing Fran and Holly's belongings for the movers. They aren't taking much. Then Fran asked us to choose something to remember her by. I chose a black leather jacket I have always loved. Lynda chose a painting of Fran drawn by Holly when she was ten, titled 'Best eva arntie'. Then we did a lot of crying and talking and drank too much and ate too much sushi and cake. The plan was to break things, but we didn't because it seemed wrong to break useful possessions. Lynda and I slept over in Holly's room – Holly was visiting a friend. In the morning we nursed our sore heads and packaged up all the breakables we didn't break to distribute through Buy Nothing."

"I'll tell Felicity about the sad party idea," I say. "It could be helpful for the people she supports in the hospice. Get all the sad out in the open."

"Stephen, you're quite the sensitive new-age bloke," Julia says, looking directly at me.

"Not really," I say, as I hold eye contact for that second beyond normal and my neck turns red.

She takes my hand, and I don't see anything out the window as our intertwined fingers take the whole of my attention.

We get off the bus on Ferry Road and walk, still hand in hand, past where the rugby stadium used to be before it was irreparably damaged in the Canterbury earthquakes. The green space left behind after the stadium was demolished is crowded with vans, motor homes and tiny houses in a grid pattern. Many of the vehicles are surrounded by outdoor furniture and plants in pots. On the opposite side of the road, housing units in rows are crammed onto small sections. We find Miranda's address, a middle unit.

"What should I do?" Julia asks.

"You go for a wander. I'll text when I've sorted things with B."

"I wish you could have sorted them beforehand."

"Yes, I know," I say. "But B is a little tricky." There's so much I haven't properly thought through.

Miranda opens the door. "Hi, Stephen, nice to see you again." She moves back so I can fit in the tiny hallway. "B's upstairs. Just follow your nose. I'll be in the kitchen if you need me."

I open B's door. "Hi, B, how're things?"

"Pretty shit," B says.

"Good thing we're singing a song about shit, then." This kid is hard work. However, this kid is extremely sick so I should cut the kid some slack.

"Have you worked on your words, B?"

"Yup."

"Can I see them?"

B unfolds an arm from the black fabric hiding B's form and thrusts a phone towards me.

SHITKICKIN' LIFE

Feeling lost, down low
Nowhere to go
A kid fighting for my life
This crab's got me down
Pincers cutting like a knife
She, he, it, they, don't know who I am?
I'm me, breaking free
I'm B, Queen B

Maybe young, but not weak
I'm tough, I'm unique
Not confined by my disease
I'll rise up, I'll seize
My life, my destiny
Show the world what's meant to be
I'm me, breaking free
I'm B, Queen B

"Excellent, B. You're a songwriter and a half. Shall we try them with backing music?"

"Yup," B says.

"We also need to think about clothes for your performance. I've asked a friend of mine to come by who is good at sewing. Can she come up and see you?"

"I guess," B shrugs.

I text Julia to come in thirty minutes.

B sits on the bed. I sit in front of the door on a stool and hope Miranda won't suddenly open the door and knock me to the ground. I've already created a chord framework. Minor key for the verse related to the major key of the chorus. I throw in a few extended chords to add dissonance. I get B to speak her words over the chords. B sits upright and speaks in a surprisingly confident manner for a monosyllabic young person who hides behind layers of black clothing. B's got performance built in.

We're immersed in the music when I hear "Hello," from Julia outside the door. I pass the guitar to B to open the door. As Julia and I manoeuvre around each other in the hall, I hear B playing the guitar. She's replicating the chords we played earlier by ear.

I poke my head back through the door. "B, you're as good on the guitar as with lyrics." In the folds of the fabric, I glimpse an approximation of a smile.

"Julia, this is B. B, this is Julia your costume designer."

"Want a cup of tea, Stephen?" Miranda calls from downstairs. I descend to the open-plan living/kitchen space where I can almost breathe – although the crowded buildings make the place claustrophobic. I like my space a lot. My space with no one else within my hedges.

I've finished my tea before Julia comes downstairs with my guitar.

"B's tired," Julia says. "But I know what B'd like to wear and I've measured B, as far as B will let me. I'll sketch something up and send it through to B. When do we need the costume?"

"Maybe two weeks?" I say.

"Good thing our ideas weren't complicated then," Julia says. "Miranda, is that a cup of tea for me? You're wonderful. I love tea."

"Could B come to Sumner, Miranda?" I ask. "I would like her to meet the Maximinions – that's the name of the band I've organised."

Miranda hesitates. "B doesn't do well with people she doesn't know. In a place she doesn't know. Couldn't they come here?"

This is too hard. Will the Maximinions be allowed? Can they afford it? How will I manage them on the bus? They won't fit in this room.

"Of course," Julia says.

I stare at her.

"It's important not to tire B out, Stephen. I'll help bring the Maximinions. It will be fun."

"Yes," I say. "Of course. It will be fun." And, if Julia is involved, it will be.

JULIA

25–26 May 2030

It's Saturday morning, and I'm thinking about what to bake for afternoon tea with Stephen when my calendar pops up a message. It's time to open my brain box and deal with the fact I have to leave my home. I didn't consider my timing carefully, did I? On the other hand, perhaps Stephen can help me think the problem through? It's really nice talking with him – he has such a kind manner when he's not apologising awkwardly. I heard that when I listened to him talking with B from the hallway.

I settle on cooking mini pumpkin pies because I have one last pumpkin from my very poor autumn harvest. Making pumpkin pie reminds me of Gran. I feel happy when I think of her. This last week has put me on an emotional rollercoaster – facing losing my home, Fran's sad party, going to see the very troubled B with Stephen … yes, Stephen. There's so much I'm losing. I need something to balance the scales. For once, I want to be spontaneous and enjoy this fun ride rather than slamming the brakes on before I pick up too much speed. Stephen's only coming round for tea, I remind myself. *Why stop at tea?* fun ride Julia responds.

Partway through making pumpkin pies I remember I made them for my birthday party at Lynda's and the Humans with Stories workshop. I don't want to look like I can only bake one thing, so I start on brownies to discover, partway through mixing the dough, I've run out of dark cocoa powder because I used it all in Fran's velvet cake.

I cycle to the Fresh Choice and back, thankful I didn't put liquid in the brownie mix.

I get the brownies in the oven and set my flower-in-the-box timer to spring open to let me know the brownies are cooked. The timer was a collaboration between Robbie and me; you set the mechanical timer and, when it counts down to zero it opens a lid, and a bouquet of flowers leaps out. We thought about making them for sale, but realistically no one would pay for the time they take to construct. I'm waiting for the flowers when there's a knock on the front door.

I rush to the door, forgetting I'm in my cocoa-smeared apron. "Hi, Stephen, great to see you. I won't give you a hug because I'm still in my cooking clothes."

Stephen's face falls slightly, and he steps back. Damn. This wasn't a carefully constructed ploy to keep him at a distance. It was just a mistake.

"Come in, come in. I've made pies and brownies which are nearly ready. Here, you can watch my timer. When it opens, take the brownies out of the oven."

I hurry down the hall to my bedroom. What to put on? My clothes look so shabby. I put on a loose top covered in flowers I bought second-hand at Time and Time Again in Sumner, then pull it off in case I look like a mad flower lady. I find a rose-coloured merino long-sleeved shirt which works over a tan ankle-length skirt. I'd like to wear Fran's leather jacket, but it hardly makes sense to wear a leather jacket inside.

When I return to the kitchen, the brownies are on the bench. Stephen has even put them on a wire rack.

"Julia, I love your timer," Stephen says. "You are so amazingly creative."

"I try," I say, blushing. "Now I'm dressed more respectably, I can give you that hug I omitted at the front door."

We stand with our arms around each other for longer than is necessary. I look into Stephen's eyes, and he looks back at me. I release my grip, but Stephen holds on.

"Julia, there's something I need to tell you," he says.

"Is it about Cynthia?"

"Yes, it is." Stephen shuts his eyes and takes a deep breath. "Cynthia's dead."

"Well, actually, I knew."

"You knew?" Stephen lets go of me and steps back into the table with such force he ends up sitting on the baking supplies strewn across it.

"Yes. I don't normally kiss men who I know have wives. In fact, I have never kissed a man I knew to have a wife." I don't go into detail about the small number of men I have ever kissed.

Stephen looks like a deflated balloon with a dusting of cocoa powder and icing sugar.

"It's okay, Stephen. I know what it's like to hide important things. I spent years keeping my daughter's death a secret because I couldn't face reality. It took Obsessives Associated and Fran and Lynda to help me see a better way to live. That's why we started up Dolls with Stories and Humans with Stories. To help people tell their stories so they can find new narratives."

Stephen puts his face in his hands and tears leak between his fingers.

I put my hands on his arms to pull him up from the cocoa-covered table, then enclose him in a hug. We stand in each other's arms for a long time until I say, "Would you like a cup of tea now? With a brownie and a pumpkin pie?"

Stephen replies by holding me more tightly and kissing me again, hard. The direction my rollercoaster should go seems obvious. I take Stephen's hand and lead him along the hallway to my bedroom. It still has my cocoa-covered apron on the floor, together with the other clothes I dropped in my rush to find my best clothing, which no longer seems necessary.

It's early evening by the time I put my dressing gown on to boil my red kettle for a cup of tea. I take my Indian tray laden with Temuka teapot, mugs, pumpkin pies, and brownies back to the bedroom. We drink the tea and eat the food, trying unsuccessfully to avoid dropping crumbs in my bed. Rain is hammering on the roof. There's an orange heavy-rain warning for tonight.

"Was that okay? I mean, should I have? I mean, should I go?" Stephen's face and body are shifting back into his tense, uncertain mode.

"Stephen," I say, "I wanted to. And no, you shouldn't go. There's no one waiting for you, after all. And it's raining cats and dogs."

He sighs and relaxes. "I had a French client tell me in France they say, 'It's raining like a peeing cow.' Rain on the roof is strangely comforting, isn't it? I suppose it's because you aren't out there getting wet. I haven't sat in bed drinking tea with someone since ..."

"Do you want to tell me about Cynthia?" I ask.

"Not now. But I will soon," he says.

I am woken from the depths of sleep by someone banging on the front door. It must be the middle of the night – who could be knocking? I can also hear the sea siren whooping in the distance. I grope for my dressing gown.

"Should I come to the door with you?" Stephen asks.

"Thanks, but no. I have looked after myself for years; I'm sure I can defend myself against a midnight caller. Or, if I can't, you can explode from the bedroom in your blanket waving whatever handy implement you find."

When I reach the front door, my bravado reduces. "Who's there?" I call.

"Rosemary," comes the answer.

I open the door in astonishment to see a wet, muddy, and bloody Rosemary on my doorstep. Behind her, torrential rain is falling.

"Can I come in?" Rosemary says.

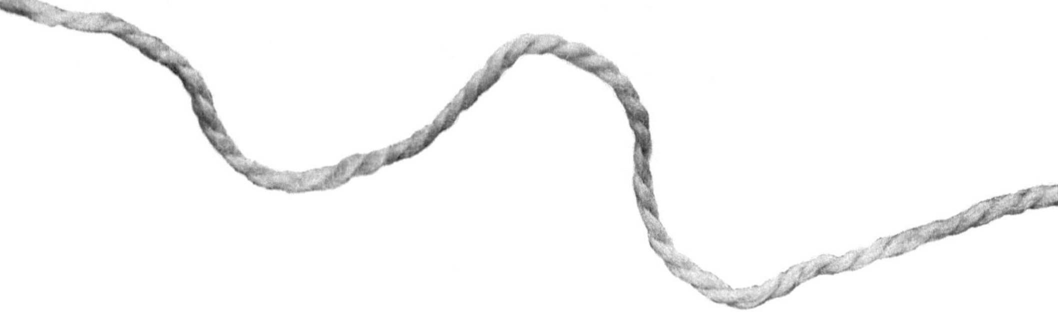

JULIA

26 May 2030

"Of course, come in," I say to Rosemary, finding the manners Gran would have expected I use with a visitor, however unwelcome. "I'll get you a towel. Are you injured? Do you need me to call emergency services? Not that they would come, given the siren."

"No! Don't call anyone! Don't tell anyone!" Rosemary's eyes flare.

"Okay, I won't. A shower? Tea?" I say as Rosemary drips in my hall.

"A shower, yes," Rosemary says.

I lead her to the bathroom and give her a purple towel from the top of my rainbow-coloured stack. I assume it's the purple towel because it's on top of the pile – we can't see much because there's no light – the power must be out.

"Do you need some clothes?" I ask. "Put yours in the machine in the bathroom."

"Clothes, yes."

"You get in the shower, and I'll drop clothes through the door."

Rosemary is no longer the svelte biker who pedalled through earthquake-damaged Sumner. My clothing will be too small, although she's a lot shorter than me. However, beggars can't be choosers. As I return to my bedroom, I remember Stephen is in it. And Rosemary doesn't want anyone to know she is here. This won't work.

"Stephen, I'm sorry, but I need you to go home," I say. "Rosemary has turned up and she's behaving strangely. You can leave while she's in the shower. It's awfully wet out, though."

Stephen's face falls, but he gets off the bed and fumbles on the floor for his clothes. "That's fine, Julia. I might have overstayed my welcome, anyhow."

"No, absolutely not!" I say. "It was lovely. I want to see you again. But I need to find out what's going on with Rosemary. Even though she's not my favourite person." I turn away as I mumble, "But you might be."

"Good thing I don't go anywhere without a raincoat," Stephen says. "I'll make a quick retreat and call you tomorrow, I mean, later today."

We needn't have worried about Rosemary coming out of the shower soon. She stays in so long my small cylinder has probably run out of hot water.

I drop an old pinafore dress through the bathroom door, together with a mohair jersey I knitted years ago out of ochre-coloured wool of a shade I can't remember why I liked. I put on warm clothes because it's chilly and I don't want to talk to Rosemary wearing a dressing gown. Waiting for her, I boil my red kettle on the gas stove, grateful as ever for its utility when there's no power.

Rosemary finally comes into the kitchen, her hair in wild corkscrew curls around her face. My pinafore and jersey don't suit her.

"Cup of tea?" I ask.

"That would be lovely." Rosemary reaches for the mug with trembling fingers. She steadies the mug with both hands. "Thank you for inviting me in. You must wonder why I'm here," she says, staring into the cup.

I didn't exactly invite her in. "Would you like to tell me?" I ask.

"Not really, but I ought to because now you're involved," Rosemary says.

"Involved in what?"

"The bombing."

"Bombing?" What is Rosemary talking about? Has she lost her mind and gone wandering the streets imagining a bombing? Did she experience a bombing in the UK when she was young and is having a flashback?

"We bombed the ship," Rosemary says dully. "So it would sink in the harbour. We had it all planned so the blast wouldn't hurt anyone but the shipment would be lost, and the coal port blocked by the sunk ship. We'd go home and no one would have any idea it was us. It didn't turn out how we hoped."

"Who's 'we'?" I ask.

"That I'm not telling. Better for you and them you don't know," Rosemary says.

"Fair enough," I say. I'd actually rather Rosemary had never come. "Why did you need to bomb the ship? And what went wrong?"

"Can I have another cup of tea?" Rosemary asks.

I brew another pot, a strong one. This night feels very long. I give Rosemary more tea and offer her pumpkin pies and brownies from this afternoon.

Rosemary chews through the smiley face on a pumpkin pie mechanically. "Why a bombing? It was a coal ship. Someone has to do something about climate change. Something that people notice. We have to stop using coal. This was a way to make a statement without hurting anyone.

"The coal ship was scheduled to finish loading late last evening and leave Ōhinehou today on the outgoing tide. We boated along the harbour and past the port in the early evening, just another group heading home after having weekend fun on the water. There are no cameras pointing out to sea from the port, which is funny, given the attack on the *Rainbow Warrior* so many years ago was from the sea. You'd think ports might have learnt. The boat slowed down to let divers roll over the side. Then we swam to the coal ship, while the boat continued on. That was the hardest part – visibility in the harbour is terrible. We used compass navigation, and rebreathers to prevent bubbles at the surface. We planted multiple charges on the hull below the waterline, then swam up the harbour, helped by the incoming tide. The plan was for the divers to rendezvous with the van driver, who'd take them home, then dispose of the gear and the vehicle. Once we were long gone, team members would contact the ship's crew and Port Authority with enough warning to clear the ship and the area, but not enough time to find the charges which were set to detonate at high tide in the early hours of the morning. We set three warning charges and then three detonations to hole the hull."

"Sounds like a reasonable plan," I say, although I'm not particularly conversant with good bombing plans. "What went wrong?"

"A car crash is what went wrong," Rosemary says.

"Did your driver crash the van?"

"No. As we were driving home in the rain, headlights glowed around a corner, and we realised they were coming directly towards us. At the last second the car swerved towards its own lane, over-corrected, then slid off the edge of the road and rolled down the hill. I yelled to our driver to stop. I had to attend the accident – I'm a doctor."

"Of course," I say. "You had no choice."

"We were still getting out of our dive gear in the van," Rosemary says. "I climbed down through the tussocks and rocks with my wetsuit arms tied around my waist with a basic first aid kit from the van. Another diver came with me while the driver stayed with the van. I told her, I mean them, to call emergency services.

"The driver protested. 'We can't call. We've got to get out of here before anyone else turns up.'

"'Okay.' I said. 'Wait till I've assessed the people and then I'll tell you to call if necessary.' That was wrong of me. I know never to delay when there might be a medical emergency."

"So two of you went down to the car, and then …?" I prompt.

"We found the kids as we climbed down. Five of them. Young, just teenagers. Joy-riding a stolen EV. Two thrown through the windscreen of the vehicle as it rolled. Three jammed together in the rear, hemmed in by airbags."

Rosemary takes a big swig of tea and looks into her cup like her tea leaves could tell a story other than the one in which she is engaged. She breathes in deeply and continues.

"I checked the children. The three in the car were breathing, with no signs of bleeding. One was mumbling and semi-conscious. The two on the ground were unconscious and bleeding profusely. I yelled up to the van driver to call for help. The other diver and I each worked on a child to stop the bleeding. By the time we heard the ambulance sirens we'd got it under control, but they were still unconscious. They needed full assessment and proper medical care."

"You did everything you could," I say. "What happened next? Why do you think you will get caught?"

"We had to wait until the ambulance officers came down. I had to show them the children who'd been thrown from the car. They'll have guessed I'm a doctor from what I said. They asked for our names, of course. I said we didn't want to be involved. We were visitors to the area and just wanted to do our civic duty. That hardly rang true."

"How would they know you had anything to do with the bombing, though?" I ask. "It was dark. The ambulance staff won't remember details."

"For a start, we were wearing wetsuits. Then, as we climbed up the slope, we heard the police and fire sirens approaching from Lyttelton. Our van was pointing towards Lyttelton, and the road was far too narrow for a quick U-turn. We had to drive towards the police vehicle. They'll have recorded our number plate as a matter of routine and questioned the ambulance staff about us. When the bombs go off, the first thing they will do is check any data logged in the area."

"What happened to the van?"

"I don't know – that wasn't my job." Rosemary is gripping her mug so tightly her fingers turn white. I notice I inappropriately gave her the 'Lighten up, sunshine – it could always be raining' mug. "I got dropped off in Sumner. I couldn't go home. Home's the first place the police will look. I should have had a plan for if things went wrong. But we were so sure we wouldn't be caught."

She's forestalled my next question. Why here? Why me? Rosemary must think I'm expendable. If the police turn up at my house and I'm implicated in the bombing, no great loss. Not like your partner being locked up and your children being taken into care. Who'd miss Julia if she did a stint in prison? What will I say if the police knock on the door and ask me about Rosemary? If I don't tell them, I'll have lied. If I do tell them, nothing good is going to happen to either of us. I could ring the police and tell them Rosemary is here and get myself off the hook. Would Rosemary know it was me who'd rung if the police arrived? Would it matter? This is all too hard on an hour of sleep.

"Rosemary, you need to rest," I say. "And so do I. I'll show you the guest room and we'll figure out what to do in the morning. Everything looks better in the morning, right?" I put my hand on her shoulder. "Let's get you into bed."

Rosemary looks up at me, like a child handing over responsibility to an adult. "Thank you, Julia," she says. "I'm exhausted."

Once I've installed Rosemary in the spare room, I go back to my rumpled and crumb-strewn bed to find sleep an impossibility. Groping for my phone to check the time, I find Stephen's reading glasses on the side table. We weren't doing anything requiring reading. He must have found them in his pocket, wanted to keep them safe, then forgotten to take them. I'll return them to him, but when can I next see him? Can I go to Stephen's house once it's light and leave Rosemary here? If the police come I won't be involved and can plausibly say I'd spent the night with Stephen. Say how surprised I am by Rosemary being in my house.

I circle round to thinking I should ring the police now and end my dilemma. Based on what Rosemary told me, it's highly likely she'll eventually be found. Why did Rosemary tell me what happened? She could have said she was splitting up with her husband and had walked here in the rain because she was so upset. She's never thought about me much.

Then again, if I'm being fair – and I don't want to be fair – I asked Rosemary to tell her story. It might be a reflexive behaviour, from Humans with Stories. Our stories are what bind us. Damn. I'm implicated every which way, whether I like it or not. Rosemary is part of our group and she's a human being, like me, with her reasons for doing what she did. Running away from emergency services without giving them your name isn't good, but it's not like she caused the accident, and she helped the joy-riding children until the ambulance arrived. What about bombing a coal ship? Is that bad if no one was injured? Of course, it's not legal. However, we all know burning coal is a big contributor to climate change and we know climate change is a bad thing. If you are doing an illegal thing to stop a bad thing, can it cancel out from a moral, if not a legal, point of view?

Perhaps the bombing didn't even happen, so there's nothing to worry about. The charges might not have gone off. I check my phone to look for reports of the ship bombing. However, there's no Wi-Fi because of the power cut and no cell reception. The unreliability of communications is frustrating. Though it might be a good thing tonight because I can't call the police. I'll take the advice I gave Rosemary and go to sleep. Everything will be clearer in the morning.

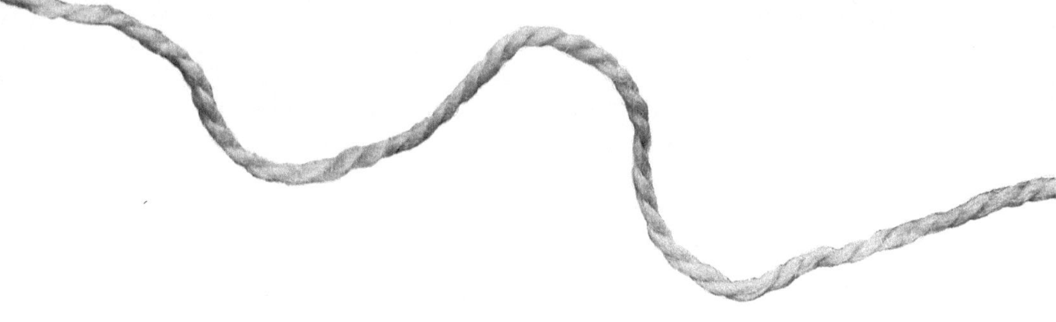

STEPHEN

26 May 2030

As I walk out Julia's door rain sledgehammers my jacket and water floods my shoes. I didn't bring my over-trou, so my jeans soak through in a few steps and hang cold about my legs. I slog up Scarborough. Julia sent me home like she was embarrassed by me being in her house. Why did she care about what Rosemary might have thought? It's not like they get on particularly well, which makes it even stranger Rosemary turning up. Could her car have broken down when she was on a call-out? Possible, but why would she not want anyone to know? Maybe she's having an affair? It still doesn't make sense for her to go to Julia.

When I finally slosh through my gate between the macrocarpa trees, I see a faint glow coming from the open door of my container. That's odd – there's no light in the container and I always close the door.

I walk to the container with a peculiar feeling of something like hope. Maybe someone has stolen all the things in the container I can't throw out because they remind me of Cynthia? I swing the door fully open, looking forward to an empty space. I see something far less welcome. There's a person, bundled up in Cynthia's last quilt, in the gap between the boxes and the door. The glow is from their head torch, and the person is Andrey.

"What the fuck are you doing in my container? Get out!"

Andrey holds his hands up. "I'm sorry, Stephen. I didn't know where else to go. I thought I could spend a short time here figuring out what to do next."

"Figuring out what to do next? What do you need to figure out? Why can't you go to your tiny home?"

"I need not to be found," Andrey says. "Just for a short time. Then I will leave Aotearoa."

"Leave? But you're part of our workshop. You never said you were leaving."

"I hadn't planned on leaving but now I must." Andrey sneezes loudly.

I'm shivering and there are dark wet splotches on the quilt so Andrey must also be wet and cold. "Let's talk inside," I say. "You can explain what's going on when you're wearing warm clothes and drinking a cup of tea. Leave the wet quilt here." I'm upset by Cynthia's quilt getting dirty because some Russian decided to wrap himself in it.

Cynthia says, *Don't be ridiculous, Stephen. Of course he should have used my quilt. Quilts are for people who are cold.*

"Actually, just wear the quilt to the caravan."

Andrey follows me quietly as I unlock the caravan door and light a fire in my tiny log burner. I put my kettle on the gas stove and pull spare clothes out.

"Put these on." I leave Andrey in the living room and change my clothes in the bedroom. I take all our wet clothing to drop out the door. There's no space inside for wet, muddy clothes, and they won't get any wetter outside. Then I see the blood on his jacket.

"Are you hurt, Andrey?"

"No, it's not my blood."

"Whose blood is it then?" Has Andrey committed some crime and, now I've found out, will he attack me?

"Children who were in a car crash."

"You attended an accident? But why do you need to hide then? People must be grateful. Did you cause the accident?"

"No, we … I didn't cause it. A long story. It might be better if you don't know."

"You're at my place together with your bloody clothes so I might as well know why." This night, that started off so well, is ending far worse than I could have imagined. First Rosemary knocking on Julia's door, then Andrey turning up here. Could there be a connection? Surely not. Why would Rosemary and Andrey be out together on a miserably wet night?

I find the bottle of rum I keep for special occasions that never come around. This occasion is pretty special. "Want some rum in your tea?"

"On a night like this, a Russian can drink rum rather than vodka," Andrey says. "*Za vernykh druzey.*"

We clink teacups.

"So, to explain. We have bombed the coal ship."

"You what?"

"We bombed the coal ship in Lyttelton Port. To make a difference without hurting people. To make a statement. To stop coal being used. The world must stop using fossil fuels. Most importantly, we must stop using coal. We should have finished with coal long ago. The world is dying, people are dying, but rich people still want to get richer using dirty coal. We decided it is time to end coal. Sink the ship."

Of course. The end of coal. Sink the ship. It was real. It *is* real. Should I have done something to prevent the bombing? Now Andrey started talking he's not stopping.

"We planned our bombing to not hurt people. Just the ship. We planted underwater charges on the ship's hull to sink it in port once it was fully loaded. Perfect. Coal ship stuck in harbour. Coal company losing money because they are not paid for their shipment. Port company losing money because a sunk ship is stuck and no more can come. Ship owners angry. Media releases to the world saying coal shipments must end. Local communities around the world inspired to do the same thing. Ports not wanting to ship coal because of the risk. Ship owners not wanting to carry coal because of the risk. The end of coal."

"Aha," I break in. "You weren't telling the truth last workshop, were you? You knew exactly what you were planning. Your gifts were goodbye presents. Now you've created a mess which you want to leave behind after hiding out in my house."

"Wait, Stephen," Andrey says. "There is no mess. Unless we get caught, which is why I need to hide."

"Why would anyone catch you? And what does the car crash have to do with the bombing?"

"We were unlucky. There were children in a stolen car. They crashed. We helped them. The authorities came. They saw our van."

"It sure was unlucky. You need to talk to the police, explain what happened." As I say this, I recognise how stupid it is. The police will not be sympathetic to people who bombed a ship because they helped children who crashed a stolen car.

I'm outraged. Why did Andrey come here? I don't mess with other people's lives, and I don't expect other people to mess with my life. I don't want a bloody Russian who says he carried out a bombing hiding in my caravan. He's an okay guy, but I only know him from the workshops. I also don't want the police invading my space or thinking I'm associated with a bomber other than meeting him at a workshop.

"Why did you come here?" I say. "And how did you know where I lived?"

"I came to you, Stephen, because you are kind. There's a fishing vessel with a Russian crew docking in Lyttelton Port this week. I will soon get on that boat and disappear out of your life."

Andrey hasn't explained how he knew where my house is, but I let it pass. "Why should I put myself at risk to help you?" I say. "You could be telling me a story to get my sympathy and you've done something terrible."

"Check online, Stephen. I'm sure there will be news about the bombing soon. Just give me a few hours. Then, if you are still unhappy, I'll go."

He's your guest, Stephen, Cynthia says.

No, he's not my guest. I didn't invite him in; he invited himself.

He's your guest, and you know his story, Cynthia continues. *You know why he's done this. If he truly hasn't hurt anyone isn't this protest a good thing? Isn't it time people took real action? Time you took real action rather than staying safely at home?* That's a low blow from Cynthia. I've never been an action sort of person.

I'm too tired and too confused. I want to ring Julia to ask her what she thinks, but it's way too late to call. I need to find out what happened when the bombs exploded. I look at my phone but there's no reception. I can't call. I close my eyes and rest my head in my hands.

"Fine, you can stay the night. But that's all. This seat by the table turns into a bed. You can't use that quilt – it's all wet. I'll give you a blanket."

When I get into bed I think my mind will whir for hours, but I instantly fall deeply asleep.

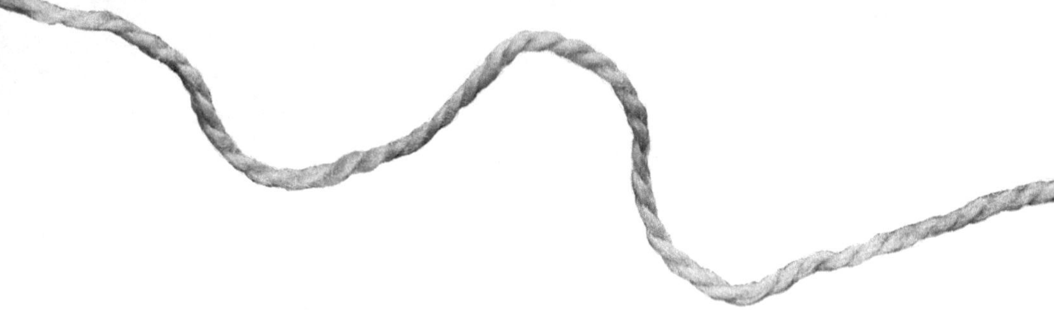

JULIA

26 May 2030

I wake up with a start from dreams of my clock sculpture exploding when the hands hit the 13th hour. My heart is beating fast, and I breathe in the familiarity of my room to calm myself. Then I remember last night. Rosemary is in my house. Rosemary, who the police will be searching for because she bombed a ship. I look at the reading glasses on the bedside table, not mine. Stephen was here last night too. I'll call Stephen. Two heads will be better than one to solve the Rosemary problem. She doesn't want anyone else involved, but Stephen already knows she's here.

I'm relieved to see my phone has reception and it's 8.30am. I wait so long on the ring tone I think Stephen's voicemail will kick in. He finally answers in a groggy tone.

"Did I wake you up?"

"Yes, but it's lovely to hear your voice this morning," he says.

"It's great to talk with you too, Stephen. I enjoyed last night. Till Rosemary …"

"So did I. We should do it again."

"Yes," I say. "But it's tricky with Rosemary here. How about I come up to your place? Although I don't know exactly where you live."

Stephen hesitates. "It might be best if we meet somewhere else. How about Coffee Culture in half an hour?"

"Oh." I try not to let disappointment show in my voice. "The flooding was bad last night – not much will be open. They'll still be cleaning the floors." Some Sumner businesses are doggedly staying in place by installing concrete floors and waterproof surfaces up the walls. When there's a flood warning they put everything on the tables and hose the floor off after the water subsides.

"How about a walk?" Stephen says. "Is the flooding near your house still bad?"

I pull the curtain. My garden is a pond with my mosaic sofa proud in the middle. I tiptoe along the hallway to the front door and open it to see water from the street lapping on the pavement, although it has stopped raining. "Pretty bad. Walking needs to be on the hill."

"Okay, let's meet at the bottom of Flowers Track, then walk through Nicholson Park towards Taylors Mistake Beach," Stephen says.

"In half an hour?" I say.

"Nine am. Looking forward to it," Stephen says.

I try to soundlessly dress and eat a bowl of porridge in the kitchen. I hear nothing from Amanda's room where Rosemary is sleeping. Last night I promised her we'd figure things out in the morning. Is it rude to leave before talking with her? Perhaps she will think of a plan in my absence and go somewhere else. Then everything will be sorted without me having to do anything. I leave her a note saying I've gone for a walk.

I walk to the base of Scarborough Hill in bare feet to keep my shoes and socks dry and exclaim at the cold. As I head towards Flowers Track, the high tide waves break over the rip-rap protecting the edge of the road. High tide is good; the flooding will recede before I go home.

I see Stephen in a blue rain jacket and quicken my steps to almost a run. "Hi!" I fling my arms around him and kiss him, and we keep kissing until a runner descending the track says, "Excuse me," as she tries to avoid us.

"What a night," I say.

"Yes," says Stephen, "and my night kept on going."

"Mine too," I say. "Tell me what happened to you."

"Why don't you tell me about Rosemary first?" Stephen says.

"It's probably best I don't," I say. "It's not something you need to be involved in."

"Julia," Stephen says, "anything you're involved in is important to me. And I'm wondering if what happened at my house last night is connected to Rosemary."

"Why are you being so secretive?" I say.

"Look who's talking," Stephen says.

"Okay, though you might be sorry you asked. Rosemary did something illegal. Very illegal. She couldn't go home so she came to my house. She didn't explain why she picked me."

"Was Rosemary involved in a bombing?" Stephen asks.

I step back. "How could you possibly know that?"

"Because Andrey turned up at my house, drenched and bloody, saying he'd been part of bombing a coal ship at Lyttelton Port and then been at a car crash."

"Rosemary told me the same thing. It's so strange. They carried out a bombing together?" I say.

"Maybe it's not as strange as it seems, Julia," Stephen says. "I had some warning there might be a bombing involving local people."

"A warning? Someone told you? Why didn't you do something about it?"

"No one told me. I read something online," Stephen says. "It wasn't clear, and the messages were on a scrolling Rappit channel, so they disappeared. It could have been people just talking about bombing a ship, rather than actually bombing a ship. I don't like to interfere in other people's lives. And how stupid would I have looked making a fuss about a bombing if it wasn't going to happen? There were no names, or dates, or anything concrete. I don't need to draw attention to myself as some mad old guy living on the hill and snooping on people."

"Fair enough," I say. "People say all sorts of stupid stuff online they don't mean or won't do. The police mightn't be impressed by someone ringing up about people talking about a bombing in messages that have disappeared. It's not like bombings happen frequently in New Zealand."

"Talking of which," Stephen says, "do we know if the bombing happened? I haven't looked online, have you?"

"No, we should," I say.

"Let's wait till we can sit down in Nicholson Park. I'll tell you the rest as we walk up there," Stephen says. "When I got home, Andrey was at my house. I need to explain about that too. He wasn't at my house – he was at my caravan. I don't have a wife and I don't have a house. I am widowed and I live in a caravan."

"You're a widower in a caravan," I say. "And a nice one. Anything else I should know? I can cope with those two things but much more might be a problem."

"Nothing, absolutely nothing. I swear. Gosh, this is such a relief. You don't know how much of a relief. Being able to talk with someone without getting tangled up in my lies. It's been so long."

"Humans with Stories is doing what we intended – helping people tell their stories. But keep talking." I want to hear what happened with Andrey.

"Andrey was shivering in the container beside my caravan, soaked and bloody. He told me about the bombing and said he needed somewhere to stay, but only for a few days. Then he's going to get on a ship and leave."

"This is crazy," I say. "I thought I had problems with my house being flooded and my letter from the council. These problems are a whole new scale."

"Letter from the council?" Stephen says. "What letter?"

"I was going to tell you yesterday. I got the letter a week ago, but I gave myself a week's breathing space to not think about it. Then yesterday wasn't about talking. The short story is, I have to leave my home. They'll pay me four hundred thousand dollars to leave and there's no choice."

"That's so sad for you, Julia," Stephen says. "But it might be an opportunity. Councils won't be able to afford to keep paying people to leave for long. You're one of the lucky ones. The money gives you options."

"Maybe," I say. "I'm not feeling lucky right now. I can't think of options I want. It's not enough money to buy another house."

"It's enough to buy a caravan, or a campervan. Or what about a tiny house?"

"Where would I put any of those? I can't stay on my land."

"You could put something on my land," Stephen says. "I have a lot of land."

I can't see Stephen's face because we are walking uphill and I'm focusing on slippery roots and muddy bits of track where the gravel has washed off. Does he mean it? Is there a possibility leaving home doesn't equate to leaving Sumner and Lynda and Hermione?

"Thank you so much for your offer, Stephen," I say. "I've got more thinking to do about what I want and now is not the time. We both need to sort out our guests. I know I don't want Rosemary staying in my house. I'm co-leader of the workshops she's attending. If the police find out Rosemary was involved in the bombing, they'll ask me and Lynda what we know. The police could come to my house. I can't lie with Rosemary there. And you've got the same problem."

"You're right, Julia. But where can they go?"

"First," I say, "we need to check whether there's a need for them to go anywhere. Hopefully, the bombs never went off. We may be worrying over nothing."

We reach Nicholson Park and Stephen lays his raincoat across the wet seat for us to sit on. I pull out my reading glasses and remember I didn't bring Stephen's. "We'll have to share glasses." Then I lean against him as I bring my phone up. My calendar screen is open, and I see red dots on Monday and Wednesday and Thursday. What am I supposed to be doing this week? My brain is too full of Rosemary and Andrey.

Thursday is Humans with Stories, of course. I can't cancel on the workshop because if the police get involved I need to behave normally.

Monday is singing with Pauline and Grant. I'd forgotten that. "Something else I meant to tell you yesterday, Stephen. We're booked to sing at the retirement units tomorrow night. I can always make excuses, though."

What's Wednesday? Oh, no. Wednesday is Fran's happy leaving party. How could I have forgotten that Fran and Holly are catching the train north at the end of the week? One of my best friends is leaving and I forgot something so important? Fran, Holly, and I will all stay that last night at Lynda's.

"Right, enough delaying," I say. "We need to know what is going on." I type in 'Bombing Lyttelton'.

The number of hits makes it clear we all have a problem.

TERRORIST ATTACK IN LYTTELTON HARBOUR

COAL SHIP SUNK: Desperate Times Desperate Measures

TERRORISTS BOMBED, HIT AND RAN

HUNT ON FOR PORT TERRORISTS

COAL SHIP SUNK, ELEVEN MISSING

GREEN PLANET DENIES RESPONSIBILITY, EMPHASISES ECOTAGE

I hand my phone and glasses to Stephen. "This is worse than I thought," I say. "There are people missing."

Stephen clicks on a headline. "Eleven crew members," he reads.

"But Rosemary said they were careful," I say. "The group contacted the crew and the port before the explosions. The divers set small charges first to scare everyone away. Surely no one would have stayed on board?"

"Andrey said the same," Stephen replies.

"The reporting might not be accurate. Clickbait. It's always hard to be sure what's real online," I say. "I don't know whether this story stacks up. Look down there. Supposedly the ship has settled into the mud and will be difficult to move, given the weight of the coal. It's not like it's underwater. If people slept low down in the hull, perhaps they could have drowned. But not if they were warned. And not all of them."

"You might be right," Stephen says. "But do we trust Rosemary and Andrey's story? And, even if we trust them, should we hide them?"

"Yes, I trust Rosemary and Andrey to tell the truth. In the workshops they told us about themselves and their motivations. They've trusted us. Andrey took Lynda to hospital when he barely knew her. He cared about her. And they're trying to do something. Make a difference. The rest of us talk about wood-fired stoves, solar panels, moving to escape floods and we make retirees cups of tea. Rosemary and Andrey, and whoever else is involved, have taken an enormous risk to make a big statement. That's important."

"I get your point. What they are trying to do is significant and if we don't make big statements ourselves, perhaps we should help others who do. However, where can they hide?" Stephen says.

Puzzle pieces are connecting in my brain. Cups of tea, retirees. I'd wondered about finding Rosemary and Andrey a tornado-damaged house to hide in. But what about Pauline and Grant's community of retirees? A couple of extra people won't make the units look more crowded.

"What about the retirement units?" I almost shout, as the idea forms in my head.

"Keep your voice down," Stephen says. "We don't want to announce our plans to anyone who might be listening. And didn't you offer that Andrey could help fix the roofs at the retirement units? They'll know him."

"No one walking in a park is going to be listening to us," I say, trying to be quieter. "Did I say he could help?"

"Yes, when we visited. You said you'd send a message when the power came back on."

"I must have forgotten. Forgetting can be useful! We're scheduled to sing with the retirees tomorrow night. We can take Rosemary and Andrey, disguised somehow. It will be hard for the retirees to say no when there are desperate people on their doorstep."

"I'm not sure, Julia," Stephen says. "I wouldn't be pleased if two people wanted by the police turned up on my doorstep and asked if I'd take them in."

"What do you mean, Stephen?" I say. "One person already did turn up and you took them in. So did I."

"Yes, but we knew them."

"Pauline and Grant know us. It's about trust. Anyhow, it's the best option I can think of. If you come up with something better, please tell me."

"Okay, for now, but we need to watch for reports about missing crew members. If people died in the bombing we can't keep helping Rosemary and Andrey. Agreed?"

"Yes, agreed. Thanks, Stephen." I give him another kiss and we sit on the bench for a while, holding hands and looking towards the Southern Alps, where the white of fresh snow blankets the outlines of jagged peaks.

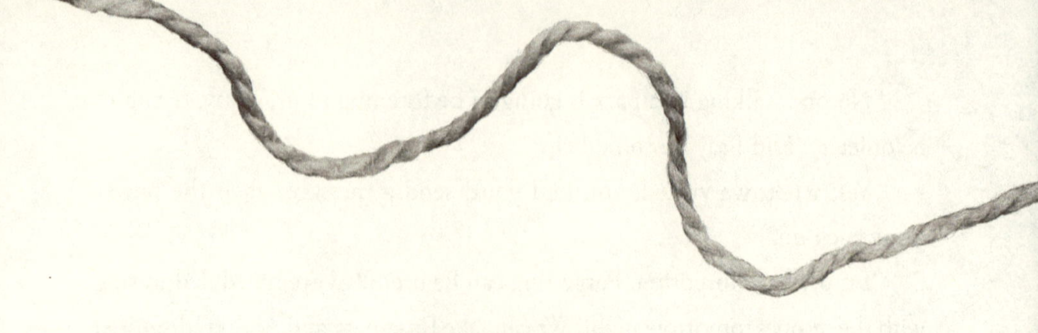

STEPHEN

26 May 2030

Julia and I walk from Nicholson Park, over the top of Scarborough Hill then down to Taylors Mistake Beach. Neither of us is in a hurry to return home. The Taylors Mistake car park is full of driftwood and plastic debris. We skirt the piles hand in hand, then walk single file on up the narrow track through the tussocks towards the top of the hill.

"I want to see where you live," Julia had said. We agreed it wasn't a good idea for her to surprise Andrey, though. I believe he didn't hurt anyone deliberately, but his size makes me nervous.

Julia looks through the gap in my macrocarpa hedge then we hug on the footpath. "Soon you can come visit," I say. "I'll tell you more about Cynthia. And how I got myself in such a mess. Do you want to go for a walk again tomorrow morning?"

"Another walk would be perfect. Tell me whatever you want about Cynthia whenever you're ready," Julia says. "No rush, but let's make it happen." Then she turns and strides down the hill. We walk at a similar speed. I've never wanted to walk with people after Cynthia, because it's so uncomfortable when you go at different speeds and are out of step.

I feel relief as Julia walks away, as much as I want to be with her. I am suddenly buried deep in people. I'm attached to Julia, and Julia has attached me to other people, and now there's a string of connections from which I cannot extricate myself. I wish I'd never gone to Humans with Stories. No, that's not true. If I hadn't attended the workshops, I wouldn't have met Julia and she's the best thing that's happened to me since Cynthia. Am I so pathetic

I need a woman to complete my life? I won't answer that question; I might incriminate myself.

Andrey is in the caravan having a cup of tea when I go in. A shame he hasn't vanished.

"Can you tell me what's happening with the bombing?" Andrey asks.

"Can't you look it up online yourself?"

"No, because I no longer have a cell phone," Andrey says. "I broke my phone into tiny pieces and threw it away."

"Here, feel free." I hand him my phone. However, I watch the screen so he doesn't feel too free, even though I know my anonymous browser means his searches can't be linked to me.

Andrey gasps when he sees reports of the missing crew. "We planned to make sure this did not happen," he says. "They were warned. The crew isn't below decks in the night – they're asleep in their bunks on the top level, or at a brothel. Even if there was an engine problem, all the crew would not be down below together. Only three are engineers. The chef won't do mechanical work and the watch and captain always stay up top. Someone's feeding the media lies. Or the media try to make a story out of nothing."

This is all logical and a relief. Media don't want to calm the public down. They want clicks and emojis. The police want upset people to ring up with information on the terrorists.

There's a new article about the car crash. The kids were private school children from three families on Cashmere Hill. The car will have belonged to a parent – you can't hot-wire an EV; you need to steal the keys. And energy quotas mean people are careful about who can drive their car.

A parent is quoted: 'Sebastian is our only child and such a caring and able person. It will take him months or years to recover from his injuries. How could those terrorists drive away, leaving him on the ground? We ask that anyone who knows about the crash contacts the police.'

"Media say we made the crash happen. That is not true," Andrey says. "The children crashed the car, and we helped them. We didn't leave until the ambulance was there. We want to make the world a better place for children."

The bombing is plastered across international media. *The Guardian*, *New York Times*, Al Jazeera, Reuters, *Washington Post*, BBC News – headline after headline. There are two themes. There's excitement about a terrorist attack in Aotearoa New Zealand, a backwater at the bottom of the world. The terrorism articles point to the supposedly missing crew members. The other theme is the need for ecotage to help end the coal trade and fight climate change. The ecotage articles argue that destroying property without loss of life is not terrorism. Some point out the hypocrisy of Aotearoa New Zealand portraying itself as a climate leader, establishing the TEQ scheme and abandoning its national airline, but not preventing coal from being mined and shipped offshore.

There are quotes from Green Planet and Enough is Enough. 'We do not condone acts of violence against humans. However, in this case, we believe only infrastructure was damaged. Coal is poisoning the people and the planet. Coal shipments must end.'

'Coal is poison. Poisoning our planet. Poison in our atmosphere. Sales of poison must be stopped.'

There is also national and international outrage about the circulation of a handbook on the web – the 'how to' of coal ship ecotage. The police want people to remember the huge fines and potential prison sentences for circulating objectionable material.

I make a cup of coffee for Andrey and myself. I rarely drink coffee, but tea isn't strong enough and rum seems inappropriate at 2pm on a Sunday.

"Andrey, we … I mean I, have thought of a good place for you to wait for your ship."

"We? Who are 'we'?" Andrey says, his voice rising.

"We was a slip of the tongue. No, dammit. I'm done with lying. We are me and Julia."

"You and Julia? You told Julia about me?" Andrey launches onto his feet, towering over me.

"Hang on, Andrey. I told Julia, but she already knew about the bombing."

"How could she know?"

"Because Rosemary turned up at her house."

Andrey subsides back to his seat. "Oh. We didn't share our plans for afterwards, of course. Then, if one of us got caught, there'd be nothing to tell."

"Our plan is that we'll take you and Rosemary to a place where there are lots of people staying together. Where extra people aren't obvious."

"I do not think Rosemary and me being in the same place is good."

"It isn't the best idea, but we have no others," I say. "If the police identify either of you in relation to the bombing it's likely they will question people from Humans with Stories."

"Will the other people take us in?" Andrey asks.

"I'll make sure before we go there." I won't, but I need Andrey out.

My caravan feels claustrophobic with the two of us in it. There are thirty hours to count down until we go to the retirement units. I evict myself to the container with my laptop; it's nastily dark and cold.

I look for any evidence people died in the bombing – that would let Julia and me off the hook. We could tell Andrey and Rosemary to sort themselves. However, there's nothing more about the sailors, missing or not.

I check The Republic of Sumner Rappit channel. There's a brief message scrolling through. "Success!" it says. The message could be about the coal ship, but it could be about something else. Like creating a new online forum for exchanging energy units. Except then there'd be no reason not to say what it's about. There's another message saying, 'Rasta Rapping Russia'. Could someone be wanting to communicate with Andrey? Or am I in a very suggestible state?

I look up terrorism legislation and terrify myself. Bombing the ship is clearly terrorism, given the intent of the bombing was extensive destruction of infrastructure. It doesn't matter how careful you are to prevent people being hurt, it's terrorism. You can be sentenced to life imprisonment for a terrorist bombing. That's what Andrey and Rosemary face. However, that's their problem. My problem is the penalty for harbouring a terrorist is up to seven years in prison. Seven years! I could call the police now and tell them a terrorist turned up and forced me to let him in, and now I'm hiding in my container while he has taken over my caravan. Except I can't, because that might lead the police to Rosemary, and then to Julia. I hide the computer in the container and head out for another long walk.

JULIA

27 May 2030

Rosemary and I are ready to go to the retirement units. She's wearing a shapeless, dull-blue pinafore dress and a grey raincoat with the hood pulled over her head. Underneath the hood, she is covering her red hair with the tornado hat I knitted. I cut her hair very short around her face. The hat is more recognisable than I'd prefer, but when I brought out my hat selection, that was the one she wanted. Rosemary isn't talking much, mostly sitting with her head in her hands or clasping the latest mug of tea I've brought her until it goes cold. She doesn't want to eat.

I questioned Rosemary about why she got involved in the bombing.

"Because I felt desperate," she said. "Although now I feel even more desperate. Will our statement have made a difference? It has to make a difference. Something has to make a difference! I want there to be a decent world for my children to grow up in, even if it's a world I'm not part of."

"Does your whānau know what has happened?" I ask.

"When I went out, I told my husband I was attending a sexual assault case for a sick colleague and I'd be back by morning. I left him a letter in the coffee plunger in case I didn't come back," Rosemary says. "In the letter, I told him how much I love him and the kids. How I was doing something for them, but I couldn't say what. I asked him not to ring the police, or anyone else, or look for me. I'd come home if I could. I don't think I'll be going home." She put her head back in her hands.

I turned from her to look at my phone. I've restricted myself to looking at news twice a day. I want to check all the time and see if anything new has been reported. However, in the COVID pandemic I learnt listening to bad news repeatedly makes you a nervous wreck. I found nothing suggesting the police know who the bombers are.

Police believe at least 5 terrorists were involved. Remember to CALL 0800 BOMBING with any information. Terrorists still at large. Remember to CALL 0800 BOMBING with any information.

The good news for Rosemary is there's a rapid spread of international action – something major is happening.

BREAKING NEWS

Coal ship sunk in Tanjung Bara Coal Terminal, Kalimantan, Indonesia

BREAKING NEWS

Coal ship sunk in Richards Bay Coal Terminal, South Africa

BREAKING NEWS

Coal ship sunk in Puerto Bolivar Coal Terminal, Colombia

BREAKING NEWS

Coal ship sunk in Rotterdam Port, The Netherlands

BREAKING NEWS

Coal ship sunk in Gijón Port, Spain

How could the copycat bombings have followed on so fast from the Lyttelton bombing? Was there an orchestrated series of attacks underway, and Lyttelton was the first strike? There was still no organisation claiming responsibility, though.

I told Rosemary what was happening online, and she said, "Great," in a dull voice. I also told her I would take her to a safer place to stay with a big group of people and Andrey would be there too. Rosemary said, "Fine."

"How long might you need somewhere to stay?" I ask. "Andrey will only be staying till the weekend because—"

"Don't say anything more," Rosemary interrupted. "No details of where we are going. I will also leave this weekend."

Is Rosemary leaving on the fishing vessel with Andrey? Although she said they didn't talk about escape plans. Presumably they have been in contact with each other. It would be better if she could go now, but if she's going by the weekend that's good enough.

"I need to introduce you to the group," I say, "but you can't use your real name. What will I call you?"

"Rhiannon," Rosemary replies.

I recognise that name – it's a song. Who sang it? I must ask Stephen; he'll know.

Rosemary and I walk down Nayland Street in the dusk. I see Andrey and Stephen walking ahead of us, Andrey with Stephen's guitar on his back. We catch up with them at the gate of the retirement complex and I notice the cabbages and cauliflowers are getting big.

Andrey pulls me aside. "Julia, thank you for your help. And, you know the little pot stand I gave you? Take it to my friend Theo who lives in the tiny house community in Redcliffs. Ask him to show you my tiny home."

That's weird, but I have no time to ask him more because Pauline is already opening the door. "Hello, Julia and Stephen, we've been waiting for you. I see you've brought more friends to join in our sing-along. How nice!"

The unit is full of people on chairs, holding mugs and glasses and looking at us expectantly. I hadn't thought there would be so much enthusiasm for a sing-along. I'd envisaged taking Pauline aside from a small group to explain about Rosemary and Andrey.

"Hi, Pauline," I say. "What a turn-out. Can we talk in private for a minute first?"

"Of course, dear. This place isn't very private, though. Grant, come here. Julia wants to talk to us. Let's go into the bedroom."

The bedroom has four beds in it. Pauline and Grant sit on one and Stephen and I sit awkwardly on another, given there's only forty centimetres between the beds. "My friends, Rhiannon and errr…"

"Pekko," Stephen interjects.

"Of course, Pekko. Bit of an unusual name, that's why I forget it. They need somewhere to stay," I say. "Rather urgently, but only till the end of the week."

"Michelle's daughter took her down south to live with the family last week so there's a spare bed here Rhiannon can sleep in. The boys can find some floor space for Pekko. Can I ask why Rhiannon and Pekko need a place to stay?"

"To be honest, it's best you don't know."

"Well, dear, you've been helping us since the tornado, so I trust you. And we're just a pack of pensioners with little left to lose. Last week the council told us we'll be moved out of these units by Christmas. Given how hopeless the council is it'll be next year sometime. Who knows where we'll be sent and whether we'll all go to the same place? What would be worse than our current situation? Being sent to prison for doing something wrong? In prison we wouldn't have to share four to a room. Or cook our own dinners!"

The prison topic is not one I want to engage in. "That's so sad you have to move, Pauline. I got a notice too, saying I have to leave, and I don't know where I'm going either. Thanks so much for agreeing to host Rhiannon and Pekko."

We return to the main room, where there's a debate going on about what song to sing. The men are arguing for 'Song Sung Blue' while the women are shouting for 'Gloria'. Rosemary and Andrey are silent at the back, perched on walking frames because there are no spare chairs.

"You're a bunch of soppy old men," Pauline says. "We'll take turns. First the men and then the women pick a song. Okay?"

No one counters Pauline.

"And, while I'm telling you all what to do, we've got guests staying till the weekend. Welcome Rhiannon and Pekko, who are in urgent need of our hospitality."

Mugs and glasses are waved towards Rosemary and Andrey, then everyone looks at Stephen, who is tuning his guitar. He launches into 'Song Sung Blue', and the room follows along, more or less. We spend an hour singing until voices grow tired.

"Enough!" says Pauline. "Men, off you go. Take Pekko with you. Ladies, it's time for bed. Rhiannon, you can be last in the toilet queue because you are the youngest."

Stephen and I say hurried farewells to Andrey and Rosemary. It's a ridiculously low-key way to say goodbye after the intensity of the last two days. Is there ever a right way to say goodbye?

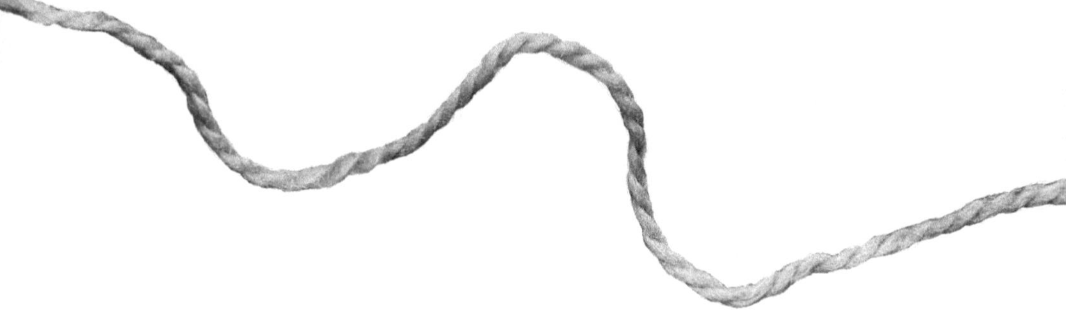

JULIA

30 May 2030

Stephen and I stride swiftly to Humans with Stories in a chilly drizzle. Neither of us has gone anywhere near Nayland Street since we left Rosemary and Andrey at the units on Monday. We don't want to know what is happening. Pauline has my number if there's a problem. In another two days, Andrey will have left the country and Rosemary gone somewhere. Somewhere that is not either of our homes. We're still hopeful the police won't track them down, despite the person-hunt still creating media headlines.

BREAKING NEWS

Wreckage thought to be from terrorist van discovered near Greymouth

BREAKING NEWS

Hunt for terrorists expands offshore

There's nothing more about the supposedly missing sailors. Five days later you would think they'd have found the sailors or their bodies. Stephen and I hypothesise the government wants to keep the pressure on to find the terrorists but won't specifically lie to the media.

Stephen and I have spent much of the time together since the sing-along, other than last night when I went to Lynda's for Fran's farewell. Lynda rang and asked if I'd like to bring Stephen, seeing how well we seemed to be getting on, but I made excuses. Stephen was too new to be part of Fran and Lynda and my last get-together. It's the three of us who've been there for each other since 2020. I was determined not to think about Stephen, or Rosemary, or Andrey, but to make Fran the focus.

Robbie was at the party, of course, seeing it was at Robbie and Lynda's house. He played cards with Holly for most of the evening, letting Fran and Lynda and I talk and cry and laugh and take turns holding Hermione, who is now grinning broadly around the room like she loves everybody in the whole world. It turned out the sad party wasn't enough for us to get our crying done, though I'm sure it helped. Lynda let Hermione stay up way past her bedtime, until she started pursing her mouth and winding up towards a howl, at which point Robbie whisked her away.

We all woke at 6am with Hermione's first cry and had tea together on the deck, wrapped in blankets, waiting for the sun to peek over the horizon. We had no tears remaining and nothing left to say. We sat quietly on the outdoor sofa with Fran and Holly in the middle and me and Lynda on either side, Lynda nursing Hermione. We watched the line of red spread out over the sea and the glowing disc of the sun rise into a perfectly clear sky, then shrink and brighten against its blue background.

"It's time, girls," Fran said. "Come on, Holly. Let's get ready to go."

Robbie had organised a car share to take Fran and Holly to the train station with their luggage. Fran had stipulated neither Lynda nor I could go with them. "We'll say our goodbyes, have final hugs, then Robbie will be a stoic and drive us to our train while talking about the weather," she said, and that was what happened. We'll talk again, of course, but only on Fran's terms. She wants to use her final energy getting Holly settled up north.

I'm in shock now – Fran's gone. Except I've no time for shock. I'm concerned about the number of problems I need to box up temporarily in my brain. Rosemary and Andrey. Losing my home. Losing Fran. I can't cope with more.

When Stephen and I climb the stairs in the fire station no one else has arrived. We knew we would be down two participants, of course, so there's only four more to come. I hear footsteps on the stairs, then Lynda and Eeman come in, chatting.

"Lynda, we must stop meeting like this," I say. I explain to Eeman, "I slept over at Lynda's last night because our friend Fran left for Northland today. Remember Fran, who was at our first workshop? She's terminally ill. She found her birth whānau, like she talked about at the Surf Club. So she's taking her daughter Holly up north to settle her in with the whānau before she dies."

"That's very sad for you, Julia," Eeman says.

"Yes," I say. "I will miss her so much." My eyes well up with tears and Lynda gives me a hug.

"Four people late tonight. That's unusual," Lynda says.

"And not even me," Eeman smiles.

I look at Lynda in surprise until I remember she's completely ignorant of the tumult since last Saturday.

"Might they be sick?" Lynda says. "But why would they all be sick at once? It's Zahra's turn to talk. We won't have anything for the workshop if she doesn't come. I sent her a reminder."

I'm racking my brain for what to say when I hear more voices in the stairwell. It must be Victoria and Zahra because it won't be Rosemary and Andrey.

"Good evening, folks," a policewoman says through the door. She looks down at her phone. "Is this the Humans with Stories group?"

"Yes," Lynda and I chorus, while my stomach sinks.

"I'm Senior Constable Gladys Nguyen and this is Constable Malosi Williams," she gestures to her male colleague. "We're community constables. You may have seen us walking around – or wading around – the area. We'd like a quick chat. We're visiting groups in Sumner and Redcliffs because we believe people involved in the Ōhinehou Port bombing may be from these communities. We're interested in whether you saw anything out of the ordinary last Saturday evening or early Sunday morning. And whether you heard anything relevant to the bombing in the last few weeks?"

My brain is freezing over, although it's still fluid enough to notice how old Gladys's name sounds for someone who looks like they are barely out of high school. Stephen and I talked at length on Tuesday and Wednesday about what we'd say if questioned. However, Fran and Holly's farewell has driven much of our preparation out of my head. Luckily Lynda steps in.

"Of course you can ask us questions. Though I'd like to point out this group has nothing to do with any sort of activism. Our purpose is telling each other stories from our lives, to create connections between people. We're all about stronger community bonds for resilience."

"What a great goal for a group," Gladys says. "Could we talk with you one at a time, so we don't interrupt your meeting?"

"No, that won't work," Lynda says. "We're here as a group so we should talk as a group. Let's all sit down, shall we?" She looks at Gladys and Malosi until they join us sitting in the small circle of chairs.

We don't look like much of a group. Will Gladys ask if we are missing any members? I can't lie about that.

Malosi takes a tablet and stylus from his bag. "Do you mind if I record the conversation?" he says. "It's more accurate than taking notes."

"I have no problem with that. Does anyone else?" Lynda says.

The three of us shake our heads.

Gladys says, "Could each of you please tell me your names, where you were on Saturday evening and Sunday morning, and whether you saw anything unusual?"

"I'll start," Lynda says. "I'm Lynda Greenwood. On Saturday evening I was home with my husband Robbie, and my daughter Hermione, aged ten weeks. We live on Scarborough Road. It was an ordinary evening. Robbie and I cooked and ate dinner together ridiculously early. I fed Hermione. He bathed and put her to bed. Then we tried to watch a movie but went to sleep after the first fifteen minutes."

Lynda looks to the person on her right, which is me. I have to say Stephen and I were together on Saturday, but I don't want to tell the group Stephen and I are in a relationship. Are we in a relationship? We are definitely in a something. However, it would be stupid to complicate matters by lying about our whereabouts on Saturday. It is a good thing it's my turn to speak, because Stephen's habit of telling untruths about Cynthia might cause problems.

"I'm Julia Stout and I was at my house in Head Street with Stephen John here, who was visiting," I say, watching Lynda smile and Eeman's eyebrows rise. "Stephen stayed till fairly late. I didn't check the time he left as I don't wear a watch. There wasn't anyone visible in the street when I said goodbye but the weather was terrible so I couldn't see more than a few metres." I turn to Stephen.

"I'm Stephen John. As Julia said, I was at her house the whole evening, then I walked home late to my place on the top of Scarborough Hill. The streetlights were out, and it was miserably wet, so I wasn't looking at anything other than the path to ensure I didn't slip and fall." Stephen looks at Eeman.

"I am Eeman. I have no surname. I was at home, too. I live at the back of Sumner valley, on Truro Street. My wife and I cooked our traditional cabbage and carrot stew for dinner, like every Saturday. Then we prayed together before going to bed."

"Saturday was very wet and stormy, wasn't it?" Gladys says. "More flooding in the centre of Sumner yet again. One last thing. Has anyone heard people talking about a bombing? Or seen anything online about a potential bombing?"

Stephen is tensing up beside me. If he mentions what he saw online the police will want to talk with him more about the Rappit channel. However, because he goes online anonymously, he should be safe from discovery. I try not to hold my breath in the growing silence.

Gladys and Malosi sit quietly, with relaxed faces. However, none of us speaks and Gladys finally closes off. "Nothing out of the ordinary and nothing seen? Thank you all very much for your time."

The constables descend the stairs, and we hear them chatting to the fire station crew for too long. Finally, the outside door opens and closes, and everyone lets out a sigh of relief. Surely we don't all have secrets about the bombing? Or is tension a normal reaction to a police visit?

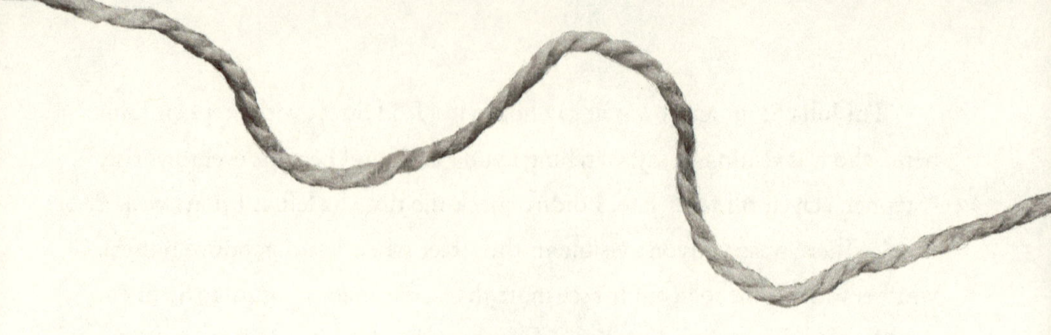

JULIA

30 May 2030

As I relax, footsteps start to climb the stairs. The police are coming back? Victoria appears in the room with eyes wide and face grey. Her hair is escaping its stretchy, and baggy clothes hang off her body. She stares at us from the top of the stairs.

"Victoria, come and sit down." Lynda walks to Victoria, puts a hand on her arm and guides her to one of the chairs vacated by Gladys and Malosi. "Are you unwell? Where's Zahra?"

"I'm fine. No, I'm terrible. But not sick. It's Zahra. She's gone."

"Gone? Gone where? Not dead?" Lynda says.

"No, not dead. I don't know where she's gone." Victoria bursts into choking sobs, clutching her face with her hands. "But it's because I told her to go."

I shift to the chair on the other side of Victoria. "Did you have an argument?"

"It wasn't safe for her to stay," Victoria says. "Because of what she'd done. I shouldn't tell you. But who can I tell? She was part of the coal ship bombing. I haven't told anyone up till now. I called in sick to work. I thought she might come back home. Come back and tell me everything is okay. It's not only her. Rosemary and Andrey were involved too."

This is not helping. Lynda and Eeman didn't need to know about Rosemary and Andrey.

"Zahra helped with the bombing?" Lynda says, taking her hand off Victoria's arm. "But she's six months pregnant!"

"Being pregnant didn't stop Zahra. Nothing stops Zahra," Victoria says. "Not when she wants to do something. She said she was doing this for our babies. Unless someone does something, there won't be a world our babies can grow up in. But I couldn't risk her hiding at home. We could both go to prison, and what would happen to our babies then? They might be given to someone else. If Zahra ends up in prison at least I can look after our babies and visit her. I had to tell her to go."

"There was no good choice for you," Lynda says. "What a terrible situation. You must be so worried about Zahra. Are you sure about Rosemary and Andrey? We need to call the police and ask Gladys and Malosi to come back. We should tell them our group members were part of the bombing. People died on that ship, and children were hurt in the car crash the terrorists were seen at."

"Yes," Eeman says. "We must tell the truth to the police. Lying is a sin. And I will have to leave Aotearoa if I commit a crime. I do not yet have citizenship."

I look at Stephen and he is staring at me.

"No," Victoria says. "I don't want to help the police find Zahra. They might not find out who carried out the bombing. Zahra might be able to come home."

"Victoria," Lynda says gently, "of course you don't want Zahra to be caught and charged, but it's wrong to kill and injure people."

"She was trying to do the right thing!" Victoria says. "To stop coal. Stop climate change. Climate change is killing and injuring millions of people."

"This is awful," Lynda says. "Did the three of them plan the bombing together because they met in our workshops?"

"I don't think they planned it after meeting here," Stephen says. "Someone was recruiting people online. I saw it."

"Online?" Lynda rises from her chair and steps towards him. "You saw someone recruiting people for a bombing online and said nothing about it?"

"Er, yes," Stephen says. "I don't like to interfere in other people's business. And the messages disappeared. They might not have been real."

"You just lied to the police!" Lynda says.

"I didn't lie. I didn't say anything," Stephen says.

"You're playing with words," Lynda says.

I break in. "I don't believe people died or were injured in the bombing. The ship was attacked, but people weren't."

"How can you know?" Lynda demands.

"Because Rosemary came to my house the night of the bombing and told me about it."

"What?" Lynda says. "Rosemary came to your house? Why?"

"I don't know," I say. "I wish she hadn't. It's not like we're friends. Maybe that's why – because we aren't friends. Anyhow, she arrived, dripping wet, in the middle of the night. I gave her a shower and a cup of tea, and she told me about the bombing. The car accident was nothing to do with it. She helped the children who crashed until the ambulance arrived. That's what messed everything up. If they hadn't stayed to help the children they'd have been long gone with no trace when the bombs exploded."

"Okay," Lynda says, "they supposedly didn't cause the car crash. They supposedly helped the children. But what about the ship's crew?"

"I think the crew are fine," Stephen says. "It's five days since the bombing and there are no reports of actual deaths or injuries. Maybe the crew's disappearance is being used to pressure people to out the bombers. The bombers were careful to warn the crew."

"How do you know?" Lynda asks. "Were you involved too?"

"No, I'd never do something like that," Stephen says. "Andrey came to my house. Not to my house – to my caravan. I don't have a house, like I told you earlier. In the interests of getting everything out there, I don't have a wife, either. Well, I did, but she died a long time ago."

Stephen looks around, like he's expecting people to react to him finally telling the truth. His big reveal and everyone has other things on their minds. Maybe this will help him move on and tell his real story.

"I found Andrey wet and cold and gave him a cup of tea. Then he told me the same story of the bombing Rosemary told Julia."

"Now I wish I hadn't heard any of this," Lynda says, which is unfair because she asked. "I don't want to know anything more. We have to call the police. We're harbouring terrorists."

"No, we aren't harbouring terrorists," I say. "And you never were. Rosemary and Andrey are no longer at my house or Stephen's house. They left. Like Zahra.

"And, like Victoria said, Andrey, Rosemary and Zahra were doing something real. We all do lots of talking and worrying. They took action.

Aotearoa shouldn't be mining or using coal or selling it to other countries to use. Look at what's happening around the world as a result – lots of coal ships being blown up and coal ports put out of action. Lyttelton was the start of a huge protest the world needs and is now paying attention to. It's a good thing."

"I agree with Julia," Stephen says, and I smile at him. "There are people dying everywhere because the climate is changing. Starving because droughts kill their crops. Dying from cold or disease when floods wash their houses. Drowning when their islands submerge. There's a whole generation of young people terrified about whether they have a future. We aren't talking about the bombers hurting people – only property."

"Good God," Lynda says. "You knew about the attack beforehand and did nothing. You had terrorists at your houses and did nothing. This is insane. I need to go home. You need to go to the police."

"No, Lynda. Wait." I stand up and push my chair back. "Do you remember when we had our big argument about COVID vaccinations, and I left after yelling at you? We nearly lost our friendship because I wouldn't stay and listen. I know I made a mistake then. Right now, I need you to stay and listen. This world is collapsing in so many ways. Our friendships and relationships are the threads that keep us hanging on. They give us hope when it seems like there's no hope."

"That was different, Julia," Lynda says. "You weren't wanting to break the law. What's going on here is illegal, even if no one died."

"Actually, I did want to break the vaccination requirement and it was a law," I say. "I tried to get a false vaccine passport so I could still go out for coffee and into shops without being vaccinated. The only reason I didn't break the law was I never managed to get a false passport. I never told you that."

Lynda looks at the door, then at me. "When you didn't want to be vaccinated you weren't risking anything for your child or your partner. Hermione needs me. Robbie needs me. I can't go to prison for a principle."

"None of us wants to go to prison," I say. "We all have people relying on us. We need to make our own decisions – but Lynda, please hear us out. Eeman, of course you're worried too. The police won't come back this evening because they've already been here. Let's keep talking, then we'll act on consensus. If the group still wants to inform the police, I promise I will go to them. Actually, first let's get a cup of tea. Then let's keep talking."

It was Zahra's turn to both talk and bring snacks, so there's nothing to eat. I go downstairs and beg the fire crew for some biscuits. We all make cups of tea, avoiding eye contact, then return to our chairs.

"Maybe Rosemary, and Andrey, and Zahra, haven't done anything morally wrong. No one's hurt. However, bombing a ship is still illegal," Lynda says. "They're going to get caught in the end. Everything will come out and we'll all be guilty of hiding terrorists."

"Not necessarily," I say. "There's no evidence the police have made progress towards finding the bombers. More importantly, they will leave the country very soon, at which point there's little risk the police will find them or us. We only need to stay quiet for a couple more days."

"Zahra is leaving?" Victoria says, staring at her hands splayed over her stomach. "She didn't tell me that."

"I'm not sure, Victoria," I say. "I only know Rosemary and Andrey are leaving soon. Maybe she is too."

Victoria drops her head and starts sobbing again.

"A couple of days?" Lynda says. "When exactly?"

"By Monday," I say. "I know it's a big ask, but I'm asking. On Monday morning, if anyone wants me to, I will tell the police we know Rosemary, Andrey and Zahra were involved in the bombing. But can we please wait till Monday?"

The five of us sit back in our chairs and look at each other. It's only Lynda and Eeman who have a decision to make.

"Stephen, are you asking us to wait till Monday?" Eeman says.

"Yes, I am," Stephen says. "And I will go to the police with Julia if that's what everyone else wants. We will keep the rest of you out of this. You have families to think of, where we don't."

I smile at him again. Having someone back me is beyond wonderful and I'm not going to hide what's going on between us anymore.

"Stephen, I see you with the boys," Eeman says. "You are a good man. I know you want to help people. I can wait until Monday. But then you and

Julia must tell the police what you know about the bombing without involving the rest of the group. We cannot be seen to have lied to the police."

Lynda swallows. "I'm terrified," she says. "But we need the coal shipments to stop. Hermione needs a future. So I agree to wait until Monday."

"What will you say to the police about Zahra, Julia?" Victoria asks. "You can't tell them she came back to me!"

"That's tricky," I say. "We could say Andrey and Rosemary told us Zahra was involved, but that's all we know."

"If you and Stephen are putting yourselves in the firing line, it's up to you how you tell the story," Lynda says. "Just make it convincing and watertight."

"Thank you Lynda and Eeman. I will call the police on Monday," I say. "Now, let's have another cup of tea. If Gladys and Malosi are still nearby we don't want to look like our meeting finished early."

Everyone sits quietly, drinking a second cup of tea. I want to go home with Stephen, go to bed and wake up in the morning to find there was no bombing and we can get on with the business of figuring out if our lives are jigsaw puzzle pieces which interlock.

We all watch the hands on the clock face tick around to 8.30pm, then stand and leave with perfunctory goodbyes.

JULIA

30 May–3 June 2030

Here I was, like Lynda, thinking our group was doing going so well – telling stories, developing relationships. Instead, we were creating a terrorist cell. You set out to do good, but don't necessarily achieve it. Or not how you intended, anyway. For all that Stephen says there were messages online seeking participants in the bombing, I don't think it's coincidental three people from our group were involved.

Stephen and I spend Thursday night at my house, then go up to his caravan on Friday. Too many problems rattle around my mental box, trying to escape. Going to the police will probably resolve many of these; no need to put dates in my calendar to open them up. If I'm in prison I won't need a house. I might as well accept the money from the council and schedule my departure from Head Street. Can you still get payments from local government if you are in prison?

To pass the time until Monday, I start on costumes for B and the Maximinions. I haven't yet met the Maximinions and probably never will. If Stephen and I aren't around there might not be any performance or need for costumes. I shelve those thoughts. Stephen helps me carry fabric from my place up to his caravan. He says I can use Cynthia's sewing machine and there's a lot more fabric in his container. If I wasn't going to prison soon, I could get excited about the project.

What else should I finish up before Monday? I completed my 13th hour clock last week and asked Robbie to deliver it. Lynda will have to manage Dolls with Stories without Fran and me. She won't have enough time to keep Humans with Stories going, but it's been such a disaster that hardly matters.

I Cast Johnno in case I can't contact anyone from prison. I should have got in touch earlier to talk through what's happening about my house, but I haven't had a lot of spare time.

"Hi, Johnno, it's your favourite twin calling." I'm always surprised to see Johnno ageing at the same rate as me. He shaves his head these days, but he hasn't tamed his eyebrows. His face is lean, with a big, relaxed smile.

"Hey, Julia, how are things? So sad about Fran."

At Fran's request, I'd emailed Johnno about her illness, her going up to Northland and her resignation from Dolls with Stories, given Johnno's a trustee.

"Yes, really sad. I don't know how we'll manage, and I still can't believe she's gone. We gave her and Holly a great send-off last week at Lynda and Robbie's. But there's more bad news. The council sent me a notice; I've got to leave my house. They will pay me four hundred thousand to leave, half the value."

"You should take the money, Julia. You can come live in Golden Bay with me and Kannika. Put a caravan on our land."

Johnno's never been attached to Gran's house in the way I am. Why do people think I should live in a mobile unit when I've been living in a house?

"Thanks, Johnno, but all my friends and community are in Sumner. I would miss Lynda and Hermione too much."

"The offer's out there if you change your mind, Julia," Johnno says.

"That's very kind. And ... errr ... I'm sort of seeing a guy. His name is Stephen."

"Sort of seeing Stephen?" Johnno says. "I hope he's nice to you."

"Yes, he is. Very nice," I say. "We should all get together on Cast soon."

"Let me know a good time," Johnno says.

Stephen and I immerse ourselves in the process of creation. I inveigle Stephen into helping me with costumes. For B, I create a hooded dress with voluminous sleeves and a long train. The fabric is all black, but I sew in conductive thread with LEDs. When B moves, the LEDs will glow silver and gold and she will become a universe of networked constellations. When she stops moving she will be black again. I get Stephen to dye T-shirts and I make denim overalls for the Maximinions. I make a variety of children's sizes because Stephen can't give me accurate information on the size of the boys. I'm picking the Maximinions will be jealous if B gets all the lights, so I also insert LEDs on the overalls.

Stephen programmes the Maximinion's LEDs to run through red, orange, and green with all the overalls showing the same colour at any point in time, controlled by a remote.

Neither Stephen nor I feel much like dinner on Sunday night. Should we have our favourite meal, like death row prisoners before they receive their lethal injection? We get into bed and lie rigid on our backs, breathing quietly to fool the other person into thinking we are asleep. It doesn't work and we reach for each other simultaneously in the early hours of the morning. Desperation is an appropriate emotion.

We wake again when the sun rises and get up for the breakfast of the condemned. It turns out condemned people only want a cup of tea, which we drink on Stephen's caravan bench seat, device free, for a last few minutes of peace.

"It's time," I say, and Stephen brings his computer screen to life to discover the state of play before we call the police. Please let there be no reports of actual dead people in the sunk ship. I sit on my hands as Stephen runs a search.

BREAKING NEWS

Coal ship bomber apprehended

BREAKING NEWS

SinkingTogether claims Lyttelton bombing

BREAKING NEWS

UN international summit for cessation of coal trade to be held in Brussels 10 June 2030

Stephen and I stare at each other, goggle-eyed. Who has been apprehended? The headline only refers to a single person. He scrolls down to the article below.

Dr Rosemary Barne of SinkingTogether turned herself in at Christchurch Police Station this morning, claiming responsibility for the sinking of the coal ship in Lyttelton Port. Dr Barne is a psychiatrist employed by the Christchurch District Health Board and lives in Moncks Bay. She is a mother of two young boys.

The international group SinkingTogether simultaneously issued a press release. This secretive group only carries out communications via Rappit chat. When queried about other people involved in the sinking, SinkingTogether's comment was that Dr Barne is the only person involved in the bombing who remains in Aotearoa New Zealand.

It is assumed the delay of SinkingTogether's media release was intended to allow the other members of the bombing party to flee. SinkingTogether states that the sinking of the coal ship was a deliberate and careful act of ecotage, in which no people were injured or killed, distinct from terrorism.

The Port Authority has confirmed the crew, described as missing from the ship, were in fact on leave and there was confusion as to their whereabouts.

SinkingTogether has claimed responsibility not only for the Lyttelton bombing, but for the series of sinkings of coal ships in many ports worldwide.

"We are proud to have impeded the movement of coal and brought about a world summit with the goal of ending the coal trade."

The Aotearoa New Zealand Government has agreed to an urgent sitting of Parliament to debate and vote on national cessation of coal mining, with shadow

Environment Minister Tui Greenwood suggesting, "It's
a travesty it has taken so long for Aotearoa to face
the unacceptability of coal as an energy source. Coal
companies have been living on borrowed time. We are
calling in that loan."

"Does this mean we don't need to go to the police?" I say.

"I think so," Stephen says. "There's nothing more they need to know. We have to assume Andrey left with the Russian crew, like he was planning. I wonder how Zahra left the country?"

"Maybe on the same ship. Who knows?" I reply. "As long as she's gone, I don't care!"

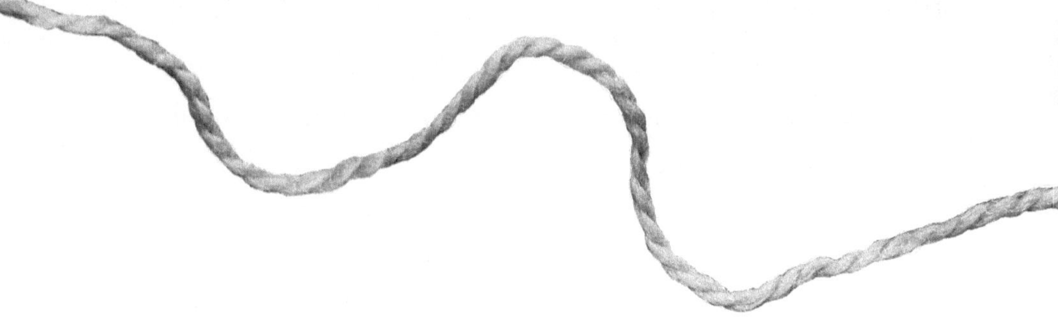

JULIA

3 June 2030

I call Lynda immediately. "Have you seen what's happened? About the coal ship? Rosemary has handed herself into the police!"

"We shouldn't talk about this on the phone, Julia," Lynda says. "How about you come round? I'll get Robbie to take Hermione for a walk."

"Can I bring Stephen?" I ask.

"You're that inseparable now? Yes, you can both visit," Lynda says.

Stephen and I walk along the top of Scarborough Hill, down the road, then up the steps to Lynda and Robbie's. It would be good to find a more direct route to Lynda's from Stephen's place. There might be one through the tracks. I'll ask Lynda.

"Hi, Lynda," I say as we reach the deck.

"Hello, Julia and Stephen," Lynda says.

"It's all good," I say. "All the reports state Rosemary is the only person left in New Zealand who was involved in the bombing."

"She might tell the police about your and Stephen's involvement," Lynda says.

"Why would she do that?" I ask. "She has no reason to get us in trouble."

"She doesn't," Lynda says. "But that doesn't mean she won't. Who knows what sort of questioning she'll get? For Robbie and Hermione and me to be safe, the two of us need a friend break – I have to protect my whānau."

"I thought I was your whānau," I say, under my breath. Out loud I say, "A friend break?" with my voice and heart cracking.

"Yes. I'm extremely upset by how you risked so much, for so many people, through taking Rosemary in. And the same for you, Stephen, with Andrey.

You should have told Rosemary and Andrey to leave as soon as you found out what they had done, and then called the police. You probably still should call the police to tell them what happened, but I'll leave that up to you.

"Julia, we need to sort out business arrangements for the time being. I can wrap up 'Humans with Stories' – that group has run its course. I will contact Eeman and Victoria. You're still a trustee for 'Dolls with Stories'. We will keep in touch about governance matters as necessary, but strictly at a business level. I can manage nearly everything about the organisation on my own and I can talk with Johnno. There's 'Broken is Beautiful', too – obviously you will have to be in contact with Robbie but I'm asking that your exchanges are business only as well."

"How long is a 'friend break'?" I ask.

"Until Rosemary is convicted, so we're sure nothing more will come out about the bombing and who knew about it."

A conviction could take years. There's nothing quick about the Aotearoa courts. "Can I say goodbye to Hermione?" I ask.

"She's out with Robbie," Lynda says. "I don't know when they will be back."

Tears run down my face as I turn to leave, taking Stephen's hand as a consolation prize. He hasn't said a word the whole time we've been at Lynda's, and we descend the steps in silence.

"I think I'll go home for a bit," I say when we reach Scarborough Road.

"If that's what you want, Julia," Stephen says. He kisses me goodbye so tenderly I almost change my mind and ask to go with him. But I don't.

STEPHEN

Early June 2030

We've lived through an eternal week. Now Julia and I need to find a new normal to inhabit. I'm still making sense of no one caring about my telling the truth at the last workshop about Cynthia and the caravan. I worried for so long about something that didn't turn out to be a problem after all.

Julia is in a much worse space. She is devastated by Lynda's wanting a friendship break, and it's clear I can't make up for that loss. I am trying not to feel hurt, but it's hard. Distraction might be a good tactic.

"Why don't we go visit the Redcliffs tiny home community and have a look at what they are doing? You could consider building a tiny home for when you leave your house."

"I don't want to think about leaving my house right now," Julia says.

"I'm sure you don't. But you could look at options."

"I guess," Julia says. After a pause she continues, "Funny, Andrey told me to take the little pot stand he gave me to his friend Theo there. I don't know why. I suppose we might as well go visit."

We walk to the tiny home community, which is much larger than I was expecting. It's not visible from the main road so I'd never paid it much attention. The community must have been developing for some time, given the number of tiny homes, gardens, and children's play areas. There are several tiny homes being constructed, interspersed between the inhabited homes.

Theo is easy to find. His tiny home is beside a meeting space in the centre of the community. "So nice to meet Andrey's friends," Theo says. "It's such a pity he left because he helped so many people here. Everyone loved Andrey and his big personality. I was surprised his visa application was denied. I thought the government had an amnesty for anyone in the country, given how difficult it is now to arrive and leave."

"Yes, it was sudden, and we'll miss him too," I say. "He told us such a sad story about his partner and dog in Slovenia."

"What happened?" Theo says. "He told us he had to leave Slovenia, but no details."

I look at Julia, who has taken the mini pot stand out of her bag and is turning it in her hands. "Theo," she says, "Andrey told me to give you this and ask to see his house. He was in a rush the last time I saw him and didn't explain. Do you know what he meant?"

"Aha," Theo says, "the puzzle piece. Yes, let's go see Andrey's tiny house."

Theo guides us between the tiny houses. "Where do you get the materials from?" I ask, looking at piles of stacked timber and roofing iron.

"We try to get as much as possible from houses being deconstructed – recently from tornado-damaged houses," Theo says. "Often, people deconstruct their own places so they can keep something of their homes. There's far more timber and windows and doors in a normal house than a tiny house needs, so people share materials."

Julia looks interested. "People are re-creating their houses as tiny homes?"

"Exactly," Theo says. "Making something smaller, relocatable, more resilient. And sharing at the same time."

"I like that idea," Julia says. "Re-creation is what I know. Stephen, maybe I could do the same with my house. I don't have to leave it for the council to knock down. I can build a tiny home and donate building supplies to other people. My house is made out of beautiful native timbers."

"Here's Andrey's place," Theo says.

Andrey's tiny home is more like a gypsy caravan than the standard rectangular model people use to maximise space. The roof and walls are clad with cedar shingles. It has a miniature porch at the back as an entrance, with a balustrade made out of weathered driftwood. The doors and windows are wooden and look like they are from several different buildings. Some are brightly painted, while others are being stripped back.

Theo ushers us onto the porch and we file into the tiny home. Like in caravans, you don't stand two abreast in tiny homes. The inside is as original as the outside with interlocking rectangles of different sizes and colours of ply on the walls. A driftwood ladder leads upstairs to a bed at one end and another ladder to a study space at the other. The table that folds out from the downstairs wall isn't yet finished. There's a piece of ply tacked onto the frame and a jigsaw of shapes with inlaid flowers on it, with an obvious hole in the centre.

"Look," Julia says. "The stand Andrey gave me belongs here." She drops the piece with its opposing curves into the hole.

"Yes," Theo says. "Andrey and his games. He was our grand champion tiny house Scrabble competitor, even though his first language was Russian. He only occasionally tried to cheat by using a Russian word. And he was always making jigsaws for our community children. He told me if he had to leave in a hurry he would give this table piece to the person he wanted to take over his tiny home."

"Oh," Julia says. "That's very kind of him. But I don't want his tiny home. I want to build my own home like my grandparents did."

I'm happy Julia is looking interested, but it seems silly to turn down an almost complete tiny home when you are about to lose your house.

"Hang on, Julia," I say. "You might not want it, but you might know someone who does."

"I can't think of anyone, but maybe you are right, Stephen," Julia says. "It's all so unexpected. Theo, can I leave the tiny home here for the meantime? If you have people needing somewhere to stay, they can use it. Also, if I want to build my own tiny home, out of my house, is there anyone here who can help?"

"Of course, to both things," Theo says. "We have workshops here every weekend where people share their knowledge of tiny home building and assist with other people's projects. Come and join us."

Our walk home is much more animated than our walk to Redcliffs. Julia is already thinking about designing a tiny home and how she can deconstruct her gran's house to make the most of the timber.

"Who might need a tiny home to live in?" she says. "Andrey's is lovely, but I definitely want my own. I need to take some of my past into my future."

"What about Victoria?" I say. "With a baby coming soon, she'll be wanting security."

"Good point. She could live in the Redcliffs community." Julia says.

"Yes. Or she could put it on my land. There's a lot I need to figure out, but I'm thinking I should allow other people to live on my two hectares, rather than have an empty grass paddock. You included, remember?"

"I wasn't sure if you meant it when you said I could live there. Are you sure?" Julia says.

"Absolutely," I say, and kiss her to seal the deal.

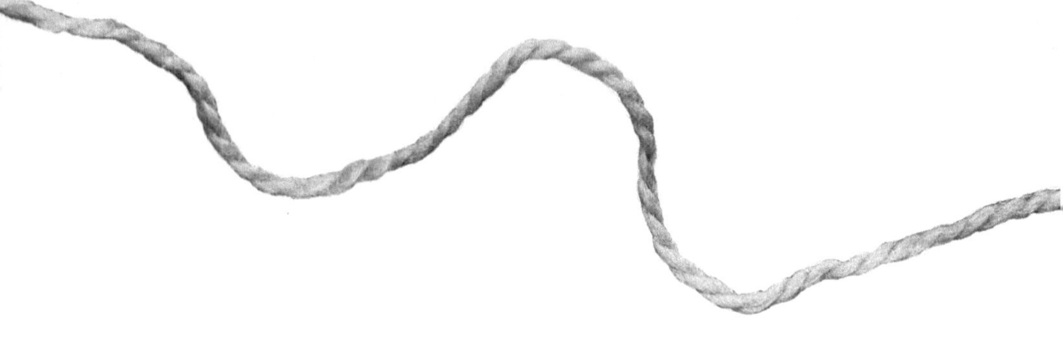

JULIA

Late June 2030

Stephen and I visit the retirement units because we promised to have regular sing-alongs. I'm nervous. Will they have connected Rhiannon with Rosemary? It's not likely, because there are few photos of Rosemary in the media; the government has a deliberate policy of minimising notoriety for terrorists. I'm hoping that by the time the court case comes round the retirees will have forgotten her face. Because, if they do recognise her, they might wonder why we brought her around and want to involve the police. Of course, that's why Lynda has demanded a friend break.

"Lovely to see you," Pauline says when she opens the door. "We enjoyed having your friends stay for a few days. What nice people. They helped out with jobs needing doing and were so capable. Well, Pekko and Phaedra were."

"Phaedra?" I say. "You mean Rhiannon, right?" I hope Pauline isn't showing signs of dementia, although that would reduce the likelihood of her identifying Rosemary.

"Phaedra came round the next morning and chatted with Pekko and Rhiannon. You must know Phaedra. I'm sure she and Pekko are an item. Then Rhiannon said she would leave so Phaedra could have her bed because she didn't want to crowd our place."

"Phaedra and Pekko are an item, are they?" I say. "We thought they were close, but …" I'm improvising because I don't know who Phaedra is.

"I love Phaedra's dreadlocks. They made me wish I had enough hair to make dreadlocks, but I've barely enough to cover my scalp. Enjoy it while you have it, that's what I say. Though Phaedra was surprisingly modest. Wore big baggy trousers and puffer jackets all the time she was here, even in bed."

"Phaedra feels the cold," Stephen says, giving me a meaningful look. "You know Phaedra, Julia – Victoria's friend."

Dreadlocks. How did Zahra find Andrey? And they're an item? But she and Victoria were having babies together. Zahra has stowed away on a ship when she's seven months pregnant? A baby could be an interesting surprise for the crew.

"Did Phaedra and Pekko leave at the weekend as planned?" I ask. "It was a shame we couldn't come and say goodbye, but we had a lot on."

"I heard Phaedra tiptoe out in the early hours of the morning. When I needed to have a pee but didn't want to get out of bed. It's so annoying. It would be much more sensible to get up and pee, but you want to be asleep, so you don't," Pauline says. "Happens far too many times a night.

"Now, let's get on with the sing-along. I'll go call Grant and the boys over. We weren't sure you were coming – I said I'd tell them if you arrived. The boys are too loud to have visit for long. They won't put their hearing aids in and constantly shout so we can't hear ourselves think. It's even worse once they start on the whisky."

Stephen and I drop in on Victoria to see how she is doing. The short answer is, not well. Everything about Victoria, other than her stomach, is drooping and her kitchen is almost devoid of food. There are wizened apples in a bowl and a couple of cans of baked beans and chickpeas in the cupboards.

"You need to look after yourself and your baby," I say. "Are you eating? Are you working?"

"I don't want another mother," Victoria says. "One is plenty. She rings me all the time because she lives in Auckland so won't visit until our baby is born. Then she'll come for too long because it's such a big trip. Maybe Zahra will be back before Mum comes. I haven't told anyone Zahra's gone, because she might come back. Our babies are siblings. They need to grow up together."

After Pauline's announcement about Phaedra, Stephen and I had discussed what we'd tell Victoria. Stephen was all for telling her like it is. He's gone from being reticent about the truth to wanting everything out there. Like a reformed smoker wanting everyone to hear the truth about cigarettes. I was more hesitant.

"Why does Victoria need to know about Zahra and Andrey?" I said. "All she needs to be told is Zahra definitely won't be coming back."

"So, what are you going to say?" Stephen asks. "You heard she got on a ship? From who?"

I sit with my head in my hands, squeezing my eyes shut and willing my imagination to kick in. Finally, it does. "I know – you can say you read it on your Rappit channel."

"But there wasn't anything about Zahra getting on the ship on the Rappit channel," Stephen says.

"Of course there wasn't," I say. "But Victoria doesn't watch The Republic of Sumner channel, does she? Otherwise she'd have known about the bombing beforehand."

So that's what Stephen does. He clumsily tells Victoria that Zahra has left the country. His doing the telling allows me to comfort Victoria as far as is possible. I hope she will achieve closure from knowing Zahra has gone permanently, but it's not helping in the short term. I suggest Stephen makes tea, although the only teabag choice is green tea, which tastes pretty bad. I pat Victoria's back as she breaks into another round of sobs and hiccups.

"Would you like some good news, Victoria?" I ask. "Though perhaps you'd rather wait till another time." I quickly add, "It's nothing to do with Zahra."

"How could any news be good right now?" Victoria says.

I've been tying myself up in knots to figure out how to explain Andrey's gift of the tiny house. Why I don't want it. Why I want my own. How I can explain my guilt for the damage done by people meeting through Humans with Stories. I couldn't say I think Andrey donating his tiny house to Victoria would be less than a fair trade for leaving with Zahra. I finally realised the easiest explanation is the simplest one. "Andrey gave me his tiny house, through his friend Theo. But I would like to give it to you."

"Why me?" Victoria is surprised enough to stop crying.

"So you and your baby have somewhere of your own to live," I say.

"Where would I put it?" Victoria asks. "I don't own any land."

"There are two possibilities," I tell her. "You can keep it in the Redcliffs community, while the red-zoned land there is usable. Or Stephen will let people put tiny houses on his land. You can think about it."

It might be nice to have someone with a baby at Stephen's in a separate dwelling. A baby we can visit, but not hear crying in the night. On the other hand, Victoria is rather emotional and that could get tiring. Lynda is so much more straightforward and pragmatic. However, I don't have the option of Lynda and Hermione.

I'd like to be able to talk with Fran about what's happened with the bombing, and the group, and Lynda. It's great having Stephen to support me, but he's not the same as someone who has known me over the last decade. Of course, talking about the bombing over Cast is out of the question. And Fran is no longer up to talking about other people's problems. Her tone tells me she's wrapping up all her loose ends and tucking them into a tight bundle; there's no space for new threads. When I Cast her we talk about the grey, damp Northland weather. We talk about how Holly is spending every weekday in te reo Māori immersion classes and cutting people's hair as her contribution to the community. "I'm so happy to see her happy," Fran says in a voice that cracks every other sentence. "Are you happy, Julia?"

I tell her how well Stephen and I are getting on. I don't talk about Lynda and Hermione, or Humans with Stories or Dolls with Stories, and Fran doesn't notice. I describe B and the Maximinions and how Stephen, B and I will go to the Maximinions' house this week for a singing practice. I've finished their costumes and am looking forward to seeing everyone try them on. Fran is sitting in bed and her head starts to droop as I enthuse about the LEDs on B's outfit and the overalls. "Time for me to be going, Fran. All my love."

"Much love to you too, Julia. And Holly says 'Hi.'"

I arrange an online tea ceremony with Johnno and Kannika so they can meet Stephen. We Cast from Gran's house because my tea set is still there. I make Kenya Bold tea in my Temuka teapot, put milk in Boris's head, get out the two gold filigree cups and put everything on the Indian tray to take through to the sitting room.

Kannika has her own tea ritual with a turquoise pot and cream-coloured, hand-shaped bowls, served at a low table which she and Johnno sit cross-legged beside. I get an internal giggle out of my brother sitting cross-legged on the floor like a primary school kid. He and Stephen toast each other with tea and call each other 'mate'. They find a common thread discussing photovoltaic systems for household power and talk about wattages and amp-hours, while Kannika and I drink our tea in the background.

Next time we'll use two screens, so Kannika and I can discuss gardening in a separate chat room. I've lost heart in Gran's dying garden, but Stephen and I are already laying out a vegetable garden at his place and I will take as many of Gran's surviving flowers as possible. I've borrowed Andrey's bike and trailer from the Redcliffs tiny home community to move plants up onto Scarborough. Plants are heavy, so it will take a while. Good timing on the move, though — early winter is perfect to get plants established for the next growing season. I'm reading up on food forests too. This might be the opportunity to take a whole different approach to growing. Stephen thinks we should push pause on the veggie garden until we decide about the food forest, but I say we should start growing food now and iterate towards our bigger-picture solution as we learn.

STEPHEN

July–October 2030

After the intense time of the Lyttelton bombing, normal life seems surprisingly manageable. Julia and I have developed a routine where I stay at her place on Mondays and Tuesdays, she stays at mine on Fridays and Saturdays, and we have the other nights on our own. Mondays we usually go to the retirement units for a sing-along. The place is emptying as their inhabitants move to relatives or other care when they get ill. The remaining retirees have been told they will be moved to Woolston in February. Pauline says she'll still plant her spring vegetables because, with the council, who knows when things will happen.

Pauline pulls me aside one evening as we are preparing tea with whisky to lubricate our sing-along. "I know, of course," she says.

"Know what?" I ask.

"About Rosemary Barne, the climate warrior," Pauline says. "I'm not that old and confused. No one else has noticed though – or not that they've mentioned. I don't think their eyesight is good enough to recognise Rosemary, so I wouldn't worry about it. I won't be saying anything to anyone. Rhiannon, that was a nice touch. Great song, if a little sentimental."

"Sorry," I say. "We were struggling to find somewhere they could go. We shouldn't have involved you."

"Don't be sorry," Pauline says. "Rosemary's a hero, not a terrorist. We need more women like her. And we love getting to know you and Julia better – you are both so gracious about running sing-alongs for old biddies and grouches."

"It's not like that at all," I say. "We enjoy the sing-alongs too. Though the men could still improve their taste in music!"

"Absolutely they could, but they seem to be past educating," Pauline says. "Too bad for them."

On the days Julia and I spend together, I help her build her tiny home. I'm learning a lot about building, and I'm impressed by how, once Julia decides on action, she makes rapid progress. Her tiny home is progressing so fast her gran's house will soon no longer be weathertight, and she'll have to join me in my caravan. I worry she may get sick of me living in such close quarters, even though it will be temporary.

Julia's building her tiny home on a trailer in the street in front of her gran's house – it's the most efficient solution given she's reusing house materials. At first, I worried someone might make a fuss about the construction, or the council might ticket her for parking a vehicle long-term on the road. However, the council aren't enforcing rules in places they are paying people to leave. And nearby residents are far more focused on their own departures than someone building a tiny home. It's not like there's any value in properties left to lose.

Julia's construction has done the opposite of annoying people. It's created a local movement – her tiny home is a gathering place for the neighbourhood. Walkers and cyclists constantly stop and ask her what she's doing and where they can learn more about tiny home construction. I make cups of tea while Julia shows people around. People are starting to work on more tiny homes in nearby streets. Theo and another tiny home expert from the Redcliffs group visit to advise them and the suburb is transforming into a gypsy caravan park with an air of excitement and energy around the structures.

Julia offered leftover materials from her house to the Maximinion families and Eeman, to build their own tiny homes. She also offered to loan them the cost of tiny home trailer bases. The Maximinion families are thinking it over because they don't want to be in debt, but they'd love to have their own places. It's looking likely Julia's street will shortly host a fleet of tiny homes cannibalising her gran's house.

Eeman thanked Julia for her offer but said construction isn't in his skill set. His church has offered him and Deb a room in a shared house in Rolleston, west of Christchurch where the city is sprawling onto the safer ground a long way from the sea. I'm secretly relieved. I felt compelled to offer Eeman a place on my land given our connection through Humans with Stories and the Maximinions. However, the religious thing will never sit well for me.

Victoria is going to join Julia and me on Scarborough. She decided there's too much risk of flooding in the Redcliffs tiny home community so will soon move Andrey's place up the hill. I need to cut a bigger gap in the macrocarpa hedge around the gate to allow her house and Julia's to get through. It won't be just Victoria joining us – Victoria and Zarita will come. Victoria's life now revolves around Zarita. Every time Julia and I visit, Julia's discussions with Victoria are all focused on the intakes, outputs, and sleep patterns of small humans.

I'm still nervous about whether a tiny home community on my land will work while thinking it's the right thing to do. Communities are not so different from communes and there are many reasons communes don't usually last long. They last the longest when run by a dictator, something I don't want to be. Instead, I have developed a contract the tiny homers and I will sign – in keeping with my new mantra of everything in the open. Tiny homers need security, and I need to know that if they don't behave well I can ask them to leave. Julia's doing everything she can to increase our chances of success – she visits the Redcliffs tiny home community on a regular basis to learn about their sharing schemes, food growing, circular use of materials, and exchanges of goods and services. However, Julia and Lynda also thought Humans with Stories was a good idea and look how that ended.

As far as I know, none of us have been in contact with Rosemary. Perhaps Eeman has. He's the most likely of us to follow his principles about caring for people. Put bluntly, Julia and I are too scared. We respect what Rosemary did, but we don't want to be associated with her because neither of us is brave enough to stand up for our beliefs in the same way. Julia's braver than me, but she says she'd rather work at the small-scale end of change – repairing broken possessions, building tiny homes, sharing land and gardens, and finding the best ways of creating connections between humans.

Without a doubt, Rosemary was part of a big thing. The UN General Assembly resolved to end international shipments of coal by January 2031, an amazingly unambiguous move and none of the big coal exporters tried to fight it. The international series of coal ship sinkings was what started it all off, with the Lyttelton bombing being the first. Ecotage is now the socially acceptable term for destruction of property in the interests of environmental protection. A member's Bill is going through Parliament, proposing destruction of property without risk to human life be removed from the definition of terrorism. The Bill has broad support because of Rosemary's case, which remains in the headlines.

MOTHER OF TWO BEING TRIED FOR SAVING THE PLANET

BARNE'S ACTS GREEN? OR BLACK? COURTS WILL DECIDE

Rosemary will be tried under the existing law, so it's pretty certain she will be found guilty of undertaking a terrorist act. Her trial is in November and the maximum sentence remains life.

We have a concert with B and the Maximinions, which becomes the first of multiple performances. I persuade Miranda to bring B to Sumner to meet the Maximinions – ten small boys really can't fit in Miranda's townhouse. B is at Miranda's all the time now – no more hospital. B had surgery to remove the cancerous bone and B's doctor says there's no further sign of disease, though of course, B will need regular monitoring. B has more energy every time I see B, although B tries to keep it hidden in her black garments – except when B's performing.

B gets on better with the Maximinions than I would ever have expected. B treats them like a bunch of annoying, but endearing, brothers. At their first meeting, the sky was blue, even if the day was cool, so we played music in the garden. I encouraged the Maximinions to go first and show B what they could do. Felicity, B, Eeman, Ruby, Julia, and I sat on folding chairs while the

Maximinions sang and danced their little hearts out. They were thrilled by the prospect of singing with a mysterious hooded character who's recovering from a deadly disease. When the Maximinions sang the roller-skating song, B started to smile, so we repeated the chorus until everyone was shouting, "There ain't no brakes on roller skates!"

Then I suggested B sing the verses of the 'Shitkickin' Song' to the Maximinions and the Maximinions sing the chorus back.

B said, "This is my song, right? We'll practise it together. Adults can go away."

We sat in the living room, sneaking glimpses of the kids out the window. B knew how to rule the Maximinions from the outset. B must have grown up with other children, the way B got them into order. Since that first meeting, they've worked on more songs to sing together – some of them covers, and some originals B has written with little help from me.

Julia's costumes remain a great hit with all the participants. When Julia first gave the Maximinions their overalls they begged to wear the outfits to bed. Ruby later told us how she went into the Maximinions' room at midnight to get them to calm down and let everyone sleep. She discovered they'd lifted the LED controller out of her pocket and were making light patterns as they danced around on their bunks.

B looks amazing in the costume, shifting between a death figure and a shower of light. B says it might be GOAT.

We give a concert to the retirees, who love the Shitkickin' song so much they want to change the verses to fit their own ailments. I give them the lyrics which prompts me to lodge it with APRA AMCOS to say we have the rights to the music. Good thing, it turns out. At B's request, I have recorded their performances, but I didn't know B had posted them online. Suddenly, B and the Maximinions are trending on NikNak, with a million subscribers and numbers rapidly rising.

The Maximinion families don't understand how their boys are becoming a worldwide social media phenomenon when they can't leave Aotearoa to visit their relatives. Maybe they can one day, though, using income from video streaming. I'm doing my best to help with this and am on a rapid learning curve in the world of online personalities and social media marketing. That our key personality prefers to hide behind a hood and not talk to anyone they don't know has turned out to be an ultimate drawcard. Despite my being a beginner at marketing, my ability to develop algorithms has translated perfectly into creating self-managing advertising campaigns and the money they get from the videos keeps growing. Even better, now an advertising company is asking for the rights to use 'Shitkickin' Life' to promote a cancer treatment.

JULIA

November 2030–March 2031

Life is moving right along, as it does, and it's already hard to remember when Stephen wasn't part of mine.

Rosemary is convicted in November, an impressive turn of speed for the justice system. However, she pleaded guilty from the start, simplifying the trial. There were lots of calls for her to plead not guilty to terrorism, given the debate about terrorism versus ecotage her case inspired. However, once the member's Bill on ecotage got pulled out of the biscuit tin she said she didn't see the need to delay her trial. Someone must have already had that piece of legislation ready to go for it to appear so quickly. Were Sinking Together involved? According to the media, Sinking Together supplied legal representation for Rosemary and supported her all the way. I should have visited Rosemary in prison but, to be honest, I didn't want to. I'm dealing with enough change, and I need to allow myself to not do things I don't want to do.

To celebrate the end of this year of change and, specifically my moving to Stephen's land in my new tiny home, Stephen and I hold a party on New Year's Eve 2030. It's as formal an announcement as we'll ever make about being together. Sometimes I think we complement each other brilliantly and other times I want to shake Stephen until he gets on with things and stops worrying. He's heavy on thinking and light on action for anything beyond music and computer algorithms.

Although I still have little faith in the council delivering what the city needs, they did extend the bus service to the top of Scarborough Hill, which helps get everyone to our party. Pauline and Grant and the remaining retirees come. They're now scheduled to move to Woolston in March; Pauline says moving is believing.

Eeman and Deb come to the party from Rolleston. Deb is visibly pregnant, and Eeman is visibly thrilled. Climate change or no climate change, humans keep wanting children and hope for their futures.

Victoria and Zarita are at the party because they're already part of our tiny home community. Once the Maximinions move in, there will be lots of children for Zarita to grow up with.

The Maximinion families all come and the Maximinions proudly show everyone who will listen where their tiny homes will soon stand. They got a stay of execution from the council, on the basis they are now building their new homes, but the last date to vacate their rentals is also March. The boys have built a bicycle track as their contribution towards property development, integrating the track into my food forest layout, which will cover the entire section other than platforms for tiny homes.

B comes to the party with Miranda. Once it's dark, B and the Maximinions perform a light-with-music show to enormous rounds of cheers and applause. The show leads on to a group sing-along which we keep going until the New Year rolls around. To avoid contention between Pauline and Grant regarding which songs are more appropriate, we choose through the Songalong app, into which everyone puts their music preferences. The app doles out a list of songs that will fit the given timeframe, allocating everyone a relatively equal number of songs they like. It then provides lyrics to multiple devices, karaoke style, so we can all sing the words. Stephen designed it and apparently sales are going well. He's branching out in all sorts of ways.

The big surprise at our New Year's Party is the appearance of Johnno and Kannika. They told Stephen but asked him to keep it a secret. I was so excited to see them because it's been three years since Johnno came to Christchurch, and the last time I met Kannika was at Mum's funeral, long before she and Johnno got together. It took them two days to travel here on the bus and then the train. Big floods took out the route through the centre of the South Island during winter, which has made the trip much longer. Johnno and Kannika are quietly happy together.

Fran wasn't at our party because Fran died in September. She had more time than she'd hoped in Northland with Holly and her whānau. The last time

Fran and I got together on Cast she was tired and gasping for breath. She ended our conversation with, "I'm going to say goodbye, Julia."

"That's what everyone says at the end of a catch-up," I said.

"No, Julia. Don't make it harder than it has to be. This is the last time we'll say goodbye. I won't be talking with the world outside my room again. I'm letting go, step by step."

I so badly wished it was Lynda and me saying goodbye to Fran together.

"Thank you for your friendship, Julia. And for Dolls with Stories, where we achieved so much and made so many people happier. And all the good times and laughter, cups of tea, tears, the whole of it. I'll always love you, Julia. You know that, right?"

"I'll always love you too, Fran," I said with matching tears running down my face. We raised our fingers to the screen as if we could hold hands one last time. When I dropped my hand, the session had ended because the power was out, again, for several hours. That's a good thing about being at Stephen's with his solar panels and batteries, we don't have a lot of power, but it doesn't cut out.

At midnight on New Year's Eve, as I hugged Stephen and then all the many other partygoers, I thought of Fran, and of Lynda and Hermione and Robbie. I'd wanted to invite Lynda and her family, but I know I must wait until Lynda wants to get in touch with me. If she ever does. Sometimes I see her pushing Hermione in a stroller on Scarborough, or in Sumner, and she raises a hand. We manage the Dolls with Stories business through formal emails, though there's little for Johnno and me to do.

I see Robbie at the Ferrymead Broken is Beautiful workshop where he is as nice to me – and everyone else – as ever. Robbie is discussing additional rental space with the owners of buildings next to Broken is Beautiful. He wants to separate the professional repair side of the business so the drop-in workshops can run every day because there's never-ending demand for them. We don't talk about Lynda. I don't know how she explained our separation to Robbie, given she didn't want him to know anything about the connection between Humans with Stories and the Lyttelton bombing. I regularly ask Robbie about Hermione. He shows me pictures on his phone; she's growing up fast and is already talking. He tells me her latest words, like 'Birdoo', when a bird pooed on his T-shirt while they were sitting outside. I remain hopeful Robbie will bring Hermione to the workshop when I'm there, but he doesn't. Maybe Lynda is stopping him.

In March, Rosemary is sentenced to six years in prison, with eligibility for parole. Her lawyers make passionate arguments regarding the desperate state of our atmosphere and environment. They point out the lack of fairness in Rosemary going to prison when leaders of companies that wreak environmental havoc never appear in court. Rosemary's sentence means she could be released in a little over two years, given she has already been in prison for nine months. Tough on her family, though, however long or short the time she is in prison. I heard they moved to Nelson, to put distance between themselves and Lyttelton.

The day after Rosemary is sentenced is a Tuesday – a night Stephen and I have dinner together in my tiny house. We've kept our routine of visiting each other's places, even though we only live a few metres from each other. We still also enjoy our own regular nights alone. It doesn't work for two people who've spent the majority of their adult lives single to be cooped up together constantly, as we discovered when we briefly shared Stephen's caravan.

On this Tuesday, Stephen comes over waving an envelope. "We've got mail!" he says.

Getting mail is such a rare occurrence, I rip the envelope open in my excitement without looking at the writing.

JULIA AND STEPHEN

Are warmly invited to Hermione's

FIRST BIRTHDAY

21 March 2031

at 11 Scarborough Road

No presents necessary although random objects covered in multiple layers of reusable wrapping materials will be welcome.

Bring food, bubble-blowing materials, and YOURSELVES.

My heart inflates like an expanding soap bubble. I'm swinging Stephen round and he's banging into my tiny house table. "She meant it," I say. "It was a break, not forever!"

We walk down Scarborough Road on the twenty-first of March. Stephen is carrying a carrot cake with cream cheese icing and two endless paper parcels with layers of brown paper all the way to a paper love heart in the centre. I'm flying a taniwha-shaped kite with a streaming blue, green and silver tail. Soap bubbles are fun, but I want something more to mark the occasion.

Stephen pointed out the difficulty of walking across Scarborough flying a kite – there might not be enough wind, or too much, or I might trip because I was concentrating too hard on kite-flying. I was happy to take the risk. When we reach Lynda and Robbie's stairs, I could swear the kite is pulling me skyward, lightening every step.

We step onto the landing at the top to see Hermione toddling around on the deck. I hesitate and Lynda comes forward. "I'm so happy to see you again, Julia. I've missed you."

"I've missed you so much too, Lynda. The whole Humans with Stories thing was quite the disaster."

"Was it ever? But you met Stephen, so not a complete disaster. And now I hear you are growing a commune on Scarborough Hill."

"Not a commune, exactly, but somewhere people can live rather than an empty paddock. With a food forest – I'm learning lots about better ways to grow food in communities. Victoria's with us too, did you know?"

"Yes, I did. There's little that stays completely secret around here," Lynda says. "Although, obviously, there are some things …"

Perhaps there'll always be a slight space between Lynda and me. We're humans, so our stories don't weave together in perfect patterns. There are always holes from dropped stitches, runs, snags, and mismatched colours no one should ever have combined. Still, here we are. Knitting together again.

ACKNOWLEDGMENTS

I'm really grateful to my beta readers for helping direct and consolidate the story – Ann Shearer, Chris Nelson, Sue Harcombe and Viv Williams. Thank you Lesley Marshall for your assessment and Stephanie McConchie for you accurate and considered editing. Big kudos to Holly Dunn who created another excellent book cover for me, as well as laying the text out.

Thanks to everyone who inspired and informed my characters, particularly Frauke John for her insights into nursing, Greg Zelenoff (whose partner Anna is very much alive in Slovenia) and Efrando of northern Sulawesi. Pete Davie provided essential insight into the workings of harbours and coal tankers.

ABOUT THE AUTHOR

Jane Shearer is a professional non-fiction writer and this is her second novel. Like Broken is Beautiful, this novel is set in Sumner, Christchurch, as a place Jane lived long term until moving to Central Otago.

www.ingramcontent.com/pod-product-compliance
Lightning Source LLC
Chambersburg PA
CBHW050249110726
47898CB00007B/2336